Praise for

Plague thoughtfull̲y̲ _____ ...a and feelings of helplessness
healthcare workers e. ,...c while caring for the sick and dying. Its poignancy
and vivid exposition highlights how little has changed over the last 100 years of
responding to pandemics.

~David Kuhn, M.D.

Sweet reminiscing and accurate historic content and events embed this story
into firm bedrock.

~Robin Densmore Fuson
author of two 2020 Selah Awards finalists:
The Encounter and *Restoration.*

Crisp writing and good storytelling. Marian Rizzo somehow manages to weave
the history-based tale of terror of the deadly 1918 influenza outbreak with the
love of a wife for her family and their faith in God. It rings true on every page.

~Frank Stanfield,
author of
Cold Blooded, A True Crime Story of A Murderous Vampire Cult.

Faith yields courage is what strikes me most about *Plague*. Marian Rizzo skill-
fully takes us back a century to remind us we are not the first to pray for God's
protection of America's brave doctors and nurses, or who had such a desperate
need of their aid.

~Gerry Harlan Brown
author of
White Squirrels and Other Monsters.

Historic fiction at its most timely! Marian Rizzo's narrative style is perfectly
suited for this clinical yet intimate perspective on how the invisible threats among
us tear at family and society. This family drama is wonderfully told from the
perspective of a nurse and mother married to the town physician as they witness
their community besieged by the deadliest flu in American history.

~Aaron Shaver
PR guide and author of
Furious and other works.

PLAGUE

Also by Marian Rizzo

Angela's Treasures
Muldovah
In Search of the Beloved
In Search of Felicity
Presence in the Pew
Silver Springs (with Dr. Robert Knight)

PLAGUE

a novel of the great influenza

MARIAN RIZZO

WordCrafts Press

Plague is a work of fiction. The author has endeavored to be as accurate as possible with regard to the times in which the events of this novel is set. Still, this is a novel, and all references to persons, places, and events are fictitious or are used fictitiously.

Scripture quotations from The Authorized (King James) Version of the Bible. Public Domain in the United States. Rights in the Authorized Version in the United Kingdom are vested in the Crown. Reproduced by permission of the Crown's patentee, Cambridge University Press.

Lyrics to *I Love You Truly*, by Carrie Jacobs-Bond, 1901, public domain.
Lyrics to *Now Thank We All Our God*, by Martin Rinkart, 1636, public domain.

Plague
Copyright © 2021
Marian Rizzo

ISBN: 978-1-952474-74-3

Cover concept and design by Mike Parker.

Published by WordCrafts Press
Cody, Wyoming 82414
www.wordcrafts.net

To my sister, Rose,
who lent me her name for this story,
and to her husband, Mike.
Together they are a good example
of teamwork in marriage.

Also to the medical professionals
who give their lives every day keeping the
world safe from disease and trauma.

Prologue

December, 1957—in the throes of the Asian Flu

A blanket of snow covers the landscape. Evergreens stand tall and proud, their feathery branches weighted by fresh-fallen snow. A cloudless, blue sky promises a break in the weather. Sunshine bathes the cobbled streets in streaks of gold.

I stand on the back stoop and inhale the cool morning air. Touches of color speak of life and hope. Poinsettias bloom on my neighbor's front porch. Others on my street have strung colored lights on the eaves of their houses and along the greenery bordering their front walks.

But I know the truth. It's a deceptive camouflage, for beneath the festive holiday cloak lies a specter of death. Once again, an influenza pandemic has circled the globe.

I'm old enough to remember a similar attack that struck us 40 years ago. Back then, we passed the disease around like Halloween candy. In time, we understood its lethal power, so we put on masks, and we shut ourselves up in our homes.

"Isolation is the key," my husband, John, kept saying. "We have to separate the healthy from the sick."

As the town's only physician, John oversaw the health of approximately 1,400 people. Though our quiet little burg wasn't hit as hard as some of the big cities—specifically Philadelphia, Pittsburgh, and Boston—we suffered several

1

losses before residents of Sawmill, Pennsylvania, began to acknowledge that John was right, and isolation helped to curb the progression of the disease.

But isolation also brought with it another set of hardships.

Shops and restaurants shut their doors. Schools canceled classes. Churches stopped holding services. Neighbors stopped helping neighbors, friends became strangers, and our youngsters were confined to their bedrooms where they played alone, apart from their friends.

Ultimately, people had to deal with the psychological effects of separation. Still the flu ran rampant, and no one knew how to stop its spread.

Now I look back at what I remember as one of the worst periods in American history. While scientists were trying to find a cure for the flu, America had entered the Great War. Two battles were being fought at the same time. One waged against a human enemy that could be seen. The other against a silent, furtive killer that ended up killing more people than those who lost their lives in the war.

Living in the country, we fared better than those who lived in crowded conditions in the big cities and the outlying military bases. Nevertheless, the influenza of 1918 found us too.

Chapter One

October 1918

By the time the sickness came to our sleepy little village of Sawmill, Pennsylvania, in the fall of 1918, the influenza had already become a worldwide pandemic. Scientists agreed, it was an influenza unlike any the world had ever experienced.

We lived in a rural community where the air was fresh and clean. Our folks were going about their usual business—farmers growing crops, raising livestock and chickens, milking cows and gathering eggs. Family-owned businesses kept the foot traffic flowing through the downtown area where David Cowell ran the general store and post office, and individual retailers sold ladies' apparel, men's work boots, and household items of all sorts. Children went to school during the week or gathered in the playground on the weekends. The Rialto held stage plays and concerts on Friday and Saturday nights. And two churches—one Catholic, the other Lutheran—hosted services and town meetings.

The ladies' sewing club met every Tuesday. The men's Rotary Club met for Wednesday morning breakfasts. Farmers attended Grange meetings. Neighbors gathered for potluck suppers and afternoon teas. With a population of about 1,400 people, everybody knew nearly everybody else. We were like one big, happy family, living in different houses, but available to each other when needed. We held barn raisings, outdoor festivals, and church picnics. You might say we lived in our own secluded little Shangri-La, never suspecting that a silent killer was about to drag us into hell.

My husband, Dr. John Gallagher, was the town's only physician. He did everything from pulling teeth to delivering babies to amputating a limb, sometimes using the same tools. The more serious cases he sent on a 70-mile drive to Philadelphia for treatment at any one of more than two dozen hospitals. As a trained nurse, I assisted John whenever needed. Most of the time, I delivered babies and handled his patients' aftercare. Together, John and I handled the usual colds and fevers with medicines he kept in his home pharmacy.

But overnight, simple coughs and sneezes turned into something worse. Our neighbors complained of chills, aching muscles, pounding headaches, and shortness of breath. Like always, John treated the symptoms. Back then we didn't have antibiotics or serums. No vaccines, no life support, no EKG's. We relied on simple medicines that sometimes worked and sometimes didn't. We watched for complications. Bacterial pneumonia was the worst. Once a patient developed lung problems the chance for recovery diminished.

We assumed the disease would pass like so many others in the past. But after the first couple of cases, the germs spread like wildfire. Sick calls kept John running from one end of the county to the other. I stayed home and kept our children safely sheltered behind closed doors. I hoped the illness would pass in a short time.

Some of us older folks remembered the influenza pandemic of 1889. I was 11 years old at the time. It had started somewhere in Russia and within four months it had made its way around the globe. But this flu was different. In time we would look back on the Spanish Flu as the worst disease to attack mankind, rivaled only by the bubonic plague of the 14th century.

If the media had done its job, we would have had some forewarning. Until the flu became a worldwide pandemic, the American newspapers were writing about the Great War, women's fashions, and baseball games while neglecting to warn us about a furtive evil that was about to change our lives forever. By the time the press decided to focus on the influenza it was too late. The Spanish Flu was no longer a threat to the big cities and military bases. It had crept into Sawmill.

I didn't know how bad things were until the night John stumbled into the house, hunched under an invisible weight. He'd spent the entire day trudging the streets on foot and taking our horse and buggy out to the farthest reaches of the county. It was after dark when he entered our little cabin.

Releasing a long sigh, he stopped in front of his pharmacy cupboard and dropped his bag on the floor. It landed with a muffled thump, empty. Then he shuffled into the kitchen and collapsed in a chair at the table.

I approached him, offered to take his coat. He struggled out of it and handed me his scarf.

"What's going on, John?" I suspected the worst, had seen those troubled lines on his brow before. He'd had that same look of despair when Oskar Schmidt died a few years back.

He stared at me with sad eyes, like he was about to tell me something so painful he couldn't find the right words. I steeled myself for what was coming.

"Little Robbie Wilson died today," John's voice broke. So did my heart.

I pressed my hand to my chest. Robbie's mother was my best friend. She was godmother to our baby girl Lily. Releasing a groan, I dropped into a chair, John's coat and scarf still in my hands.

My husband shook his head with an air of despondency. "The poor boy fell into convulsions and then he was gone. It happened so fast, I couldn't save him."

Tears flooded into my eyes. "Dear God, I should have been there for Emma. I knew Robbie was sick, I should have gone to the house and helped somehow."

"No, Rosie. You did right by staying away. You had to think about our own children."

"But I'm a trained nurse. It's my duty."

"Doesn't matter. Believe me, you couldn't have saved him. And Emma? She was so grief-stricken she didn't want to see anyone." He wiped a tear from his eye. "What's more, darlin', you might have exposed yourself to the germs. You could have brought them home with you."

I raised my eyebrows in disbelief. "You're afraid I might bring the germs home? And what do you think you're doing, John? You've been visiting the sick for weeks. You've spent every hour of every day at the bedsides of the sick. Did you ever think you also might bring the germs home?"

"I take precautions, Rosie. I wear a double layer of masks and I use disposable surgical gloves. After every visit I discard those items, then I sterilize my medical equipment with carbolic acid. By the time I walk in our front door I'm as germ-free as an operating room surgeon."

"Don't you think I can do those things too? I can wear masks and gloves. I can disinfect my nurse's instruments."

"No, Rosie. One of us out there is enough. I'm a doctor. I

can't turn my back on our neighbors. But you're a mother now. You have other responsibilities." He shook his head. "This illness is like nothing we've ever experienced before."

I rose from my chair and hung his coat and scarf on a hook near the front door. Then I went to the sideboard and retrieved last Sunday's copy of the "Philadelphia Inquirer." It had arrived in the mail that morning. The front page headline told the distressing truth. Influenza remains unchecked; city officials call for quarantine.

At last, the newspapers had begun to publish the truth about the illness, and the government leaders had begun to devise a plan of action. The influenza pandemic was no longer a secret.

I spread the newspaper on the table in front of my husband. As he read the article he kept nodding his head and groaning.

"They should have warned us sooner," I told John. "They should have prepared us."

They were calling the disease "The Spanish Flu," a misnomer because it hadn't originated in Spain at all. The warring nations had suppressed the information in order to prevent a panic. As a neutral country, Spain was the first to publicize details about the flu. The Spanish government didn't restrict the press as other European nations had. The number of their deceased was climbing and their king, Alfonso XIII, also became ill, making the flu newsworthy to the Spanish.

John looked up from the page, his usual calm facade hidden behind wrinkles of concern.

"It says here, nearly 12,000 have died in Philadelphia. The hospitals are overloaded and the morgues are filled to capacity. The Red Cross is begging for doctors and nurses to come and help. There's a terrible shortage of medical workers." He shook his head. "Many qualified physicians and nurses have gone off to serve as medics in the war. The city leaders also are calling for volunteers to help transport the sick to the hospitals and to make gauze coverings for the nose and mouth. The Red Cross has already distributed more than 100,000 masks. They're taking precautions, Rosie. Philadelphia's officials have shut down all schools, churches, and public places."

"I know, John. I read the report three times."

He turned his attention back to the paper. "Well, well, well. It looks like Rupert Blue, the surgeon general, has issued a mandate requiring people to wear a mask whenever they go out in public. Better yet, he's ordered those who are coughing or sneezing to stay home."

John looked up at me. "That makes sense, Rosie. Stay home. Stay away from the sick."

"And what if the sick live in the same house with those who are well?"

"Separation," John said with a shrug. "Keep the sick in bed, away from the healthy, as much as possible."

He went back to the newspaper. "Blue's recommendations are simple. Avoid overcrowding, cover your coughs and sneezes, wash your hands regularly, and he says, 'remember the three C's: clean mouth, clean skin, and clean clothes.'" John chuckled over that one.

"The man's advice is coming too late," he said, his voice turned serious. Then he pointed at the third paragraph and snorted. "Look at this, Rosie. They're threatening to arrest people who appear in public without a face mask, and they've imposed a $5 fine for spitting on the sidewalk." He chuckled again, but a cloud of concern diminished the sparkle in his emerald eyes. "I'm afraid their response comes too late," he said, shaking his head. "This thing has already gotten out of control."

"How long?" I searched his face, needed him to tell me the truth, no matter how painful.

"What do you mean?"

"How long before it's out of control here?"

"I can't say, Rosie. Emma's little boy is my sixth fatality." His green eyes darkened to almost black, and I knew. Things were going to get a whole lot worse before they got better.

He took my hand and held it tight. "The flu is spreading faster than any of us anticipated. I no sooner take a person's temperature when someone else in the household gets sick. Family members are coughing and sneezing on each other. One minute they're shaking with chills, the next they're burning up with fever. I'm at a loss what to do."

His defeated tone sent a chill through me. "This disease is unpredictable, Rosie. Some of my patients rise from their sickbeds within a couple of days, and I think, How wonderful. Maybe they're out of danger. Then a patient takes a turn for the worse. Oddly, the elderly and infirm seem to be coming through with few complications. The more vulnerable victims have been the young and the healthy, particularly pregnant women. Connie Johnson fell terribly ill, almost lost her own life and the baby inside her as well."

I thought over what he'd just told me. "The elderly come through just fine, and the young and healthy succumb? That's strange."

He nodded. "Many of the older folks lived through the last influenza attack twenty years ago. It's possible they developed an immunity. I can't say for certain, it's a theory of mine. The truth is, we're dealing with something far more lethal and erratic than anything we've ever seen before. I'm afraid no one is safe. We have to do our best and pray for God to work a miracle, because that's what we need right now—a miracle."

I thought about my neighbors. I knew their children and their grandchildren. We were friends, members of the same church and the same clubs. We passed each other on the street every day. Now we'd locked ourselves behind closed doors.

"Is there anything I can do?" I asked in my innocence.

He responded with a sympathetic smile. "You can pray. Pray for our friends and neighbors. Other than that, you can do what everyone else needs to do. We all need to disinfect our homes, wash our hands often, and most of all, keep our distance from the sick. Isolation is the key, Rosie. More than anything else, everyone needs to separate from those who are infected." He puffed out a troubled sigh. "I'm afraid our neighbors have not been following my recommendations. People go out on the streets, running errands like nothing's wrong. The farmers are still coming to town selling their produce. Many of our friends are still going to church and to meetings. Mayor Barnes has requested that the people of Sawmill do what they've done in Philadelphia. He wants a complete shutdown until this disease passes. But he hasn't insisted, so few people are complying. What makes things more difficult is the healthy ones are caring for the sick. They feed them and bathe them and hover over their sickbeds. Then they also fall victim."

My dear Irish husband's usual blithe spirit had all but disappeared. He looked like a defeated man. For weeks he'd been fighting this battle alone out there, relying on reports coming in from the city, and trying to come up with a cure out of his own store, only to fail.

"I'm just one man, Rosie. I'm the one physician within 50 miles. What can I do?"

I stepped up behind him, rubbed the back of his neck and massaged his tired shoulders. "You need to rest, John. Give yourself a day or two to regain your strength. If you want to help your patients you'll have to take care of yourself first."

He buried his head in his hands. His voice muffled, he poured out his heart. "I can't stop, Rosie."

"You must."

He raised his head and gazed at me as hopeless tears spilled from his eyes. His forehead was creased the way his father's used to do when he was troubled. In that moment he resembled the older man, tired and defeated, and ready to retire or go to his own grave. The image frightened me. My husband was 42 years old, yet he looked like an old man.

I mumbled a prayer for God to give John the strength to go on and the wisdom to know when to quit.

Yes, I said to myself, quit.

It was no sin to quit, to know when you've lost the battle, to give up trying to save the world and take care of your own health and your own family.

But John, being a humble man, and a strict adherent to the Hippocratic Oath, had always been a giver, not a taker. He'd never quit as long as someone needed him.

I wanted to help him, the way I used to when we first met—John as the doctor, me as his nurse. But I'd given up my career 16 years ago when Amy was born. After two miscarriages, and then the birth of young Johnny and baby girl Lily, I settled into motherhood. By the time this influenza came around, I'm ashamed to say I had forgotten much of what I'd learned in nursing school.

John rose from the table and shuffled over to his cupboard. I settled in the chair he'd vacated and kept my eyes on him.

He opened the cupboard doors and checked what remained on his shelves, turned over empty bottles that once held medicines and tinctures, sifted through limp bags that at one time bulged with herbs and powders.

I strained against the lump in my throat. If we could hold our own, if we could wait it out, perhaps our little village would avoid the devastation felt in the big cities. Separation. Like John said, that was the key. We needed to stay separated. From sick people and from places where the illness was the worst. Like New York, and Boston, and Pittsburgh. And, yes, Philadelphia. Word was the city had been hit harder than any municipality in the nation except for Pittsburgh.

John faced me and shook his head, hopelessness weakening his resolve. I held my breath. I knew what was coming. I read it in his eyes and in the way he sighed, like he had no other recourse.

Don't say it, I thought. I stared at him with intensity and tried to sway him with my gaze. Please, John, don't say it.

Another sigh, a sad smile, and he spoke the words I didn't want to hear.

"I need to go to the city for supplies."

Chapter Two

A myriad of arguments swirled around in my head. I could beg him not to go. Could remind him how much worse things were in Philadelphia. But he already knew that. He'd read the newspapers. He'd gotten reports from other doctors who worked in the city.

As though reading my thoughts, he stepped toward me and raised his hand, stopping me, the way a gate at a railroad crossing stops people from pulling their carriages onto the tracks when a train is coming. A sorrowful smile tugged at the corners of his mouth.

"I'm out of alcohol, Rosie. And aspirin, quinine, digitalis, ammonia—pretty much everything. The hospitals in Philadelphia have what we need. They also may have some new experimental serums, perhaps antitoxins that might give protection against complications from the flu. Such medicines could mean the difference between life and death for our people."

He paused, his steady gaze quenching my resistance. We had entered a battle of wits, and I was losing.

"You want me to try, don't you, Rosie?" His voice was soft and pleading.

I opened my mouth to speak, but words didn't come. I took a deep breath, tried to alleviate the tightening in my chest. All I could do was nod with acceptance. Not that my husband needed my approval. He was going, with or without it. The man was a marvel. Though he stood a mere 5 feet, 6 inches tall, he'd been my pillar of strength, my rock in the storms of life. He'd stayed by my side through two miscarriages and had nursed me back to health—both physically and emotionally. From the day we married, John assumed his rightful place as head of our home, and he never wavered. He made decisions for the two of us and later for each of our children as they came along.

"You'll never have to worry about anything, Rosie. I'll take care of you," he'd promised on our wedding day, and then he went on to prove it.

There was no question, John's will was far stronger than my frail arguments. Despite his meek and mild nature, my husband possessed a tenacity unlike anything I'd ever seen. He stuck to his commitment to heal the sick no matter what the cost, and he rarely gave in to my self-indulgent pleadings.

"This illness isn't going to go away on its own," he continued in that convincing way of his. "We have to put up a fight, darlin'. The two of us are an army of sorts. Like our brave, young soldiers who joined the war in Europe, so also must we engage this enemy. If we don't unite we will lose."

His words frightened me. The battle already had reached our village, even our very doorstep. We hadn't been prepared. Now my dear husband had become a soldier and was doing everything in his power to wage a war against this unseen force.

At that time no one knew where it came from or where it might go next. Once the scientists admitted the influenza hadn't started in Spain several other theories arose. Some said it originated in Asia, like so many diseases that begin in overpopulated areas of the world. For one thing, China had been battling a bird flu at about the same time the flu raised its ugly head. Other medical professionals insisted a similar illness was already present in France in 1916 and that U.S. soldiers had carried it home with them as they returned from the battlefield.

Eventually, however, all eyes had turned toward Camp Funston, an army training center in Fort Riley, Kansas, where, in early March, one of the trainees stumbled into the base infirmary with a severe headache, sore throat, chills, and raging fever. Within the day a hundred more of the Fort Riley soldiers visited the infirmary with similar symptoms, some with fevers as high as 106 degrees. Most recovered within a few days, but because of the severely overcrowded conditions the infected soldiers spread the disease from one to another. By the end of the first week more than 500 were sick, and that spring 48 soldiers died from complications of the flu, most of them from bacterial pneumonia.

One news report pointed to a nearby pig farm where a swine epidemic had resulted in the slaughter of millions of pigs. The stench from the burning of contaminated pig manure reached Camp Funstun, but medical professionals decided to look at other possibilities. In the end they paid less attention to the source of the disease and gave their full attention to finding a cure. They set up individual labs and began conducting tests.

Despite the efforts of the scientists, the government was ill-prepared to stop the spread of the disease. Through military orders, army leaders continued to send seemingly well soldiers to other bases all over the United States. Many more troops carried the disease overseas through their deployments to encampments in Europe.

Woodrow Wilson, our president at the time, didn't appear to be concerned that the disease could turn into a worldwide pandemic. The escalation of war in Europe had consumed his attention. When the Central Powers and the Allies first entered into conflict in the summer of 1914, Wilson declared that the United States was going to remain neutral. Then Germany became more aggressive. By 1915, the German emperor, Kaiser Wilhelm II, declared the waters surrounding the British Isles as a war zone. German U-boats sank several merchant and passenger ships that ventured into the area, including those belonging to the United States. Many civilians, both merchants and vacationers, lost their lives. It was becoming more difficult for America to stay out of the war.

Congress responded to the attacks by passing a $250-million arms appropriation bill as a threat to ward off further German aggression. Instead, like such bills generally do, this one went beyond a simple warning and prepared us for battle.

America entered World War I on April 2, 1917. It was like we'd been caught in a whirlwind. One day we were neutral, the next we were involved in a conflict that would come to be known as the "Great War." *Great* because of the massive number of countries that became involved, and *Great* because it was the first world war to be fought on land, sea, and air. Then there was the enormous number of casualties. More than 8 million military personnel and 6 million civilians were killed worldwide.

Wilson expanded the draft, increasing the number of soldiers, and transported them overseas. About the same time, the influenza had spread to the military bases. We'd gotten on an out-of-control merry-go-round. Many of the deployed troops were coming out of training camps where the flu had infected thousands. Even those who appeared healthy carried the germs to coastal American cities and ultimately to overseas locations, first to Brest, France, America's main entry of disembarkment and later to other parts of Europe. By August, more than 62,000 U.S. troops had settled in Brest or in a nearby army encampment. By September, 15,000 deployed servicemen had come down with the flu and 370 had died.

Many soldiers never made it to Europe but died aboard one of the overcrowded vessels, and were buried at sea. Ultimately, 1.5 million soldiers carried the germs to battlefronts in France, England, and Germany. From there, the disease circled the globe striking Africa and Asia and leaving India with the highest death toll of more than 12 million people. Eventually, a second wave of the invisible monster returned to the good ol' U.S.A., borne there by troops returning home from the various battlefields.

The second wave was far more lethal than the first. After striking Camp Devens military base near Boston, it traveled by seagoing vessels to Philadelphia's Navy shipyard, the largest in the United States at the time. With a loss of 12,000 of its 1.7 million citizens, the City of Brotherly Love would later be credited with one of the highest death counts in the nation, second only to Pittsburgh. Ultimately, nearly 675,000 Americans died from the flu, five times the number of our nation's casualties in the Great War.

As the fall weather descended on the northeast, we began to feel the brunt of the disease. We were going about our usual business when the second wave brought the flu to

Sawmill. A few people came down with coughs and fevers, nothing unusual, or so we thought.

Our little village was situated in the country about 70 miles west of Philadelphia, far enough to give a false sense of security but too close for us to avoid the flu. The infection could be transported by merchants and farmers as they traveled back and forth between the two locations.

Our neighbors were already lining up at our door pleading for medicine and begging John to come to their homes to care for their sick family members. He went from house-to-house on foot and from farm-to-farm by horse-drawn buggy, rarely getting a good night's sleep and eating most of his meals on the run.

Small-town doctoring hadn't been John's first choice. He'd finished medical school in three years instead of four, and as soon as he satisfied his required hours at the hospital, he took to the streets where he could care for the helpless. He'd found contentment in serving the people of Philadelphia, many of them living in the slums. Then his father decided to retire, and he offered John his practice.

Though his older brother also had followed their father in his chosen career, Martin Jr. hadn't wanted any part of what he referred to as a "thankless ministry," for that's how John's brother described the work of a country doctor. Such a calling didn't promise the usual pats on the back and high salaries the big city physicians enjoyed. Marty chose instead to work in a Philadelphia hospital where the wages were high and the accolades abundant.

We'd been married almost two years when John took over the medical needs of the people of Sawmill. Naturally his brother thought he was wasting his time. But their father saw potential in a young man who'd chosen the profession out of altruism rather than for selfish gain.

The village of Sawmill turned out to be a similar arena for pretty much the same thing John had been doing in Philly. Such a calling couldn't promise the kind of lifestyle the big city doctors enjoyed. Most of our neighbors paid John a reasonable stipend, but it was far short of the steady income the city doctors received. A few of the wealthier citizens, like Tom and Grace Duncan, insisted on paying double. It was as if they knew John was settling for meager payment in favor of helping his neighbors. Then there were the farmers who paid with butchered pigs and bags of vegetables. I never knew what John would carry home with him at the end of a long day. Sometimes it was a hind quarter of beef. Sometimes a homemade pie or a sack of corn.

"Sacrificial service has other rewards," John reminded me on several occasions.

To our disappointment, it took a while for the people of Sawmill to accept my husband as their physician. After all, his father, Dr. Martin Gallagher, had served them for many years. They were accustomed to seeing the old man's weathered face at their door. They'd learned to trust him.

Meanwhile, many of the older villagers had vague memories of John as a young scalawag who swam naked in the river and ran barefoot through their flower beds. They weren't open to having him take over their health care. In the beginning they preferred, instead, to drive their sick relatives by horse and buggy 70 miles over a network of rough and dirty roads to Philadelphia.

But John didn't give up. Like many country doctors back then, he continued to visit people in town, whether they were sick or not, just wanting to check up on them. Then he'd either saddle up old Flossie or he'd hook her up to his buggy and drive out to several outlying farms, some of them more than twenty miles away.

Emma Wilson was the first to make us feel welcome. She brought casseroles and cookies to our door and convinced the other ladies in her sewing club to do the same. Even the men started offering John cigars, which he kindly refused, and shots of their homemade cider, which he heartily accepted.

But it took time—too long, in my opinion—and I sometimes wanted to ask why he didn't just close up his office and move us back to the city.

Eventually our neighbors started calling on John for simple ailments, like stomach bugs and minor cuts and bruises. It was as if they were testing his competence. He conducted exams in the privacy of our bedroom. More often, he dropped whatever he was doing to brave the rain or the snow to answer a call to a sickbed. As a trained midwife, I counseled expectant mothers through their pregnancies and often went along with John when one of them went into labor.

Most of the time, the majority of John's patients came down with simple colds and, in recent years, the measles and diphtheria. He used the latest medicines of the day to cure their ills, and they learned to trust him more and more with each passing month. Hadn't lost a patient. The first was our next-door neighbor, Oskar Schmidt, an 84-year-old German immigrant who'd been suffering for years with a bad heart.

Oskar's wife, Greta, was the oldest woman in town. The two of them had lived long past the median age of longevity. We rarely saw Oskar, but Greta had a grandmotherly air about her. She fawned over young Amy and brought homemade candies and German pastries to our door. But our friendship didn't last long. Oskar died while under my husband's care. It didn't matter to Greta that her husband had suffered for years with heart issues. Didn't matter that he was 50 pounds overweight. The stubborn man ignored John's advice. He refused to give up his daily helpings of bratwurst, pork knuckles, and dark beer at every meal, sometimes even at breakfast. He also chain-smoked cigars. He always had a stogie in his mouth. Even after it had burned out, he kept chewing on the end as if it were made of candy.

John made the usual doctor recommendations. "Cut back on sweets and fatty foods, quit smoking, and take a two-mile walk every morning. You'll extend your life by at least ten years."

Did Oskar listen? Hardly.

Nevertheless, John did what he could. He provided digitalis and he often went next door to check Oskar's heart rate and blood pressure. In those days the medical world didn't have pacemakers and artificial hearts. But the Philadelphia hospitals had some of the latest tools, such as electrocardiograms, bottled oxygen, and x-ray machines. My husband suggested on several occasions that Oskar make a trip to the city. He even gave him the name of a prominent physician he remembered from med school.

But it was to no avail. Oskar refused to leave the comforts of home but wallowed instead in his own self-appointed misery. He died in his sleep one night when my husband had gone to see his father in Philadelphia. Greta blamed John, and she never spoke to us again except to hurl expletives at us from her front porch.

A few days after the funeral we caught sight of her sitting out there in her cane-backed rocker, it's rhythmic motion emitting a resounding scritch-scratch against the floor boards. She stopped rocking and glared at John.

"Miracle worker? Hah! Physician, you need to heal yourself!"

John simply smiled and gave her a friendly wave.

I swallowed my bitterness and managed a simple, "Good Morning."

"Halt deinein mund!" she shouted back.

I turned to John. "Did she just tell me to shut up?"

"I think so," he said with a chuckle.

Sadly, our two younger children, Johnny and Lily, never got to taste Greta's German chocolate bars, nor did they experience the grandmotherly hugs Amy had enjoyed. After moving to Sawmill, we rarely visited my mother anymore. Greta became the closest thing to a grandparent for my children.

We tried to make peace with the widow Schmidt on several occasions. I brought her some homemade sunflower breads. She shut the door in my face. John rapped on her door to see if she needed any medicines. She refused to open it. I left a bouquet of flowers from my garden on her front porch. Later that day I found them in our trash barrel.

When America entered World War I, Greta closed herself off even more, not only from us but from everyone else in town. Her homeland was part of the Central Axis Powers along with Austria-Hungary and Turkey. When the U.S. entered the war, our boys became affiliated with the Allied powers—France, Italy, Great Britain, Russia, and Japan. The ladies in my sewing group agreed it was a senseless war. Nevertheless, we knitted socks and sweaters to send to the troops overseas.

Greta acted like the whole town blamed her for what was happening on the other side of the world. I doubted anyone considered her the enemy. Though she was the only German-born resident in our little community, we weren't concerned about nationalities. It's true our town was comprised primarily of Italians and Irish families, plus a couple of Polish men who worked at the sawmill. But Greta had lived there far too long for anyone to shun her.

The poor woman shut herself up in her house with her three cats. She rarely stepped out her front door except to shop at the general store. Even then she wouldn't speak to anyone. She avoided people along the way, sometimes crossing the street to avoid contact. She also dodged people in the aisle of the store, then hurried back home and locked the door behind her. Kids on the street started calling her "Grumpy Greta." A couple nasty boys threw mud and stones at her house. I hollered at them, and I forbade Amy from doing such things. The adults learned to leave the old woman alone. But living as close to her as we did, right next door, I couldn't completely ignore her, nor did I want to. I often spotted her looking out her window. I'd no sooner lift my hand to wave, when she'd let the curtain fall, then she disappeared into the darkness.

Concerned for her well-being, I kept an eye out so I might catch her in her backyard hanging clothes on the line or sitting on the front porch with her knitting. I was always looking for an opportunity to start up a conversation with her. But at the first sight of me, she slipped inside the house and stayed there until I went away. Sometimes I left a fruitcake or some homemade bread on her doorstep. It disappeared, and I assumed she'd brought it inside. I hoped she didn't throw it away like she'd done with my flowers. After many frustrating attempts, I finally gave up, like everyone else.

John continued to minister to the rest of the town and the people who lived on farms. In the beginning I took time away from my cooking and cleaning, and dragging Amy along in her baby carriage, I assisted in the delivery of a baby now and then, and I checked up on some of John's recovering patients.

But once our other two came along I stayed home. Then when the influenza hit our village I hunkered down with the children even more. John increased his time on the streets, and I, driven by panic like everyone else, plunged into a self-imposed disinfecting project on the home front.

I flew about the house scrubbing the floors and every piece of furniture. I washed the curtains and throw rugs in lye and hung them over the line outside so they could dry in the fresh air. I turned ordinary household chores, like washing dishes and scrubbing bed sheets, into major sterilization projects. Back then we homemakers didn't have rubber gloves. My poor hands spent so much time in harsh detergents they began to look like those of a charwoman, raw and with blood oozing from the cracks in my skin. I applied gobs of lard to no avail and tearfully said good-bye to ever having dainty hands again.

Now I was facing yet another challenge. John had decided to go to Philadelphia. Though I didn't like the idea of my husband leaving me alone with the children, my greater concern was that he was about to travel to a place where the disease was said to have been even more virulent than most other places in the land.

In spite of my unease, I set about helping him prepare for the journey.

The night before he left I packed a small bag with his toiletries and a change of clothes. Though he planned to be gone for only a day, things could change. Such was the fatalistic mood that had descended on our home. We simply went with the flow, and the flow was controlled by the flu.

I slept poorly that night. A myriad of possibilities roiled around in my head. His buggy had a bent wheel. What if it came off during the journey? What if he suffered an injury, or worse? And what about our poor, old horse, Flossie? What if she could get John to Philly but couldn't get him home again?

I must have tossed and turned that night because my bones ached when I arose the next morning. So did my head. I nudged John awake. He appeared well-rested. He stretched, grunted, and rolled out of bed, ready for a day on the road.

Again I pondered the near impossible journey that lay ahead of him. His sole means of transportation was a 12-year-old nag and a buggy with a bent wheel.

"Oh, John, do you think this trip makes sense? Old Flossie does well enough in town, but that decrepit, old horse—"

He raised a hand and cut me off. Then he gave me one of his half smiles, the kind he usually reserved for surprises. "I have other plans," he confessed. His smile faded. "As you already know, Greg Thompson passed away last week. A sorry loss for our community." He looked me in the eye. "I offered his widow $50 for his truck."

I frowned in puzzlement. "Thompson's truck? $50? Is it even worth it?"

"It's a good investment. You'll see. Old Flossie can go out to pasture, and I won't have to stop on the road and pound the wheel back in shape. Thompson's truck will save precious time."

Resigned to my husband's plan, I headed for the kitchen. He went into the bathroom.

I drifted about the kitchen, like a turtle caught in a mud

bog. I had no energy, no will to take part in my husband's plan. Nevertheless I knew the man had to eat. He couldn't go all day without food and water. I packed a sack with a hunk of raisin bread, a wedge of cheese, two jars of peaches, and several strips of dried beef—enough to last for two days if needed. I also included a flask of water along with a small tin of almond cookies. Then I set about making his breakfast.

He came out of the bathroom, got a look at what I'd packed for him, and released a little chuckle. "I expect to be home on time for supper, Rosie," he said still laughing softly.

I shrugged sheepishly. "You never know..."

John started for the door. "I'll load all this in the truck," he announced.

"You need to eat something before you leave," I insisted. "It's a long ride to the city. Even in Thompson's truck it'll take at least three hours."

He looked at my anxious face and smiled with sympathy. The man could see right into my heart. "It'll be all right, Rosie." His leprechaun eyes sparkled with intensity. "Don't you worry about me, darlin'. I'll spend very little time in the city—just long enough to purchase what I need for my pharmacy—and before you know it I'll be home with medicines to help our neighbors." Then he cocked his head to one side. "Have I told you how much I love you?"

I nodded. "Every day." Unchecked tears ran down my cheeks, but I managed a weak smile.

John grabbed a chair at the table. "I suppose a hardy breakfast will do me good."

I set before him a plate of scrambled eggs and toast, poured his coffee—strong and black, the way he liked it. Then I sat across the table from him and watched him eat.

He was scraping up the last of the eggs with a wedge of toast when a soft voice drew our attention to the kitchen doorway. I turned. For an instant I saw a younger version of myself standing there. It was our 16-year-old daughter Amy. Damp black ringlets trailed to her shoulders and she had the same skinny, reed-like physique I'd been stuck with all my life. There I was—no stomach, no bustle, and almost no breasts to speak of. My firstborn daughter had been cursed with her mother's genes. I would pity her when the time came for her to seek a beau.

But my pity turned into abject concern as I surveyed her standing there. Her face, usually flushed with the flower of youth, was as pale as a bowl of flour. Her rich brown eyes had clouded over and were half hidden behind drooping lids.

Intense foreboding flooded into my heart. The front of Amy's nightdress was soiled with last night's supper. We'd had lamb stew. Now a large, brown splotch stained the front of her clothing, and she looked like she might drop to the floor at any moment.

I lunged out of my chair and hurried over to her. I placed my palm against her forehead. It felt like a burning coal. Suddenly she went limp and fell into my arms. John tossed down his fork and rushed to her side. He lifted her like a dry leaf and carried her to the sofa. She sank into the cushion with a moan.

My poor girl reeked of urine and vomit. John leaned close, felt her face, pressed his ear to her chest, gently ran his hands over her arms and legs. She moaned again beneath his touch.

He straightened and turned toward me, a hint of alarm in his eyes. "Wet a towel with cool water, Rosie. And hurry."

I knew the routine, had followed his orders multiple times

during visits to the homes of the sick. I raced to the bathroom, came back with a damp towel and thrust it in John's hand. He touched it to her forehead, then to her throat. I quickly fetched his medical bag, set it on the floor beside him and opened the clasp.

Without having to be told I went to the refrigerator and chipped some flakes off the block of ice in the freezer. Returning to the sofa, I slid tiny slivers of damp coolness between Amy's parched lips. John was going through the typical doctor routine, stethoscope in one hand and thermometer in the other. "Her temperature's 104." He shot a troubled glance at me.

I ran to the children's bedroom and went through Amy's bureau. Clean underwear. A fresh nightdress. Socks for her ice cold feet. I returned to Amy's side, removed her soiled clothing, bathed her with a damp cloth, patted her dry with a soft bath towel, then I dressed her in the clean garments. She flopped around like a rag doll, didn't make the slightest effort to help me put her clothes on. Her eyes, vacant and searching, stared past me into nothingness.

John took over again. He ran his hands through her hair, pulled the damp strands away from her face. Then he eased her back against the pillow. He grabbed a quilt from the back of the sofa and draped it over her.

Frowning, John turned toward me again. "What about the other two?"

My heart pounding, I hurried back to the children's room and checked on them—Johnny on the top level of their bunk bed, Lily on the bottom. They were sleeping peacefully, undisturbed by the trauma that had taken place across the room where Amy had spent a troubled night.

I pulled the soiled sheets and comforter from Amy's bed, carried them to the bathroom, and dropped them in the bathtub. I ran the water and tossed in some lye soap, then shoved the folds of cloth into the suds and gave them a quick scrub against the metal washboard. Satisfied, I left them there to soak. The solution stung my hands, already raw from disinfecting everything in our home.

Moments later I was back in the kids' bedroom scrubbing the places where Amy had released the contents of her stomach. I tried to ignore the relentless irritation between my fingers. It had to be done. Such was the way we confronted illness. Sterilize everything and treat the patient.

Medicine. We needed a few bottles of *something*. But John had run out of medicine. No quinine to bring down Amy's fever. No aspirin to take away the pain, no morphine or opium to help her sleep.

I returned to the living room and stood beside the sofa, wringing my burning hands. Amy gasped for air, then settled back against the pillow, her breathing shallow. In that instant, panic flooded into my heart. With my daughter struggling to breathe, I was in full agreement with my husband. At that moment I *wanted* him to go to the city, *wanted* him to bring back as much medicine as he could carry. And he should hurry.

But where had he gone?

Frantically, I looked around for him and found him at the sink filling a pot with water.

"You need to leave, John." The panic had surged from my heart to my throat.

He nodded quietly, then taking care not to spill a drop, he carried the pot of water to the stove.

"John, please. Shouldn't you be on your way?"

He ignored me, just lit a match and set fire to the cluster of wood beneath the burner.

"Fill more kettles," he said, an urgency in his voice. "Get two or three of them going. Saturate the room with steam. It will keep the air moist for Amy—and for all of you."

I eyed him with impatience, but I went to the cupboard for two more kettles. Maybe if I complied he'd get moving. I ran water into the pots. "You're still going, aren't you?" I repeated over my shoulder.

He didn't respond.

One by one I placed the kettles on the other two burners. John stood very still and hovered over Amy, regarding her with such intensity I held my breath.

I turned my attention to my daughter. Even without any drugs, she'd fallen asleep on the sofa, then I turned my eyes back on my husband. He was still standing there, motionless.

"I'm fine, John. I can take care of our daughter." Anxiety tightened my throat.

He breathed a heavy sigh. "To be honest, I don't *want* to leave now. I can't leave you and the children, not with Amy like this."

"You said they have life-saving medicines."

He pursed his lips. "Yes, they do." Still, he didn't move.

"I'm a nurse, John. I can handle things while you're gone."

A moan from the sofa drew my attention to Amy. I hurried to her side and placed my hand against her forehead. The fever had lessened a little. The three kettles rattled on the stove and poured more steam into the air. I smirked at the noisy chorus. They may be helping Amy, but they could turn the rest of us into drowned rats. My hair was already kinking into tight spirals, and my blouse had begun to cling to my back.

"You still have your nurse's kit, don't you?" John said thoughtfully.

I nodded. "I have a few essentials—a jar of Vicks VapoRub, another of Vaseline, and a handful of gauze masks." Oh yes, and a pack of Chesterfield cigarettes, but I didn't tell him about that.

John drew closer. "Keep our daughter drinking as much as she can handle. Water, of course, and tea, and a little of that apple cider in the pantry. Small sips, you know the routine. When she's ready, give her some broth, a few spoonfuls at a time. And try feeding her some apple sauce." He paused and shot a glance toward the children's bedroom. "And keep them away from her."

My husband had mentioned exactly what I already had in my head. My heart was pounding like a jackhammer. I wanted him to hurry.

"Yes, John," I said as calmly as I could. "I know what to do."

He planted a kiss on my cheek. Then he grabbed his medical bag, the pack of food on the table, and an empty burlap sack that he would fill with medicines once he got to Philadelphia. I beat him to the front door, opened it and let in a blast of cold air.

"Hurry home, John. And stay safe."

Then he was gone.

Chapter Three

After John left that fateful morning, I stared out the front window and watched after him until he was out of sight. For a while I couldn't pull myself away from that pane of glass, transfixed by the nearly leafless branches reaching out like fingers of death across the October sky. Beyond them the gathering of dark clouds promised another spray of icy rain or perhaps an early dump of snow to clog our streets and obstruct our walks. Beyond the town's quiet thoroughfares stretched miles of open spaces and a scattering of farmers who would also need medicine if they were to keep producing what the rest of us required to survive the coming winter.

We were like most Americans who lived in rural communities in the early 1900s. In our day, farms defined the American landscape. You could stand on any intersection, and no matter which way you turned you'd see acres of plowed fields, fenced pastures, apple orchards, red barns, silos, and three-story farmhouses. Horses and oxen provided power for plowing, sheep provided wool for warm clothes, and cows and goats provided milk and other dairy products like butter, cream, and every kid's favorite—ice cream.

The Industrial Revolution had begun to alter that landscape. As factories went up, cities grew. Workers flooded in from rural areas. More immigrants flocked to America.

Farming communities began to shrink. Sawmill, Pennsylvania, held on, with its flourishing sawmill and rock quarry, but many of our young men had been drawn away by the city's higher pay and exciting night life. Then there were those who'd gone off to fight that senseless war. Still, the population had remained close to 1,400—minus the few who'd died of the flu in recent days.

We lived in the little stone cottage John's parents had owned for 60 years. Martin and Elizabeth Gallagher raised two sons in the two-bedroom, one-bath dwelling. John and his older brother, Martin Jr., shared a bedroom. They also shared the chores, like cleaning out the horse stall and maintaining the garden tools, plus the outdoor work, like trimming the lawn and weeding the vegetable garden. As a reward they also shared every last piece of pie and every last cookie in the jar.

John admitted that they clashed now and then like most brothers do, but they also would run to the other's defense when threatened. Martin Jr. was the first to follow in their father's footsteps and chose city hospital work over the drudgery of small-town medicine. Strangely, that's exactly what appealed to John. He loved the challenge, loved getting his hands dirty. To say he was the more humble of the two was an understatement. Martin moved up in higher positions of authority in one of Philadelphia's finest hospitals, and he and his wife, Cecilia, set up house in a country estate along the city's Main Line with easy commute to his work in the city.

After Elizabeth passed away, Martin Sr. kept working for another year. Then he retired and moved in with Martin Jr. and his wife, Cecilia, and their four children. They had more than enough room in that five-bedroom mansion. The old man could lose himself among the flowering gardens or rock for hours in uninterrupted peace on the front porch.

John had no problem moving into the old house where he had grown up as a boy. For me it was a step up, considering where I'd come from. I willingly made the move, thrilled to be able to transition from the claustrophobic atmosphere of tenement living and grateful for a daily breath of fresh air.

The tiny four-room structure was built out of cobblestone from the nearby quarry. One window in each room let in a sufficient amount of daylight, and there were two entry doors, one leading to the front porch and the other opening to the backyard. To one side of the property Martin Sr. had framed out a large shed as a place to keep yard tools, and a separate horse stable for the short line of horses the family owned. He also had installed a 50-foot clothes line with T-shaped wooden poles at each end. In the early morning, when the sun was just coming up over the horizon, the shadows of the poles looked an awful lot like two of the crosses on Calvary. I sometimes imagined the cross of Christ positioned somewhere in the middle, protecting our yard from harm. Such thoughts often set me off with a song and a prayer, a good way to start my day. I often wondered if Greta could hear me belting out "Rock of Ages" or "The Old Rugged Cross" as I pinned our laundry to the line. I figured it might do her some good, might even draw her out of the house to join me in song.

The inside of our home—all of the walls and the ceilings—were built out of boards hewn at the local sawmill. We had an attic, but no basement, not even a crawl space, only a foundation of solid rocks. The little house provided all we needed—a wood-burning stove, a small refrigerator, a bathroom the size of a closet—but nevertheless a *real,* working bathroom—and two bedrooms, one appointed for the children, and the other containing a four-poster bed, a large bureau, and a free-standing closet for John and me.

I once asked John if we could turn our attic into a third bedroom for Johnny, an ideal spot for a young boy to dream in, whether awake or asleep. John adamantly refused.

"Johnny's too young. He might fall from the ladder and hurt himself," was his argument.

I shut my mouth about it but planned to bring it up again someday.

Our home had many conveniences some of our neighbors still did without. Just before we moved in John's father installed indoor plumbing and electricity.

It might have been a simple life for some, but for me it was sheer luxury. I'd grown up with six siblings crammed together in a run-down tenement in south Philly. The Italian immigrants had flooded into that section and called it "Little Italy." My father was a brick layer. He worked at menial jobs in different parts of the city earning 65 cents an hour or $28.60 for a 44-hour workweek. If not for my two brothers quitting school and taking construction jobs we might have starved. There were too many of us for my father to feed on his meager salary.

As it was, Papa didn't spend much time at home, except for Saturdays when he hid behind a newspaper or took a much-needed nap. On Sundays he made his presence known, insisting we all go to church together. Immediately after mass, we all rushed home and settled around the largest piece of furniture in our house, the red oak dining table that could seat Mama and Papa and all seven of us kids, plus my older sisters' husbands and any children they'd brought into the world.

Growing up with four sisters and two brothers, I learned to share not only my bedroom, but clothing, food, and anything else that crossed our doorstep.

During the early years of her marriage, Mama had given birth to two boys. Her first child, a premature baby, stopped breathing when he was a month old. The other, my older brother Joseph, died at the age of 17 of a bowel perforation from typhoid fever, a terrible disease that struck Philadelphia's crowded tenements in 1876. In those days the city drew its water supply from the Schuylkill and Delaware rivers. All sorts of industrial runoff and human waste had polluted those waterways and was getting into the drinking water. The residents soon learned they needed to boil the water, but not before most of the people became ill, including my brother Joseph who died two years before I was born. Sadly, after 20 years of typhoid attacks 5,400 people died, making Philadelphia's death toll from the disease among the highest in the nation.

For years afterward, I listened to Mama mourning over Joseph and how hard she'd struggled to save his life. For what must have been the 90th time, I sat on the floor at her feet and listened to her reminisce. I was getting ready to enter nursing school at the time. She used Joseph's illness to teach me about her personal methods of healing. She wanted to make sure I knew there were other ways to deal with symptoms besides little white pills.

I remember how she looked me in the eye, her face as serious as I'd ever seen it.

"First he had a fever." She shook her head and turned her attention to the wall, like she was seeing something there that I couldn't see. "I applied cool compresses and made a hot drink from the herbs on my windowsill." Then she looked me in the eye again and continued her monologue. "He complained of a headache. I soaked his feet in hot water to draw the blood away from his head. He vomited something awful, couldn't hold anything down. I fed him a few sips of ginger tea." She began to weep then, and she shook her head. "Nothing worked. Your brother kept getting worse. I called the doctor. And what did he do? He recommended a mild diet of soft-boiled eggs and beef broth. We didn't know his insides were messed up until it was too late."

There was little I could do to soothe my mother. It was as if she had to repeat the entire scene over and over again, and then she could cry and let it all out and be done with it until the next time.

One day Mama opened her jewelry case and pulled out a tattered, sepia-toned photograph of a teenage boy with a sparkle-eyed grin that had the power to melt any mother's heart.

"Your brother Joseph was going to be a priest." Mama stared off past the photo, her eyes filling with moisture. "He got good grades in school, read books all the time, especially his Bible. And he always helped me around the house. Not like Angelo and Tommy. Those two are into themselves. My Joseph should never have died."

Of course my mother didn't mean the other two should have died, only that she missed Joseph so much a part of her heart must have died with him.

As it turned out, more than a decade after Joseph died, the city installed a filtering system and several large reservoirs, all of which helped reduce the number of people who were dying of typhoid fever. Mayor Samuel Ashbridge had gotten things moving with a $12 million bond, but in the end the entire project of sand filtering and pipe construction ended up costing the city more than double that figure.

It was too late for Joseph, but the rest of us got to drink clean water without having to boil it. The clarity of our water got even better after they started adding chlorine, although it was hard to get used to that bitter, metallic taste.

I wish Joseph had lived. It would have been pleasant to have a nice older brother. I never knew him, but I got to know *about* him from Mama. She inserted little comments about his amazing attributes in random conversations, with never a negative remembrance coming to mind. To her, Joseph was a saint.

"Joseph didn't have a thing wrong with his health until the day he was hit by that bacteria," Mama wailed. "If only Joseph had lived. He was a good boy, a healthy boy, gave me no trouble. Not like your brother Angelo." She frowned at me, like it was my fault Angelo had turned out the way he had.

But I knew what she meant. The cops had brought Angelo home on several Friday nights, four hours after the city's 9 p.m. curfew. He gave Mama a lot of heartache during his teenage years.

"Stupido Testa! You're a stupid head!" she'd shout at my brother in front of the police. "You break-a my heart, Angelo. You break-a my heart."

Mama continued to grieve the loss of Joseph long after the rest of us had grown up and given her grandchildren. Even Angelo had turned his life around. He landed a high-paying job in construction, married a good, Catholic girl—to our mother's relief—and fathered four healthy grandchildren for her.

Mama told me so many heartbreaking stories about Joseph,

I began to grieve over the brother I had never known. Meanwhile, I merely tolerated the other two. They were bullies, especially toward us girls. Angelo loved to pull my hair, and Tommy teased me about my weight and called me 'String Bean Rosie.'"

Even after I started seeing John on a regular basis, my two brothers refused to let up. Whenever John came to the house they surrounded him, pressed him with questions about his intentions, made snide comments about me not getting any younger and what an awful cook I was.

The day John asked me to marry him came as a total surprise. We had taken a drive in the country. He parked his horse and buggy under the shade of an elm tree, and we sat on a bench beside a little pond where we tossed bread ends to the ducks. A young man and woman drifted by in a rowboat. A flock of birds soared overhead. The sun was at its peak. Its blinding rays spread silver ripples on the water. The surrounding trees cast a glass-like reflection on the edge of the pond.

I relished the warmth of the sun on my back, and I breathed deeply of jasmine and gardenias, their scents carried through the air by a gentle breeze.

I was about to open our picnic basket, when John surprised me by sliding off the bench and dropping onto his knee. It wasn't a major production, just a young man kneeling before his love and presenting her with a tiny circle of gold and a diamond in the middle. In my mind he was offering me more than a ring. He was offering me a life away from a noisy, congested household and two bothersome brothers. But more than that, John was offering me a future at his side. I couldn't think of anywhere else I'd rather be or anyone else I'd rather be with.

I would have followed him to the ends of the earth if necessary. As it was, I only had to move to the little cottage in Sawmill with just the two of us owning everything. No longer did I have to share clothes or hairbrushes or lipstick. I had my own house, not just a place to hang my hat when I came home after a hard day's work. No more daily chores dusting my mother's furniture and all her little knickknacks. I had my own place now, and I could furnish it as I wished.

I found that I enjoyed decorating our little cottage. Our large front room served as a canvas for all my needlework. The Gallaghers' age-old furnishings came to life beneath my crocheted throws and embroidered pillows.

We had ample space. I could take a deep breath that wasn't mixed with the smell of Tommy's pipe tobacco or the regurgitated puffs of beer from Angelo's foul mouth.

A wood-burning fireplace heated the entire living room and kitchen area. One long wall held John's pharmacy cupboards that contained a variety of medicines and powders, plus his microscope and an assortment of scalpels, saws, surgical tools, and several bottles of carbolic acid for disinfecting everything. The more potent items he shoved on the top shelf out of reach of Amy's tiny hands.

We had everything we needed right there in Sawmill. There was a general store and post office in one building, plus several little shops, and a section where local farmers peddled their fruits and vegetables. We used a horse and buggy for long trips into the city, or we grabbed a couple seats on the sawmill delivery wagon and traveled the 70 miles to Philadelphia, bouncing along on hard boards just so we could buy things we couldn't get in the village. I enjoyed searching through the newer fabrics and discovering unusual items for my kitchen. John replenished his medical supplies and often added some new gadget doctors were raving about, like the three-pronged bullet extractor he brought home one year but thankfully never got to use. Few people in Sawmill ended up getting shot. In fact, it's safe to say no one did.

By the time John and I settled in Sawmill, the industrial age had taken hold in the much larger cities. The filthy dregs and polluting smoke of the big city's factories had not yet invaded our sleepy little community. Our water was still pure. We were separate and self-sufficient in those days. Except for rare occasions when we traveled to the city, we went on with our lives without so much as a thought about the smog that had settled over a good part of Philadelphia.

Whenever we did venture into the city, I was struck with the noticeable change in the atmosphere. We had left behind the serene aura of country living—the sound of buzz saws, mocking birds, and baaing sheep—and we'd entered a cacophony of clanging trolleys, rattling cable cars, and the steady drone of subways. Even the air smelled different. Instead of the familiar aromas of corn mash and cow dung, we were struck by the sharp sting of manufacturing dross, the metallic taste of fresh-cut steel in the air, and in some neighborhoods, the emanation of garbage that hadn't yet been swept from the streets.

Then there was the ongoing noisy construction of sky-scrapers and huge, glass-fronted storefronts. And hoards of people. I was never prepared for the crowds and the fast-paced activity—men in dark suits rushing here and there, but with purpose. After an hour or so of being jostled about, I often urged John to please get us home, but not until I made sure I had an ample supply of wool stockings and enough fabric to make a couple of dresses for me and the girls and a few shirts for John and young Johnny.

All those memories seemed to come alive as I watched my husband depart for Philadelphia. Then reality set in. The memories faded amidst the falling leaves and the beads of moisture trickling down the window pane. Steam filled the room. I tugged my blouse away from my back. It clung again, pasted there by the mist.

Breathing a frustrated sigh, I removed two of the rattling pots and refilled the remaining one almost to the brim. I was placing the lone pot back on the stove when a knock sounded at the front door. I paused and held my breath. Another knock. It could only mean one thing. Somebody needed the doctor. With John away and his pharmacy swept clean, I didn't know what I could do to help anyone. I walked over and cracked open the door, but only an inch.

"Who's there?"

"It's me. Emma Wilson."

I was immediately reminded of her little boy who had died. "Oh, Emma, I'm so sorry for your loss."

She began to weep. "Thank you, Rosie."

"I'm sorry I wasn't there for you."

"I understand. But now I need help. My other two boys have fevers. It's an awful lot like what happened to Robbie. Can John come to the house?"

I held the door barely open. "Oh, Emma. John has gone to the city for supplies. He'll be home tonight, I think."

"Please, Rosie." Her voice was filled with anxiety. "I can't lose my boys. You're a nurse. Can't you do something?"

"I *was* a nurse, Emma. A long time ago. I delivered babies and doctored minor wounds. Now I'm simply a mother, like you. I can't come to your home, but I can tell you what to do."

I explained how we'd made Amy comfortable, how we'd brought her fever down with cool cloths, and how we'd kept the room moist with steam from the kettles.

"If you have aspirin, give each of your boys one tablet. When John gets back I'll send him over. Will you be all right until then?"

"Yes, I guess so." Her voice cracked and she fell into pathetic sobbing.

My heart broke for her. Still, I refused to open the door any farther.

"What did you do with Robbie?" I needed to know. Had she buried him immediately to stop the spread of germs? Or perhaps she'd done like others had—wrapped his body in a sheet and placed him in a back room with the door shut until the undertaker could come for him.

Emma fell silent, but she hadn't moved off my porch. I could hear her breathing on the other side of the door.

A sudden chill gripped me. What if she pushed her way in? What if she brought her children's sickness into my house? It was bad enough Amy was sick, but my daughter might not have the influenza. It could be a simple stomach bug. Emma's boy had suffered all the bad symptoms. Raging fever. Coughing up blood. Delirium. I needed to protect my family.

Carefully, I edged the door shut and turned the lock. The loud click resounded in the crisp morning air. I stood very still, listening, barely breathing. Footsteps moved off the porch and down the front steps, then crunched along the icy path. I went back to the front window and peered between the droplets of moisture sliding down the pane. Emma's dark shadow glided down the street toward her home several houses away. A memory surfaced.

It wasn't long ago when Emma and I walked together down this very street, pushing our baby carriages, my daughter Lily in one and Emma's son Robbie in the other. We shared recipes, laughed together, talked about the funny things our children said and did.

We belonged to the same sewing circle and sometimes gathered in each other's houses for tea and scones. Besides Emma there was Grace Duncan, Marge Offenbach, and Felina Gray—an amiable group of women who threw baby showers and held charity events. Then the flu hit. If I passed those women on the street now, I'd probably run the other way for fear they might cough or sneeze in my direction. I shunned the men the same way, afraid they might spit on the sidewalk or blow cigar smoke at me.

As Emma's hunched form moved slowly down the street, I had a sudden urge to run after her and wrap my arms around her. My friend needed comfort. I returned to the door. I hated what I'd become.

I reached for the latch but stopped short of opening the door. This was what the pandemic had done to us. We'd become a self-protective, self-serving people. We wore masks. We kept our distance from friends. No more hugs. No more handshakes. No more club meetings or parties or church picnics. We fiercely guarded our homes and our families, all the while turning our backs on our neighbors. Our friends had become our enemies. Our homes had turned into fortresses.

As a trained nurse and a woman of faith, I found my behavior unthinkable. A horrible realization seized my heart.

I was no better than the soldiers who fled from the battlefield. No better than the people who stood at a distance during the crucifixion of Jesus.

I dropped into a chair, raised my elbows to the table, and put my face in my hands.

"Please, God, help me do the right thing. Show me how I can help my neighbors and still protect my children. I am at a loss without John. I beg you, remove this horrible illness from the earth. Get us back to the way things used to be."

The way things used to be? What did that mean anymore? I couldn't remember what *used to be* was like. I wept freely. Wept for my neighbors. Wept for my children. Wept for John somewhere out there, on his way to Philadelphia. Maybe he'll get the supplies he needs and head for home, eager to get back to his wife and family.

Until he returned, all I could do was continue to care for my own. I filled the pot with water whenever it ran low. I roused the little ones and fed them breakfast. The hours ticked slowly by. I helped Johnny and Lily with their lessons and allowed them time to play—away from Amy. Meanwhile, I got her sipping different liquids, checked her temperature often, and helped her to the bathroom when she needed to go. She slept most of the time, and when she was awake she lay staring at the ceiling. A terrible fear raged within me, because I didn't know which way she might go. She appeared to be improving, and at one point she even asked for a book to read. Shortly after, she dropped the book on the floor and fell asleep, her breathing labored.

Every so often someone knocked at our door. I refused to open it and gave them the same advice I had given Emma.

By suppertime another knock broke through the stillness.

Like all the other times I didn't open the door, merely responded through the weathered boards.

"Who's there?"

"Hello, Mrs. Gallagher. It's me, David Cowell."

The man who operated the general store and post office. He had the town's only telephone, a wall-hung, coin-operated box that everybody used.

"I have a message from your husband. He telephoned a few minutes ago."

I flicked the lock and opened the door. Poor old David stood there shivering inside a heavy wool jacket, his face half-hidden behind a mask. I reached for the paper in his hand, said a quick, "Thank you," and shut the door in his face. My nerves on edge, I squinted at David's scrawled notations.

Made it to Philly. No luck buying anything. Red Cross desperate for doctors and nurses. I'm going to stay and help. Love, John.

Chapter Four

Early the next morning more people came to my door—every one of them asking for John and begging for medicines I didn't have. Speaking through the closed door, I gave them the same advice I had given Emma Wilson. Disinfect everything. Boil water to put steam in the room, bring down the fever, feed the patient dribbles of water, tea, and broth, and most important of all, keep the healthy members of the family separated from the sick.

I finished each conversation with a promise that John would be sure to visit them upon his return. As each of my neighbors departed, I added more names to my list of the sick. As the list grew longer I became more anxious. My husband had a huge task ahead of him. The long trip would certainly take its toll, and only God knew what sort of horrors he was facing in Philadelphia.

I prayed that my neighbors were able to hold on until John returned. If anyone died, I would blame myself for not doing enough. The truth was ever before me. I was trained as a nurse. I had attended one of the Florence Nightingale schools of nursing. In preparation for my graduation, I repeated the Nightingale Pledge, over and over again, until it was embedded in my mind. It was the nurse's version of the Hippocratic Oath the doctors take. Once again the words surfaced in my mind as clearly as when I first learned them.

I repeated the promise in a whisper, so I wouldn't awaken Amy. "*I solemnly pledge myself before God and in the presence of this assembly, to pass my life in purity and to practice my profession faithfully. I will abstain from whatever is deleterious and mischievous, and will not take or knowingly administer any harmful drug. I will do all in my power to maintain and elevate the standard of my profession, and will hold in confidence all personal matters committed to my keeping and all family affairs coming to my knowledge in the practice of my calling. With loyalty will I endeavor to aid the physician in his work, and devote myself to the welfare of those committed to my care.*"

A tear traveled down my cheek, like a punctuation mark to the words I had shoved to the back of my mind. When had I left my calling? What had become of the dream I'd held onto from the time I was a child? Early on in my life I thought about becoming a nurse. I wanted to take care of people who were hurting, not only to deal with physical illnesses, but also psychological and emotional problems as well. The Florence Nightingale training taught us to heal the whole person—body, soul, and spirit. I had failed on all three counts. Emma had walked away from my house defeated. How many other people had I sent away feeling helpless and alone? I was so concerned about the health of my own family I had neglected my original calling.

With these thoughts pressing on my mind I went about the rest of the morning in a sort of stupor, merely going through the motions, cleaning what needed to be cleaned, cooking what needed to be cooked, and planning the day's activities for my children. Their meals. Their schoolwork.

Their playtime. Everything programmed the way people do at a worksite, with only the noon whistle to tell them when they should take a break or the five o'clock blast allowing them to leave for the day. I had my own time clock, and it didn't involve the needs of anyone outside my home.

Shoving my guilt to the back of my mind I went to check on Amy. I felt her forehead. Her temperature had returned to near normal. She opened her eyes and gazed about the room in confusion.

"How did I get here?" She frowned and looked down at her nightdress. "This isn't the one I wore to bed last night. What happened to my clothes?"

I propped pillows behind her and helped her sit upright. "You suffered a terrible bout of stomach distress," was all I told her. "You're fine now." I gathered her damp locks behind her head and fastened them there with a couple of hairpins from my pocket.

"I'm hungry," she said to my delight.

That was a good sign. "I'll fix you some breakfast." I hurried to the stove, ladled some freshly made oatmeal into a bowl and took it to her. She grabbed it out of my hand and plunged the spoon in.

"You need to regain your strength, Amy, but take your time."

She nodded, took a couple slow spoonfuls, and then steadily cleaned the bowl. Color returned to my daughter's face. Her cheeks flushed a soft pink. A hint of a sparkle settled in her dark brown eyes. I mouthed a silent thank you to God, though I wasn't certain the danger had passed. I needed to keep an eye on Amy throughout the rest of the day and be ready to interrupt whatever I was doing if she needed me.

Moments later the front room came alive as Johnny and

Lily tumbled in, roused from sleep and ready for breakfast. Johnny caught sight of Amy on the sofa.

"What's goin' on?" He took a step toward his sister. "Why is Amy on the sofa?"

I put up a hand and stopped him. "You need to keep your distance, son. Amy had a bad time of it yesterday, but I think she's better now. It doesn't matter. You stay away from her for the rest of the day. You hear me? And keep Lily away from her too."

He nodded but his face screwed up in puzzlement. My heart broke for Johnny. My rambunctious eight-year-old had been made to suppress a ton of energy since the flu struck our village. I couldn't let him go to the playground in the park. He hadn't seen his friends in several weeks. Keeping him confined to the house was like trying to stop a runaway train from running away. Yet, I had no other options.

Mayor Barnes had shut down our schoolhouse, both churches, and most of the smaller stores in town. Only the general store remained open out of necessity, so we could fill our cupboards with canned foods and purchase incidentals like Colgate Dental Cream and Johnson & Johnson Baby Power.

I let my kids play in the backyard for short periods. I was concerned that their squeals and shouts might upset the widow Schmidt. The few times when I took them out back, she glared at them through her window, her arms crossed and her lips mouthing words thankfully muffled behind the plate glass. Not only had she insulted my husband, now she was turning on my little ones.

I turned my attention to my son, and my heart melted with sympathy. "Do you want some oatmeal? Or how about some sausage and eggs?"

Johnny gave a little boy shrug and went to the table. Lily followed him and sat beside him. She stared at me, her chocolate brown eyes wide and questioning.

"It'll be all right, Lily." I pulled a link of sausage from the icebox and tossed it in a hot fry pan, momentarily distracted by the instant sizzle and spatter of grease. A tantalizing farmhouse aroma filled my kitchen. I scrambled some eggs, grated in a sprinkle of sharp cheddar, and dished everything into three plates.

I set our breakfast on the table. The three of us held hands while I said the blessing. As soon as we said, "Amen," Johnny reached for his fork.

Lily turned inquisitive eyes on me, and her chin began to quiver. "Where's Papa?"

"He's gone to the city for medicine." I looked from one to the other. "He'll be coming home tonight, maybe in time for supper."

In my heart I hoped I had told them the truth. To the kids yesterday had seemed like a typical workday. Sometimes John returned in time for supper. Sometimes he didn't get home until hours after they'd gone to bed. But now they hadn't seen him for more than 24 hours. Of course they'd wonder where he was.

"We're going to be fine, kids," I assured them. "Now eat up."

I forced a smile. The truth was, I didn't know for certain we'd be fine. Nor was I certain John would make it home that night. His message didn't say how long he planned to stay in Philadelphia. Only that he was there to help. That could mean days. Or weeks.

I ate my breakfast with a cloud of images swirling in and out of my head. John hovering over a dying patient. John racing from one bed to another. John following the orders of the doctors in charge, giving them every last ounce of strength he possessed.

I turned my attention to Amy. She'd set the empty bowl on the floor and was sleeping peacefully again. Perhaps she'd passed the worst of her illness. But for how long? I'd heard the rumors. This particular flu was unlike any other we'd experienced in the past. This one began like most influenzas. Sometimes the symptoms appeared to diminish, then they returned with a vengeance. One minute a person rose from bed, seemingly cured. The next minute he collapsed and died. More often than not, the victims had gotten well. Then there were those who stopped breathing within hours of the first symptom. Unpredictable. That was the best description for this particular influenza.

I didn't know for certain that Amy hadn't gotten the flu at all. Perhaps she'd eaten something that turned her stomach. She didn't have the typical flu symptoms. She wasn't coughing or sneezing. But she'd had a raging fever. John never gave a diagnosis, merely told me what to do to take care of her. Then he'd left. How I wished he'd come home. The truth was, having a doctor in the family didn't make me feel as secure as some people might think. Most of the time my husband was off curing someone else.

I finished my breakfast and continued to keep an eye on Amy, alert for any changes. My nurse's training had kicked in for a while. I'd gotten away from the canning and the baking, the sewing and the ironing, and had begun to think like a Florence Nightingale trainee again. The bookwork and lectures had fueled me with enough information to be able to recognize a serious illness and treat the symptoms.

I'd learned to make a diagnosis, and I'd spent long hours on my feet at the hospital caring for this patient and that patient, each showing different symptoms, each requiring a different medicine or treatment.

I found myself washing my hands often again, like I used to do when moving from one cubicle to the next. Other than Ignaz Semmelweis, the Hungarian doctor who promoted washing of the hands between patients, Florence Nightingale was the greatest proponent of sanitary methods in hospital care. Most of all, hers was the leading voice in that tender loving care we nurses were famous for.

All of a sudden, I was a nurse in my own home. But it wasn't that different from being a mother, was it? Without thinking about it, I'd been practicing nursing for the last 16 years, caring for my children the way a nurse would care for a patient in a hospital, but with a sacrificial love people don't often feel for a stranger.

Grabbing the children's schoolbooks, I called Johnny and Lily to the table. Johnny picked up his reader and started another chapter. Lily grabbed a crayon and drew purple circles on a sheet of paper. I guided her hand and tried to help her turn those circles into recognizable letters of the alphabet. At three years of age she should have moved past the circles, maybe printed some semblance of an A or a B. I left her to her scribbling and helped Johnny with his multiplication tables. Lily became bored and went off to play with her alphabet blocks in a corner of the kitchen I'd set up as a play area.

At mid-afternoon, Amy woke up and asked me to bring her a novel she'd been reading—*Little Women* by Louisa May Alcott. Except for once or twice when I helped her to the bathroom, she remained on the sofa, immersed in that book. I made sure she had plenty of liquids—water, tea, and chicken broth.

Still, I kept interrupting her reading to check her vitals. I placed my hand on her forehead again. Normal, or close to it. I pressed my fingers against her wrist and checked her pulse. It was slow, maybe too slow. If John came home he could take some blood and check her urine. He had the tools—and the training. I didn't. I knew how to bring a baby into the world, how to nurse a surgical patient back to health, how to administer anesthesia and give a vaccine for typhoid fever. But I hadn't used John's microscope and many of the other pieces of medical equipment in his cupboard; never had a reason to.

One time I peered through the lens of his microscope and asked him what I was looking for on those little slides.

He turned a crinkled eye at me and grinned. "They're blood and sputum cultures," he said, sounding much like a biology teacher. "I'm looking for bacteria."

I shook my head, stepped back, and observed from a distance as he moved one slide after another onto the little stage. He released an occasional "Hmmm," but never told me what he'd seen on that tiny piece of glass. Bacteria? If he found any germs, what might he do about them? Did they tell him what medicine to try? Or did they provide clues so he could develop a treatment of some kind?

I'd been content with the way medicine had advanced, before we thought about germs and flu bugs and death. Why couldn't we just deliver more babies? At least, those were happy times.

As it was, most of the time we treated the symptoms. If a patient had aches and pains along with a fever, John prescribed aspirin or salicin, both of which were extracted from willow bark. If pneumonia had progressed to a secondary stage, a shot of epinephrine sufficed. A patient who couldn't breath would be given bottled oxygen.

With our limited resources in those early days I sometimes found myself depending on some of my mother's home remedies. When I was a young girl living at home, my mama came up with a whole slew of cures lurking right there in her own kitchen. If I had a fever, she added a few shakes of cinnamon to a glass of milk and insisted I drink it all at once. If I had a cold, she rubbed Vicks VapoRub on my chest. She cured achy muscles with a warm bath spiked with lavender oil, and she spread the ooze from a cactus leaf over cuts and scrapes.

Now that Amy had become ill, and the threat of influenza hovered, I began to consider some of my mother's home remedies. I had a jar of Vicks in my old nurse's kit, and I was certain I had enough herbs and spices in my pantry to set up my own little homegrown apothecary.

I glanced around the room. Johnny had joined Lily in the corner of my kitchen. They were playing with her alphabet blocks, building little houses and setting them up in a row like the ones on our street outside. Amy had remained on the sofa and was well into her book. As for me, I hovered, like a nervous mother hen with one eye looking out for the fox and the other guarding my nest of baby chicks. It was exhausting.

My life was less complicated before the children came along. John and I worked from dawn to dusk and never got tired. We were doing what we both loved to do. Then three other people came into our lives. They depended on us to keep them well and safe, and we also had to stay healthy ourselves so we could continue to care for them. I'm not complaining.

I love my role as a mother as much as or more than my role as a nurse. But I haven't delivered a baby in several years. I miss the joy that such an occasion brings. I looked forward to being the first person to hold a newborn child. I saw each one as another miracle.

I learned midwifery early in life having grown up with three older sisters, all of them married and bearing children of their own. When my eldest sister went into labor, I watched from her bedroom doorway. The midwife invited me closer and explained each step as she brought my nephew into the world. When my next sister gave birth, I assisted. Then, at the birth of my third sister's child, I handled the delivery while the midwife looked on. I was 16 years old at the time—Amy's age.

The experience planted within me the seeds to pursue a career in nursing. The day I turned 18, I entered one of the nurse training programs in Philadelphia. By this time there were nearly 800 nurse training schools throughout the nation, most of them controlled by different hospitals. Many of them followed the Florence Nightingale principle of caring for the sick. Aside from reading assignments and attending a lecture now and then, we nursing students—primarily women—learned our trade almost entirely through the hands-on care of patients inside the hospital. We accompanied doctors on their rounds, then stayed behind to continue caring for a particular patient. At times we were called to the operating room where we administered anesthesia and kept track of the instruments on the surgical table.

Most importantly of all, the Florence Nightingale model of nursing required that, over and above all our other duties, we needed to make the patient as comfortable as possible.

The rules were simple. Provide plenty of healthy foods and keep the patient hydrated with pure drinking water and tea. We were instructed to keep their immediate environment dust-free, well-ventilated, and at a comfortable temperature. If the hospital room was cold, we added more blankets or turned up the heat, and for buildings that had a furnace, this also meant we sometimes had to bring in a few nuggets of coal. Not a pleasant task since black coal dust stained the front of our uniforms, and our hands had to be scrubbed clean.

Needless to say, strict hygiene practices were encouraged. The Nightingale schools also taught us to address our patients' spiritual and emotional wellbeing along with their physical care. Apart from changing soiled bandages or administering medicines prescribed by the doctors, most of our time was spent feeding, bathing, and comforting patients like they were our own little children.

Back then training was simpler. Not like today when there are hundreds of medicines to memorize, plus a whole slew of illnesses with Latin names I can't pronounce.

Most of the time patients came in with a severe cold or influenza, sometimes a broken arm or leg. Occasionally, we dealt with more serious problems such as a heart attack or a head injury. We were expected to handle everything with confidence tempered with tenderness.

The hospital I trained at had five floors, each floor divided into different wards. Each ward contained one huge common room for women and a separate common room for men. Smaller private rooms were reserved for the more serious cases or for the wealthy patients who insisted on having privacy and paid well for it.

My schooling took two years. Much of the hands-on

training took place at a hospital where I delivered babies, learned to administer ether, and cared for patients recovering from surgery. Then there was a whole slew of duties patients expected of us angels in white. Among other things, Florence Nightingale introduced the little call bell a patient was able to use for any number of requests. The tinkle of that bedside bell would get most of us flying to a room, only to find out that the patient wanted to know what kind of bird that was perched outside her window.

On days away from the hospital I went to various lecture halls where doctors explained the basics of effective patient care while also slipping in a quick primer on the authority of the doctor.

With a sense of pride I donned the traditional nurse's attire—a long white dress with a hem that skimmed the ankles and wrist-length sleeves that could be pushed back to the elbows. We wore a tri-corner cap and ugly black lace-up shoes with one-inch heels. We carried a supply of gauze masks in our pockets along with a stethoscope and a thermometer.

I plunged into my chosen career with the enthusiasm of a child unleashed on a playground. I enjoyed caring for the sick and helping them recover after an operation or from a debilitating illness. The hours were long and taxing. I was on my feet most of the time. But I didn't want to sit behind a desk and answer a telephone, or clean people's houses, or any of the other menial jobs available to people who, like me, grew up in the tenements.

At least once a day my best friend Olive and I managed to slip out of the building and catch a smoke out back by the trash disposal bins. We'd lean against the hospital wall and discuss procedures we'd learned during the day. We joked about the doctors who either snapped orders or made a pass at us with a wink or the brush of a hand. Olive inhaled the smoke into her lungs. I chose to take small puffs and released little clouds into the air. The smell of the burned out match and the smoldering tobacco masked the odor rising from the garbage bins nearby.

We didn't care, we'd taken a break, though brief. We could look up at a star-speckled sky and, for the moment, we could forget about the woman who died that morning in Room 4-B and the man in 3-C who complained about his lumpy mattress. We could step away from the operating room doctors who breathed curses down our necks if we didn't respond fast enough or if we handed them the wrong instrument.

It was during one of those smoking escapes that my career pretty much came to an end.

Chapter Five

U nable to find Olive, I went outside alone this time, my precious pack of Chesterfields in my pocket. I'd be gone for a few minutes. Just needed a break and a quick smoke. I'd left the bedside of a young boy who'd come in with a severe stomach ache. Five minutes. That's all I needed after spending nine hours going from one cubicle to another. I made a brief check on the boy. He was resting peacefully, so I left the building.

I'd been gone a little longer than I had intended, long enough for all kinds of commotion to break loose. When I entered the building, blue lights were flashing. A garbled code echoed from a box on the wall. Doctors and nurses were rushing toward the operating room at the far end of the hall. I hurried to the boy's room. His bed was empty. A cold panic rushed to my face. I gripped the bed's guardrail, caught my breath, then hurried toward the excitement.

Olive met me in the hallway, her face twisted with concern. "Where were you?"

"Out back."

"Yeah, I can smell the smoke residue on your uniform. Haven't I taught you anything? You're supposed to stand upwind."

"What's going on?"

"They took your patient to the OR. Severe appendicitis attack. I think it ruptured."

I clapped a hand over my mouth. My head began to reel. "What should I do, Olive?"

She grabbed my upper arms. "Calm down. Just wait until after the operation is done. Hopefully the boy will come through just fine. You'll need to apologize to your supervisor for leaving your watch. There's nothing you can do right now, Rosie."

"Will you wait with me?"

"Can't. I'm supposed to be getting the vitals on that old woman they brought in this morning." She stepped back and frowned at me. "Don't you have other patients?"

I nodded, but my mind was on the operating room. An entire team of doctors and nurses had disappeared behind those doors. I should have been with them.

We parted there in the hall. Olive headed off to the east wing. I hovered for a few minutes, my eyes on the double doors at the end of the hall. With anxiety building inside me, I turned away and went about my work. The time passed far too slowly. I kept checking my watch, kept stepping out in the hall, waiting for any sign of activity.

Two hours later, my supervisor called me to her office. Mary Pritchard was one of the former nurse trainees who had been asked to stay on as supervisors. Most of the other nurses in her class had left the hospital to work in private family care or for any number of doctors who had their own practices. A fresh group of nursing trainees had taken their place at the hospital. I was one of them.

Now I stood before Mary like a naughty schoolgirl in front of her teacher. She wasn't attractive, had a sharp nose and thick eyebrows, but she had a sweet spirit, always smiled at me when we passed in the hall, and often complemented my work. I silently prayed that her sweet spirit might prevail. But the wave of creases on her forehead troubled me.

"Your little patient died."

Mary's words were crisp and to the point.

Gasping, I gripped the back of a chair. The boy had died, and I was responsible. I'd neglected my duty. I hadn't even asked someone to fill in for me while I took a break. I just had to have that smoke, didn't I?

"I don't have to ask where you were or what you were doing," Mary began. "I can smell the stale odor of smoke on your uniform. The point is, you left your post and something terrible happened while you were gone."

I bowed my head and waited for the final blow. It didn't come.

Mary softened her tone. "I need to tell you, nurse Falcini, it wouldn't have made any difference if you'd been standing right next to the boy's bed. His appendix had already ruptured, and the poison had swept through his body. The poor kid didn't have a chance."

I breathed a little easier, but a web of guilt continued to grip me. For the first time a child had died while under my care. I had nursed back to health numerous people who looked like they had one foot in the grave. I later wheeled them out the door to waiting vehicles, and I received thank you cards from them after they left the hospital. I even stood at the bedside of a dying woman and held her hand until she was gone. Mine was the last face she saw.

But I wasn't prepared to lose a six-year-old boy.

"No charges are being filed," Mary assured me, "but if you're the kind of nurse I think you are, you'll carry this with you for the rest of your life."

My future changed that day. The hospital administrators decided to drop me from the training. I not only had shirked my duty, but I'd done it to smoke a cigarette, breaking still another rule. I wasn't going to graduate.

That evening, I fell on my face before God, spilled out my guilt, and pleaded with him to forgive me. Then I threw away every pack of cigarettes I owned except for one. I kept it as a reminder of that little six-year-old boy and the worst mistake I'd ever made in my life. Whenever I started to forget, "Id pull out that one pack of Chesterfields and stare at it long enough to remember. Then I'd put it away until the next time I forgot. Never again did I smoke a cigarette or even want to.

A few months later Olive graduated with honors. I knew the truth. She smoked like a chimney, but got away with it. She walked off with a diploma and was honored during the Florence Nightingale pinning ceremony. The hospital brought in a whole new batch of nursing trainees. Hopefully none of them would make the mistake I had.

Though I didn't get a diploma or a pin, I'd had enough training to want to keep pursuing my original dream. I couldn't do home-based nursing, which paid well, because no one wanted to hire a caregiver who hadn't earned a diploma. It didn't matter. Though such a position promised a little freedom it tied the nurse to the demands of the rich. Such situations often turned trained nurses into full-time servants.

Olive had chosen midwifery. With no doctors looking over her shoulder she was pretty much her own boss. She could step outside and smoke a whole pack of cigarettes if she wanted to. And she could get married, something none of the hospitals or private doctors allowed. For some reason beyond my understanding those medical professionals assumed we couldn't do both—provide sufficient care to our patients and raise families of our own.

Still hanging onto my original dream of caring for the sick and delivering babies, I signed on with a back-street shelter, where the pay was low but words of appreciation ran high. I was a shade above being a volunteer, but I was able to use my experiences from the hospital to care for people who couldn't afford to go to a doctor. Fewer rules and restrictions made up for the loss of a bulging pay envelope. Instead of being bossed, *I* was the boss. I had a small office, barely bigger than a phone booth, but it was well stocked with bandages, iodine, aspirin, and other basic medical supplies. In addition to caring for the women and children in the shelter, I went to the homes of the poor, delivered babies, patched scrapes and cuts, applied tourniquets, and most of the time I merely listened to someone who needed to talk. The more serious injuries and illnesses I sent to the hospital in the city.

I dealt with a variety of nationalities. Immigrants had flooded into the slums of Philly, giving me an entire community of patients to treat. They'd come from Lithuania, Italy, Germany, and Sweden. I responded to homes where I didn't understand a word they said. In the end I relied on simple sign language and drawings to help me diagnose whatever was wrong.

One day I was called to a home where a small boy of about seven had set his shirt on fire while playing with matches. He had second degree burns on his chest and left arm. I cleansed his skin, then I pulled out a jar of Vaseline and applied gobs of it over his wounds. I was in the middle of applying strips of clean linen, when a man cleared his throat and drew my attention to the doorway.

A stranger leaned against the doorpost, his arms crossed, a twist of amusement on his brow. Everything about him was a contradiction. He wasn't tall for a man, maybe 5-foot, 6-inches, but his broad shoulders and large hands told me he was strong. Perhaps he'd done a little boxing or maybe worked at a heavy duty job. His full head of red hair gave him the appearance of a cuddly rag doll, but his sharp green eyes spoke of deep intellectual wisdom. His approving smile belied his square jaw. He wore a doctor's lab coat with a stethoscope protruding from its pocket, yet his casual demeanor didn't match the pinch-lipped air of superiority I'd discovered among the doctors I'd trained under at the hospital. He'd completed the same medical training as the others, but I sensed he wasn't the kind who barked orders if the nurse grabbed the wrong instrument or responded too slowly in the operating room.

My heart did a little flip, something that had never happened to me before in the presence of a young man. I had two older brothers—pests, if you will—but I could stand up to them when needed. Something unseen stirred within me. I didn't feel threatened. On the contrary, I caught myself blushing.

He stood very still until I finished wrapping the boy's wounds. I nearly crumbled under his steady gaze. My hands felt like limp dishrags. It was amazing that I was able to secure the bandages. I hoped the young stranger hadn't noticed my nervousness. I waited for the usual criticism.

He didn't say a word.

The job completed, I gave the boy a loving pat and rose to my feet. Still unsure of myself, I turned to face the man in the doorway, transfixed by his piercing green eyes. The roll of gauze slipped from my fingers and bounced onto the dirty floor, now worthless. Before I could pick it up, he reached past me, grabbed it, and hurled it into a trash bin. He moved with the dexterity I'd seen in teenage boys playing catch in the streets.

"I'm John Gallagher," he said, straightening. His gentle tone and ready smile disarmed me. He extended his right hand.

I wiped traces of Vaseline from my fingers and onto my smock. Then, shyly, I gripped his outstretched hand. "I'm Rose. Rose Falcini."

"Ah, Italian. I should have guessed."

"Pardon me?"

He shrugged. "Your black, curly hair and those exotic, dark eyes of yours." His comment set me back a little. I wasn't accustomed to men talking about my eyes or my hair, except when my brothers made fun of me.

"My parents came from Italy years ago," I said, recovering. "I was born here. I consider myself an American."

His smile broadened. "I see." He turned his attention to the boy's injury, now hidden beneath the bandages. "You did a fantastic job wrapping what appeared to be a serious burn. Your little patient never cried out. Not once. You have a gentle way about you, Rosie." His eyebrows went up. "May I call you Rosie?"

My cheeks burned as if every drop of blood in my veins had rushed there. All I could do was nod. My brothers and sisters called me Rosie. So why not?

This street doctor was a refreshing change from the stone-faced physicians who were in charge in the operating rooms. Hidden behind swaths of white and masks that covered most of their faces, they ruled us trainees with unnerving superiority. When the masks came off, more disapproval flowed from their pursed lips. I often came away feeling belittled and hopeless, ready to quit the nursing field and take a job cleaning houses, or worse, learn how to type. I couldn't see myself stuck in an office from nine to five.

But this man had not criticized my work. He'd praised it. I stared in awe at someone who had earned the right to feel superior but hadn't seized it.

"Rosie," he said again, as though testing my name. I loved the sound of it on his lips.

He tilted his head. "I've been looking for a nurse, someone who knows how to keep a patient calm while providing care. Like you just did with that little boy. A real nurse. Not like my last one." He chuckled. "I sent that one away last week after she got an old woman shrieking for mercy."

I suppressed a smile. He'd called me a "real nurse." If only he knew the truth.

I gestured toward the end of the alley where the boy's family lived. His mother and four siblings had lined up in the narrow opening next to a toilet they shared with other families in the building. Two of the kids had runny noses.

"I have plenty of work to do right here," I told this doctor named Gallagher.

He nodded. "Yes. As do I."

I had a sudden desperate need to protect my heart. Dare I dream that this could become more than a casual meeting on the streets? I looked down at my bloodstained smock. I had come there directly from another tenement where I'd just delivered a baby.

Suddenly, I also became conscious of my unruly hair. I ran my fingers through it in a vain attempt to give it some order. I looked at my hands. Far from feminine, they were scarred from the lye soap I used multiple times a day. I slipped them out of sight behind my back.

I stared at those captivating green eyes and fumbled for something to say.

"Shouldn't you be in one of those city hospitals with the other physicians?" My remark sounded cold, almost like a rejection. I blinked back my embarrassment. "I'm sorry, I didn't mean—"

He shrugged. "It seems this is where God has called me." He waved a hand at the filthy tenement walls that rose on either side of us, the cement floor, wet with slime, dingy laundry clinging to a rope strung high above the alley. "To be honest, I work in the city part of the time," he admitted a little sheepishly. "I receive an adequate salary. Then I carve out a few hours to tend to these poor souls. Someone has to, don't you agree?"

I found his modesty quite endearing. I narrowed my eyes and tried to look deeper into the soul of this contradiction of mankind. I couldn't look any farther than his cocksure grin and those fascinating emerald eyes.

"You seem different from the doctors I've met in the past," I admitted. "Most of them are in it for the fame and fortune a career in medicine promises. They live in large houses with servants to do their bidding, and they prance up and down the hospital corridors like they're gods."

I could almost hear my mother's disparaging *tsk-tsk*. She didn't approve of such insolence regarding such an honored profession. But I didn't falter. Perhaps this one also did his own share of prancing when he wasn't dirtying his hands in the slums.

"I left the hospital for that very reason." His response eased my heart. Perhaps I'd misjudged him.

"This is where I belong." He waved his arm again, this time at the crowd gathering in the alley. "In the trenches, with common people who can't get the life-saving medicines so often reserved for the rich."

"They can't pay much," I reminded him.

"True. That's why I continue my work in the city. I raise enough funds to keep a roof over my head and food on the table. Then I'm free to care for the poor without any monetary expectations." He gazed into my eyes, and I was held captive by that sudden swell of green. I caught my breath.

"Are you willing to join me in my work, Rosie?"

Once again I blushed. I pondered my options. I could keep going as I had been, starving myself for lack of an income, depending on my two worthless brothers to bring the bacon home. Or I could join John Gallagher as his nurse, get paid a regular salary, and continue to help the helpless, but this time at the side of a man I could respect. I'd be able to contribute to my family's expenses—a plus to my father—and I could keep on nursing the way I had chosen, on the back streets of Philadelphia.

John gave me a hopeful smile. I caught myself nodding.

"Is that a yes?" he said, his green eyes sparkling with anticipation.

"I guess it is, Dr. Gallagher."

"No. No more Dr. Gallagher. It's John. Just call me John." He was grinning like he'd just found a cure for the measles. I couldn't help but return his smile. It was that contagious.

Chapter Six

So began my relationship with Dr. John Gallagher, rebel physician, a man who'd followed his heart instead of his wallet. Thankfully he didn't ask to see my degree, didn't quiz me about why I was working in the streets instead of in a sterile office somewhere. He offered to pay me $5 a day, but he warned me that the hours promised to be long and arduous.

He didn't lie. We worked from dawn to dusk and sometimes far into the night. But I didn't mind. Those long days kept me away from my pesky brothers. And I gleaned many valuable experiences working alongside a professional who explained things in a kind and patient manner. Every morning I flew out of bed and donned my nurse's smock, eager for another day with this captivating man. Not only was I learning *from* him, I was learning *about* him.

We worked well together. I surprised John many times by handing him what he needed from his medical bag without him having to ask for it. I knew the name and function of each instrument—scalpels, scissors, tweezers, catgut and horse hair, stethoscope, thermometer, splints, tourniquets, and several medicines. There were also tools he rarely used—an amputation saw, a circumcision knife, and a hemorrhoid severing device—gadgets that caused me to cringe at the mere sight of them.

I carried along my own kit filled with nursing items—forceps and tongs, plenty of gauze and strips of linen, plus iodine, alcohol, and some herbal compounds known for their numbing properties.

The two of us made quite an interesting picture as John drove his horse and buggy into the heart of no man's land. There I sat, perched high on the seat beside him, feeling like a queen surveying her kingdom, ready to help her subjects wherever needed. I turned my head from side to side, searching unmarked buildings with no clue where to find the sick unless a frantic relative came running up to our buggy. As soon as we entered a particular district, word spread that a doctor and nurse had come to the neighborhood. People flowed out of doorways as though a dam had broken. They surrounded our buggy, pleaded for us to stop for one reason or another and inundated us with requests for medicines. John evaluated each plea and determined our course of action. He surprised me when, more than once, he asked my opinion.

I ended each day exhausted but elated. I returned to my parents' home, and John went to his apartment, which he described as "a one-room retreat in the midst of similar dwellings in a four-story building." It was situated halfway between the hospitals and the slums. From there he had access to all of his patients, rich and poor, and none of them knew about the other.

My mother welcomed me home each night with a warm meal and a barrage of questions about the fine, young doctor, and what are his intentions, and when can he come for Sunday dinner? I introduced him to them once when he dropped me off, and the whole family hurried out to the front walk. All six of my siblings surrounded his buggy, including my three oldest sisters with babies slung over their hips. My two brothers glared at John like he'd done something wrong, and my younger sister, Annie, clung to the side of his buggy, her wide brown eyes staring up at him like he had wings and a halo.

Then there was Mama. No problem there. The second she met him she tried to pull him off the buggy.

"Come inside. Eat supper with us. Stay awhile."

John took one look at Papa and promised to come on another day.

The old man could have set him on fire using only his eyes as matchsticks.

"Gallagher?" Papa kept saying after John left. "Gallagher? What kind of name is that?"

"It's Irish, Papa," I told him. "You work with Irish men, don't you?"

Of course, my father always had it in his mind that I was going to marry an Italian, like my sisters did. To help me with that decision, he'd selected several eligible young men who'd recently stepped foot off a boat from Sicily and had found work in the mills and factories in Philadelphia. They hadn't even learned to speak English yet, but Papa didn't care. Any one of them would make a fine husband for his spinster daughter.

I hadn't said one word about having a relationship with John beyond our work, yet both of my parents obviously expected we were heading that way. While Mama was all for it—a doctor in the family!—Papa was determined to scare him off.

I soon learned that John also had been thinking about taking our relationship to another level when one Friday after we finished our rounds—he invited me to go for lunch with him the next day.

"Just a friendly time of relaxation over a meal," he pressed. "No strings, Rosie. I merely want to get to know you."

Eight to ten hours a day working together wasn't enough? I knew better, of course, because I wanted to get to know him too, beyond the doctor-and-nurse partnership, beyond discussions about drugs and the latest tools of our trade, beyond evaluations of toothaches, fevers, coughing spells, and labor pains. I wanted to know the *real* John, the personal one—his dreams, his aspirations, even his troubles and his mistakes. I wanted the flesh-and-blood John, not the doctor in a white coat with a stethoscope hanging around his neck.

All I knew about him so far came from little tidbits he'd tossed into our conversations while we worked. Most of what he talked about were memories about growing up in Saw-mill, Pennsylvania, where life was easy and laid-back. He made that little town sound so appealing. But I wanted to go beyond the surface incidentals of his past. I wanted to uncover the man's heart.

So I said yes to his lunch invitation, and I went home that night with all sorts of delightful thoughts running around in my head. Did I dare to even *think* about wedding bells? I tried to dispel the possibility. After all, it was just lunch.

The next morning, when my mother found out I was going on a date with John, she rushed around the house like a mother hen searching for a wayward chick. First to my closet where she pulled out my only three dresses fit for a date. She had something to say about every piece of jewelry—all but one came from the dime store, the one with a gold chain and a cross my grandmother had sent from Italy. Mama also checked my nylons for runs and she searched through my closet for my Mary Janes.

"These are right shoes for a date—not those ugly boats you wear to work. And here, take this shawl I got from Italy. Your grandmother made it."

In other words, Mama foresaw every detail of my preparations as if I couldn't do it on my own. My heart was pounding. In less than an hour I was going on a date with John. Not only did I have to bathe and dress before he came to pick me up, I had to contend with all the problems my mother wanted to fix, including my unruly hair. She gathered my hairbrush and pins, determined to restyle my tangles for the big event.

"No, no, Rosita, you look like a washerwoman. Here. Let me."

Grabbing my arms she forced me into a kitchen chair and stepped behind me. The first thing she did was unfurl the tight bun I wore to work. Pins flew left and right, to the kitchen table, to the floor, even as far as the sink. She brought this side up and the other side down, then she piled a few curls on top, didn't like the way it looked, and took them all down again. In the end, I removed all the pins and the little combs, and ended up with dark waves framing one side of my face and my hair on the other side tucked behind my ear with one rhinestone-studded barrette. To be honest, I even liked it that way.

From the three dresses Mama pulled from my closet, I chose the black basic. Gramma's hand-made shawl, knitted with variegated yarn, brought just the right amount of color. I surveyed my image in the mirror and didn't recognize myself.

John was already on the porch about to knock when Mama ushered me outside and nearly shoved me into his arms.

"Here she is, Johnny boy. Isn't she lovely?"

He opened his mouth to speak but didn't get a chance to say anything, because the next thing both of my brothers came charging up the front steps like they'd been waiting in the bushes all along. They crossed their arms and glared at John like two hit men. If I didn't know better, I'd swear my father had hired them.

John took my hand, and we started to leave.

My brother Angelo jumped in front of us blocking our path. "Get her home by eleven," he commanded, frowning.

"Take as long as you like," sang my mother. Then she wacked Angelo's arm with the back of her hand. "He's a doctor, you fool. Leave him alone."

Then she turned toward John, her face aglow. "One of these days you and me, we'll sit down and have a talk. I want to share my family remedies with you, things they don't teach you in medical school, things that were handed down from my mother and my grandmother, God bless their souls. You will be—"

I quickly stepped between them. "Okay, Mama. Maybe later."

I took John's waiting arm. He led me down the stairs to his buggy, helped me climb in, and we started off. The more space I could put between John and my family the better.

When we got a suitable distance from the house, we looked at each other and grinned. Then we both burst out laughing. My heart leaped for joy, and I couldn't help but imagine what great things might come from this first date. After the reception he got at the house, it wouldn't be our last.

I was smiling to myself when our first date began to fade from my mind and I returned to the reality of my life in

Sawmill, Pennsylvania. I was married to John, and we had a family. A terrible influenza had circled the globe and now had come to our sleepy, little village. I checked on Johnny and Lily. They'd put away the blocks. Lily was singing softly to her ragdoll, and Johnny had pulled out his bag of marbles. I'd trained them well, insisting they put away one toy before getting another from the box in their bedroom.

Contented that they'd be fine for a while, I went to the living room and found Amy asleep once again with the book lying open on her chest. The children didn't need me at the moment. It looked like John wasn't coming home. I had at least another hour or two to myself.

I could finish knitting the shawl I'd started last week. I picked it up, stared at it, and set it back inside my knitting basket. I'd cleaned the house so well nothing needed my attention. I'd already baked enough breads to last the rest of the week. Nothing called to me from the many projects I'd started. I didn't even feel like finishing Jane Austen's *Sense and Sensibility*, my favorite of all her novels.

With memories of our first date still calling to me, I went to my bureau and pulled out our family album. Another stroll down memory lane could be just the escape I needed. Sometimes delving into the past has helped me feel more confident about the future. I set the giant book on the table and ran my hand over the cloth cover with its little pink bows and beaded flower design. I'd inserted the photos chronologically, starting with family pictures. There was an 8 by 10 of me and my six siblings crowded together like a collection of toy dolls with us little ones squatting down front and the older kids hovering behind us. The following pages highlighted special milestones in our lives. Birthday parties, Christmas dinners, picnics, and trips to the fair with my brothers, Angelo and Tommy, riding a Shetland pony and us girls eating ice cream.

I owned one sepia-toned portrait of Mama and Papa. Like many older folks who posed for photos in their day, Papa sat in a high-backed chair, pipe in hand, and Mama stood behind him with one hand resting on his shoulder. Neither cracked a hint of a smile, but that's how people posed for photos back then, stone-faced and serious, like the fate of the world was resting on their backs.

I flipped to the next page. It was covered with nursing school photos of my best friend, Olive, and myself in our crisp, white uniforms and triangular hats. Unlike Mama and Papa we smiled with total abandonment. We'd entered a whole new world of adventure, and we were training in our chosen field.

The next couple of pages held pictures of John and me standing beside his buggy in the back streets of Philadelphia, waiting for a trolley on Girard Avenue, and posing in front of City Hall the day we applied for a marriage license. John had purchased a Kodak Brownie box camera for $1. He kept it loaded with film and often asked strangers to take our picture.

Then came our wedding photos. I wore my sister Marilyn's gown. Since we were the same size, the dress didn't need any altering. I released a little laugh over John looking uncomfortable in his high-collared, tight-fitting wedding suit. The next few photos came from our honeymoon in Atlantic City—again shot with John's Brownie. Images of the boardwalk, the crowded beach, me in my lace-trimmed, ankle-length satin dress, John in a summer shirt and his favorite linen slacks that hadn't changed style in more than a decade.

I caught myself chuckling. I had taken the time to journey into the past again. I could forget we were in the middle of a pandemic with no promise of any relief. Without reservation I allowed my mind to drift back to those happier times, like the Saturday afternoon when John took me on our first date. Up until that day, we'd spent every morning and afternoon together, tending to the sick, delivering babies, distributing medicine, always in the lower class sections of the city and surrounded by poorly clad children and parents with empty pockets.

Suddenly, it was just the two of us. We were on a date, driving John's horse and buggy into the more elegant parts of the city where women in silks and velvets and men in Chesterfield coats and bowler hats strolled arm-in-arm along the streets, where trolley cars and horse-drawn coaches cruised the main thoroughfares, and an occasional horseless carriage wove between the slower conveyances.

Philadelphia, the immaculate, brick and glass-fronted metropolis, where wealthy bluebloods ruled the government, and women of high degree took charge of the charities and social events. Where the poor immigrants faded into the oblivion of tenements and slums, like a forgotten world set apart from the pristine buildings. Where a more affluent society went about their daily business unaware that only a few blocks away someone was searching their cupboards for the makings of one more meal.

Boatloads of immigrants had flowed in from Germany, Poland, Ireland, and Italy. They gravitated to the big cities in pursuit of jobs, schooling for their children, and the opportunity for prosperity in America. They worked for low pay and more promises. Still, municipalities grew and became melting pots with a mix of languages and cultures.

I grew up in an Italian settlement of poor immigrants who labored long hours and came home speaking in their native tongues. When I entered nursing school, I was introduced to a whole different world. I trained at one of the newest hospitals in the city. For two years I worked alongside doctors and nurses and hospital supervisors. Then I went back to the slums and to the people who needed me most. Now I was on a date with John, and he'd taken me to the long-forgotten center of town.

He flicked the reins. We picked up a little speed and entered a part of the city I never visited anymore. I breathed in the occasional whiffs of jasmine and gardenias borne by gentle breezes across the lawns of the wealthy.

John inched his buggy along clean-swept cobblestone streets, past the birthplace of Betsy Ross, down to Race Street Wharf where I inhaled the salty aroma of fresh-caught fish, then over the Walnut Lane Bridge and a field of lush greenery. Closer to the Delaware, plumes of smoke rose skyward from the city's factories. John drove randomly up and down the streets, sometimes circling around and bringing us back to a familiar site. He kept glancing at me, like he was trying to see if I was enjoying our tour of the city. All I could do was smile and gawk at everything.

In the middle of town American flags protruded from tall red-brick buildings. The bottom floors contained various businesses that opened to the street, and the top two floors housed the proprietors' apartments. We moved on toward busy Market Street where fruit and vegetable sellers manned their stands, and the clatter of streetcars swarmed like bees escaping from a hive. From there we followed the broad paved road past the Academy of Fine Arts. At the far end I spotted City Hall with the statue of William Penn at its peak. He seemed to be proudly looking down over the domain he had founded more than two centuries before.

John secured his horse and buggy near Elfreth's Alley. He extended his hand and helped me to the ground. Like I'd seen the high-class ladies do, I took his arm, and we melted into the crowd of walkers. My simple black dress didn't hold a candle to the brilliant finery on the ladies who glided past us in the opposite direction. Their long, gossamer dresses swept by in a glittering wave of golds and beiges.

John didn't seem the least bit troubled over my simple frock. "You look amazing," he said with a wink.

Nor was he ashamed of his casual attire, a far cry from the ever-changing fashions of men's clothing. He stood out from the other men who'd picked up the recent trend of thick beards and handlebar mustaches. John's cropped red hair and clean shaven face went along with the antiseptic nature of his profession, or so he claimed.

"After all, I look the part," he'd said to me one day while we were at work, "What patient would want a shaggy-haired monster leaning over his bed?"

I knew what he meant. I wore my own hair in a tight bun at the back of my head. My friend Olive had cropped hers in the new, fashionable bob, but since I preferred to keep my hair long, I settled for the bun.

But that Saturday, I had let my hair down. Shiny black ringlets trailed past my shoulders. John smiled with approval and pulled me close to his side, like he was proud to be seen walking with me. "I like this look on you," he said, his voice almost a whisper. "Your hair. Your dress. And that beautiful shawl. It brightens up the entire street."

My heart leaped to my throat. We'd entered a whole new world, refreshingly different from the immigrant settlements we worked in day after day. Only yesterday we labored in dank, urine-soaked alleys, delivered babies onto soiled sheets that hadn't been washed in weeks, and doctored children who hadn't had a bath in months. Now we were in the heart of the city. Whitewashed storefronts glistened in the midday sun. Everything was clean, and new, and polished to a shine. The people we passed bore sweet aromas of bath soap, minty lotions, and floral perfumes. I leaned close and breathed in the citrus/musk scent of John's aftershave. I recognized it right away—Pinaud Clubman. My brother Tommy had a bottle on his dresser, though he always splashed far too much on his jaw.

"You smell like you've been to a brothel," my mother reprimanded him, and she gave him a sharp wallop to his left ear.

"It's aftershave," Tommy whined. "What do you want me to do, smell like sweat?"

"No, I expect you to take a bath and tone down the perfume." The rest of us kids chided him for days over it.

I chuckled at the memory. For some reason, my mother hadn't noticed John was wearing the same scent Tommy owned, or perhaps she'd chosen to overlook it. Anyway, he had used the aftershave sparingly, not like Tommy who'd gone overboard with it, like he did everything.

We walked past the glassed storefronts and peered through windows at elaborately clothed mannequins, elegant home furnishings, expensive jewelry, Turkish rugs, and other treasures of the rich. Having grown up in a home of hand-me-downs, I never developed a taste for the finer things of life, and I didn't miss them. My contentment came from simple enjoyments, like walking arm-in-arm with John.

We stopped at Wanamaker's six-story department store with different wares on every floor and eight elevators to take you there. The entire building echoed with Bach's baroque music pouring from the store's giant pipe organ.

"Do you want to eat at Wanamaker's Crystal Tea Room?" John said. "Or perhaps at one of the hotel restaurants?"

One thing I knew for certain, John would spend his entire week's wages in one afternoon if I let him. I recalled a place Olive had gone to on one of her dates away from the hospital. She'd described it as a cozy Irish pub with a reasonably priced menu.

I tightened my grip on John's arm. "Why don't we go to McGillin's Tavern?" I turned to look at him and was rewarded by his broad smile.

We went back out to the street and John slowed his step. For the first time since we'd met I noticed he walked with a slight limp, hardly noticeable at other times but growing more obvious as we continued a greater distance down the city streets. I frowned with concern but held my tongue. At some point, when the time seemed right, I would ask him about his limp.

It took us 10 minutes to reach the pub, and as John opened the door, the smell of malt liquor and dark beer wafted out to the street. We entered to an atmosphere of deep reds and golden browns, and I caught the aroma of grilled beef and potatoes.

A middle-aged man wearing a green-and-gold vest greeted us at the door. He recognized John and extended his hand. "Helloo, Doctor John." John introduced me to Harry. They chatted for a minutes like old friends. Then Harry led us to a table.

"Here's a list of our fare," Harry said dragging out his Rs with an authentic Irish brogue. I enjoyed the musical sound of it. Meanwhile, John spoke impeccable English, with no accent. He once told me his father had come to America as a child. Like me, John had been born and raised here by immigrant parents.

I snuggled down in my chair and admired the rich oiled wood of the tables. A long bar extended from one end of the pub to the other. Quaint little lanterns hung from the rafters. The bright red walls with golden accents painted cheerful colors on the patrons' faces. Scattered about the room were photos and souvenirs from the owner's homeland. Bottles of whiskey had been lined up like soldiers in front of large mirrors behind a bar that stretched the length of the wall, and in the middle was a large placard with *McGillin's Olde Ale House* written in bold script.

"They serve the only authentic Irish stout around here," boasted John after Harry walked away. Our friendly waiter went up to the bar, conversed with the barkeeper, and a minute later returned to our table with two mugs of frothy dark beer. I sat in shock. Apparently, Harry knew John so well he didn't have to ask what he wanted. I eyed the tumbler he'd placed in front of me. I'd never tried beer before. My entire family drank bathtub wine made by my father. I took a sip, then wrinkled my nose. It tasted like burnt coffee beans. John's eyes twinkled with amusement. I took another sip of the beer and tried to keep my nose from wrinkling again. I dabbed at my upper lip with a napkin, certain the foam had left a frothy mustache there.

"I can order you something else," John offered.

I shook my head. "No, I'll get used to it." I took another sip. It went down a little easier.

The next thing I knew, John ordered fish and chips for both of us. I'd found myself on a culinary adventure. In my house we ate Mama's homemade pasta and her chicken soup. Fried fish? John was introducing me to a whole new world. I stared at him downing his beer like it was water. Without asking, the guy in the green vest brought him another.

After the second glass, Harry returned, and John raised his hand. "No more, thank you," he said. "Just some black coffee, please."

Within moments we both had steaming cups of coffee. Unfortunately, mine was as bitter as the beer. I poured a large dollop of cream in mine and stirred the golden swirls with a spoon.

John was sipping his coffee, black and strong. He appeared relaxed. He'd had two beers. Perhaps this was the right time to ask about his limp. I chewed my bottom lip.

"Is something on your mind?" he said, his eyes twinkling.

"I couldn't help but wonder, John, were you injured in some way? While we were out on the street, I noticed you walked with a slight limp. It wasn't very obvious, but I thought you favored your left leg." I was rambling now. Embarrassed, I lowered my gaze to my coffee cup.

John burst out laughing. Shocked, I sat back and stared at him.

"I thought you might ask me about my limp sometime. I just didn't know when." He chuckled and didn't appear the least bit offended.

He reached across the table and took one of my hands in both of his. "Dear, sweet Rosie. We've been working together day-in and day-out for how long? Three months? And you never mentioned my limp."

I shrugged and must have blushed a little. "I'm sorry, John. I hadn't noticed it until we were walking together. Most of the time during our workdays, we're either riding in your buggy or walking short distances between our patients." I shrugged. "I simply never noticed before today."

He chuckled again, gave a little wink and tilted his head. "I wished you'd noticed lots of things about me by now." He leaned closer. "Haven't you seen the way I smile whenever you walk in the room? Or that I accidentally brush your fingers when you hand me a piece of gauze, or a scalpel, or a bottle of pills? Or that I shift closer to you when we're working on a patient?" He gently squeezed my hand. "Haven't you sensed that I've been falling in love with you, Rosie?"

I must have turned six shades of red. I was still trying to think up an appropriate response when he released my hand and pulled a tiny box from his breast pocket.

Chapter Seven

I must have looked stunned, for I didn't move at all. Just sat there, frozen like a statue. This was too soon for a proposal. We hardly knew each other. Except for working side-by-side every day other than Sundays, we hadn't had any intimate discussions, had mostly kept our conversations to the different diseases we encountered during our day.

I stared at the little box in John's hand. Still in shock, I looked into his intense eyes. He smiled sweetly and opened the box.

"I had this made for you," he said as he removed a red-and-white striped ribbon attached to a round pin with a red cross in the center surrounded by the words, *Faith, Hope,* and *Charity.*

Absentmindedly I pressed my fingers against my cheek and found it hot. Tears flooded into my eyes. Words stuck in my throat. In John's hand was a very good facsimile of the nursing pins the hospital gave to graduates. It wasn't an exact replica, but close enough for me to appreciate its significance.

"I realize it's not the one the school would have given you, but I believe it's well deserved. Do you like it?" John's hopeful eyes grabbed my heart.

Shortly after I started working for John, I broke down and confessed my failure and how the hospital had dropped me from the training. I felt he had a right to know so that he could make a decision about keeping me on. His response surprised me.

"I've known for sometime, Rosie. Don't you think I would have checked with the hospital where you received your training? They told me everything. How you left your post. How the boy died while in surgery. You have to stop blaming yourself. I certainly don't blame you. God knows I've made enough mistakes of my own."

Now I sat there stunned as he held out a pin I didn't deserve. I shook my head and tears welled up in my eyes.

"The thing is, you deserve this pin as much as anyone, Rosie," he said as though reading my mind. "You earned it during your training, and you continue to earn it every day you venture into the filth of the city and care for strangers who can't pay. You have a special touch few nurses can claim. You bring healing wherever you go. You're as much a nurse as anyone I've ever worked with—in fact, even more so because of your selfless dedication."

I found my voice and uttered a humble, "Thank you, John."

He rose from the table, came around to my side, and fastened the pin to my bodice. Then, stepping back he eyed me with such admiration I thought I might lose consciousness. I pressed my fingertips to the pin.

"This means a lot to me, John. It's beautiful." I blinked against another rise of tears.

He went back to his chair. His smile faded as did the twinkle in his eyes. He grew serious then.

"To answer your question, Rosie, I fractured my tibia falling from a barn loft when I was a boy."

He looked a tad ashamed. "My brother and I were prowling

around a barn of a farmer outside of town. Marty goaded me into climbing the ladder to the loft. He waited below and dared me to lean over the edge."

He cocked his head and produced a half smile. "Stupid kid. I lost my footing—and down I went." He gestured with one hand, like an imaginary someone falling off our table.

I shook my head. "You could have broken more than your leg."

He nodded sheepishly. "The only positive outcome is that I can relate to patients who've suffered similar injuries. I know their pain." He shrugged. "Of course that fall ended any hope I'd had of competing in foot races. Needless to say, I didn't climb any more ladders."

As I sat across the table from John in McGillin's Tavern that day, I was learning about the man, just as I had hoped. We'd gone past the doctor-nurse relationship, and we were getting into each other's heart.

He was shaking his head. "I learned my lesson that day. A brutal one. I fractured my tibia in two places." He brightened then, as another thought came to his mind. "The good thing was, as I watched my father set my leg gently and virtually painlessly, the seeds of a profession in medicine were planted in my soul. All of his urging and his accolades about the medical profession didn't impress me as much as being his patient for a few minutes. From that moment I dreamed of being able to do the same thing one day, to care for others the way he was caring for me, with kind words and a gentle touch." He held up his hands in a display of satisfaction. "My father was thrilled. He'd been praying that one of his sons would follow him in his career. In the end, both Marty and I chose the medical field."

"That's a beautiful story, John. I've seen how compassionate you are toward your patients and how diligently you work to alleviate their pain. Your father showed you the technique, but you developed it. You connect with your patients in a way few doctors can. You're one of the most gifted and considerate doctors I've ever worked with."

"You're very kind to say that, but I have to admit, I might have given up if God hadn't guided me into the right college and placed me under professors who taught me well. Then it was God who led me away from the hospital and into the streets where I was able to care for the forgotten citizens of the city." He smiled and leaned toward me. "And, fortunately, it was God who also led me to you."

The moisture in his eyes formed a halo around the green ovals within. "I think about you all the time, Rosie. When we're not together working, you're still on my mind."

I wanted to tell him I felt the same way, that I'd also been thinking about him every moment of every day since we first met. With a sudden burst of boldness, I leaned close and lowered my voice. "I'm so glad we met, John. I admire you—not only as a doctor, but as a man—and as a friend."

He shook his head. "No, Rosie. Not merely friends." He took a deep breath. "With your approval, I want to ask your parents for permission to court you."

My heart was pounding hard enough for him to hear it from across the table. I knew what courting meant. My three older sisters had gone through the courting stage. Then came their engagements, then their weddings. The whole process took a year, two for my sister Annette. Then there were babies and expectations of more children. At all times at least one of my sisters was walking around pregnant to my mother's wide-eyed joy.

But my sisters had done something I wasn't sure I could do. They had given up their secretarial jobs to stay home and be homemakers. The realization planted a real concern in my heart. I loved my career. Even if I married John, I'd want to keep on nursing. Most men in that day expected their wives to have babies and forget about working outside the home. But John didn't seem like the typical man.

"How would you feel if the woman you married wanted to keep on working?" I boldly asked him, for I had to know. His answer would help me decide whether or not to approve his request to court me.

He didn't hesitate. "Rosie," he said, patting my hand. "When two people embark on a life together, they meet each challenge together. Some things are meant to be decided when they arise. Don't be afraid, Rosie. I won't take your dreams away."

I swallowed the lump in my throat, but it returned. Blinking, I turned my attention to the broad dining area with its wooden tables and chairs now filling up with men in suits and families with small children.

I tried to avoid John's gaze, but his eyes hadn't left my face. I'd been waiting for weeks, wondering if we'd ever get past the working stage of our relationship, and now here we were, making the decision of our lives.

"I would like it very much if you would ask my father's permission," I said, shyly.

It occurred to me then that we knew very little about each other's past. While we were working together, John had shared memories of growing up in Sawmill, Pennsylvania, where his father served as the town's physician. I'd never been there, but I could picture the small town nestled in the countryside, far from the clamor of the city. As for *my* life, John was well aware that I grew up in one of the tenements among immigrants from Europe. In a way, we came from two different worlds.

"You have one brother," I said, more as a statement than a question.

He nodded. "Only one. And you told me you grew up with, what—six siblings? I have no idea what that must have been like."

"Wild," was the one word I thought of. "Everybody has a lot to say but nothing of substance to tell. Just a lot of talking and interrupting each other and nobody ever making a solid point. I haven't experienced one minute of quiet during my entire life, except perhaps in the middle of the night when everyone else is asleep. Then there's all the snoring from my brothers' bedroom."

John was laughing, and I began to relax.

"Of course, my three older sisters have their own homes now," I told him. "So it's just me, my younger sister, Annie, and two brothers who enjoy tormenting me. As soon as I walk in the house the boys make nasty comments about my nursing career. *Who did I see naked today? How many patients did I kill? What's that ugly stain on my uniform?* To Angelo and Tommy, I'm still a little girl with pigtails. They can't believe I've delivered a couple dozen babies and even saved a few lives."

I was rambling now. I looked around again and was grateful to see our waiter coming toward us bearing a tray with two newspaper-lined baskets loaded with French fried potatoes and on top, golden, batter-fried fish.

As we ate, John asked me to tell him more about my family. He seemed absolutely enthralled with my home life.

I told him about Mama's dream for me to marry well and Papa's dream that it should be an Italian, "right off the boat from Sicily, if possible," I added with a laugh.

John was chuckling between bites of fish. More funny stories popped into my head. I talked about my three aunts who whenever they came to visit brought a steaming casserole and plenty of homemade desserts. My uncles who strutted in carrying several cases of wine. Then there were my two dozen cousins, tumbling into the living room and kicking off noisy reunions that lasted well into the early hours of the morning, with the wine still flowing and the table covered with platters of food that miraculously refilled as soon as they were emptied.

"Somehow we cram everybody in our tiny dining room and kitchen," I told John. "And we eat and talk, and we eat and play games, and we eat and dance, and then we eat some more."

John burst out laughing and got me laughing too.

"It sounds like your family eats an awful lot," he said, amusement twinkling in his eyes.

I sighed and shook my head. "You have no idea."

He gazed at me with the same affection he'd displayed when he professed his love minutes before. "It doesn't look as though all that eating has affected you, Rosie. Somehow you've managed to keep your girlish figure."

I blushed openly and smoothed the wrinkles from my skirt. What John thought of as a girlish figure was, in reality, skin and bones.

"My brothers tell me I look like a scarecrow in a dress."

John laughed again and shook his head. "Not a chance."

As we continued to dine, I grew quiet and set about finishing off my fries.

John scraped up the last of his fish and settled back in his chair.

"My home life was a lot less hectic than yours," he admitted with a smile. "My father came from a small village in Ireland when he was very young. He finished public school, then he worked hard and paid his own way through college. My mother was born in America, but was also of Irish descent. They met at a little pub like this one." He gestured with one hand. "Mom was waiting tables and Dad played darts and drank beer with the men who worked in the local factories. After he graduated from medical school, he chose to settle in Sawmill. He claimed it was a lot like the small town in Ireland where he'd grown up. His one dream was for both of his sons to go to college and study medicine. Martin made it into medical school before me. His grades took him to the top of his class, and after graduation he signed on with one of the city hospitals."

I toyed with the last piece of potato on my plate, left it there and took a long swallow of my coffee. Harry was at our table in seconds, refilling my cup.

"It looks like your father's dream came true," I offered.

John nodded. "Marty's a well-known physician in Philadelphia," he said without the slightest hint of envy. "My brother worked his way to the top of the ladder. 'Surgery. That's where the money is,' he always said. My dad brags endlessly about Marty." John paused and stuffed a fried potato in his mouth. "I became a country doctor, much like my father. I think he's proud of me too."

I rested my hand on his forearm. "You've done right, John. You should be proud of your work. You're unselfish. You're a doctor who cares for people—sincerely cares. Wherever we go within the tenements the residents salute you. They clap their hands and shout words of praise in many different languages. Not many doctors can claim that kind of reward."

Tears flooded into his eyes. "You're a treasure, Rosie," he said, his voice breaking. "We're a good match, aren't we?'

I couldn't speak, could only nod and blink back the tears that now blurred my vision.

Again, I touched my fingers to the little pin on my bodice. It meant more to me than any pin I might have received at graduation.

From that moment, I wore John's pin every day. If I'd never made that terrible mistake, if I'd stayed on through graduation, if I'd hired into a private home, if I'd done a lot of things differently, I might never have experienced the rewards of working in the ghettos of Philadelphia. I might not have met John, might not have delighted in that moment when he pledge his love for me. Somehow, my life had taken the right path, despite my mistakes, despite my desire to control everything. In the end, like John had said, we both had planned our course, but it was God who guided our steps and brought us together.

And here I was, eighteen years later, leafing through a photo album and remembering moments that changed my life in a very profound way. With a sigh I rose out of the memories, wiped tears from my eyes, and marveled at how far John and I had come since that day we dined together in a little pub in downtown Philly. I had agreed to our courtship. A few months later I accepted his proposal. Then I married the man who'd taken my breath away from the beginning. We brought three beautiful children into the world. We established a medical practice, and we settled into a comfortable home in the country.

I took in the all-too familiar surroundings—the tiny kitchen, the smoldering logs in the fireplace, the kettle rattling on the stove. I'd given up my nursing career and had chosen something better.

I turned my attention back to the photo album, fingered the picture of John and me on our wedding day. I was about to turn to the next page when Johnny rose from the corner, put away his bag of marbles, and came to my side.

"I'm hungry, Mama."

I stared at my son as though seeing him for the first time. He was the spittin' image of his father—small frame, square face, reddish mop of hair, and green eyes like John's, which had captivated me 20 years before. My son's gaze almost stopped my heart. I pulled away from his cherubic face and checked the clock on the mantle. One in the afternoon, already well past lunchtime.

Where had the day gone? Somehow I'd been able to grab a little time for a much needed journey into the past. Remembering those early days with John and how we helped so many people who couldn't help themselves had given me a temporary escape from the disease that was threatening to destroy us all. But here it was past noon, and I needed to get back to work. I put away the album, grabbed my apron, and got busy with life.

I smiled at my son. "I'll fix you something, darling. Go wash your hands and get Lily to do the same."

As he scampered away from me, I went into the pantry and came out with a handful of carrots, an onion, and a potato. I got an iron pot going on the stove, added a splash of oil, a chopped onion, and a cup of lentils. Then I cut up the vegetables for a hardy stew. A little beef broth from the kettle on the stove and two spoons of flour created a nice, thick gravy.

The mixture simmered for fifteen or twenty minutes. I gave it a stir, then cut up a loaf of sourdough bread and slathered butter over the slices. I glanced at Amy. She was still sleeping with her book spread open on her chest. The book went up and down with every breath she took. I didn't have the heart to disturb her, she looked so peaceful.

I ladled the stew into three bowls, leaving enough in the pot for Amy when she awakened. I set places at the table for myself and my younger children, who'd already taken their seats, a hungry look on their faces. Johnny's eyes lit up when I slid his bowl in front of him. He picked up his spoon.

I raised my hand. "We need to thank the Lord," I reminded him.

He frowned with impatience but bowed his head. Lily already had folded her hands. She sat there with her eyes shut. The child was amazingly compliant. She never complained about anything but had settled into the routines I'd established for her. In fact, I soon learned that if I deviated from any of those routines, she would back away with a confused wrinkle on her forehead. She was almost four years old and rarely spoke except for *Mama* and *Papa*, plus a few incidental words. Most of the time she either smiled for "yes," or grunted for "no."

John had called her *special*. I didn't know why, perhaps it was a term of endearment, but there was something different about our little girl. I stored my concerns to the back of my mind and turned my attention to our meal.

My words of grace carried more than a simple gratitude for our food. I also asked God to make Amy well and to keep John safe during his journey. By this time my husband may have completed his work at the hospital and maybe was on his way home. But I knew the truth. John was never going to leave Philadelphia as long as he was needed there.

Chapter Eight

I toyed with my stew and ate very little. My two little ones gobbled down spoonfuls of the warm vegetables and savory broth. Lily's big, brown eyes sparkled with renewed energy, reassuring me of her continuing good health. Johnny showed no signs of a cold or fever. Nor had he complained about achy muscles or any of the other symptoms related to the flu.

Our meal over and the dishes washed and put away, I told Johnny to gather his schooling projects to the table. He groaned and stomped his foot. He preferred to play, of course, like any eight-year-old, but I needed to get him ready for third grade when the schoolhouse opened up again. If it ever did. As for Lily, without being told she made several trips to the corner and carried her alphabet blocks to the table. She started arranging the letters to her liking, beginning just fine with A, B, and C, but from there it was a scramble of letters and images painted on the wooden squares. With her fourth birthday coming up in two weeks, I was hoping she'd learn the entire alphabet and her numbers up to 20 over the next year.

Amy could read before she turned five, and Johnny was right behind her. For some reason my third little baby had continued to struggle with the simplest projects.

I left Lily moving her alphabet blocks around with a subtle

scraping of wood against wood, and I turned my attention to Johnny's spelling cards. He'd already mastered three-syllable words and could read anything I put in front of him by sounding out the letters. When he didn't know the meaning of certain words, I explained as well as I could.

While the hour hand continued to make its circuit on the clock on the mantle, Amy slept peacefully on the sofa, Lily was stacking her alphabet blocks in little towers, and Johnny was staring out the window bored to tears.

"You need to be able to spell all of your words if you want to move into the third grade," I reminded him.

He gave a little shrug. "Can I just read them myself?"

"I want to make sure you know how to spell them. You can't test yourself if you're looking at the cards. Somebody has to quiz you."

He breathed a sigh and slumped back in his chair. "Whatever you say, Mama." I felt sorry for my young son. He'd had to suppress his energy over the last few weeks. I was afraid he was reaching a breaking point.

I ran through the stack of cards. Johnny missed a couple of tough words, so I let them pass.

"Great job, Johnny," I said. I wanted to encourage him somehow. Glancing at him with heartfelt concern, I left to put the cards away. When I returned I found my son still sitting at the table, but now he had one of his father's medical texts spread open in front of him. Curious, I snuck up behind him. He turned the page and paused at a chart showing various parts of the human anatomy. He hadn't noticed I was looking over his shoulder.

A flutter of awareness struck my heart. Today Johnny was a child struggling with his second-grade lessons. But one day he might be setting a broken arm, or wielding a scalpel, or administering a life-saving drug. In less than a decade my son would be getting ready for college, and who knows what afterwards?

As he continued to pore over the pages of his father's medical book, I smiled with understanding. I'd been teaching my son things I thought he should learn, things he *needed* to learn if he wanted to move up in school, when all along his little mind had moved away from the fundamentals of second grade and onto a whole other level.

"Look, Mama!" He turned his face up at me. His freckled cheeks were glowing. He pointed. "Look at this drawing of the inside of a person's ear. See how many parts there are? See how they all work together to help a person hear?"

He went through the book, slowly turning each leaf, pausing now and then on a particular image. The drawings brought back memories of my own training. Now, as I looked at them through my son's eyes, I was reminded of how fascinating a medical text could be.

Many of the doctors and nurses who'd come through the training when John and I did had gone off to serve as medics in the war. Others, like my husband, were responding to a great need in the cities where the flu had struck the hardest.

As for me, I had escaped into the safety of my own home, isolated from the viral outbreak. While I was taking care of my own family, friends and neighbors had been coming to my door seeking help from the only medical professional within 50 miles.

Surely, John's books carried some answers for me too. Perhaps if I studied them, like young Johnny was, I might come up with some long-forgotten remedy. While my little boy could only look at pictures and imagine how everything worked, I could read the words. I could delve into the texts like I used to. Instead of wasting my time with photo albums and knitting projects, I could find ways to keep us and my neighbors well. Perhaps I had the ingredients for healing right there in my own pantry.

I walked to John's cupboard and searched the book shelf for the right book. A large tome titled *Gunn's New Family Physician, Home Book of Health,* caught my eye. I was about to slide it from the shelf when a loud knock startled me.

I left the book, moved close to the door, and spoke through the weathered boards. "Who is it?"

"It's David Cowell, the postmaster." Perhaps he was bringing another message from my husband.

Once again, I opened the door only a few inches, just enough to receive the slip of paper from the man's hand. David stood there shivering, the collar of his coat turned up against the chill. He wasn't holding a note, had shoved his hands in his pocket.

"Yer husband phoned and asked me to have you come to the store in an hour. He's planning to call again and wants to talk to you." His voice was muffled by the heavy mask across his mouth and nose, but I caught enough of what he said.

I glanced at the clock on the mantle. "An hour? That'll be 3:15."

David nodded. "More like three o'clock. It took me a while to get over here."

"I'll be there," I said and shut the door.

A myriad of thoughts ran through my head.

Perhaps John's getting ready to come home. Maybe he wants to know if I need anything. What if something happened to the truck? Why on earth had he chosen to call? Why hadn't he simply gotten on the road?

While the morning had slipped away like snow melting down a hillside in the spring, the next hour dragged like sludge. I went back to John's bookshelf and retrieved the thick one I had chosen, sat in my rocker by the fireplace with the heavy book on my lap, and tried to concentrate on the fine print. But my eyes kept drifting to the mantle clock and my mind was on my husband and the phone call.

Amy stirred awake. I was kept busy for a while tending to her needs. She was still weak, but color had returned to her face, and the fever was gone. I helped her to the bathroom and back to the sofa. She sat there with pillows propping her up. I served her a bowl of the stew.

"Smells good," she said as I handed her the bowl wrapped in a towel. She moaned with pleasure between each spoonful. "It tastes wonderful, Mama. Thank you."

"You haven't eaten much over the last couple of days, dear. This will make you strong again."

She handed me the empty bowl and begged for more. I went to the stove for a refill, scraped the kettle clean, and gave Amy her second helping.

She appeared to have risen from the worst of her illness. Still, I needed her to remain on the sofa where I could keep an eye on her. If it turned out to be the erratic influenza I'd heard about, it could return with a vengeance. I whispered a prayer. God could keep my firstborn well. I looked at Johnny, still absorbed in his father's medical book, and then at Lily, face down on the table, asleep, with the alphabet blocks scattered.

By the time I carried Lily to her bed and closed the door, the mantle clock showed 2:45.

"I'm going to the general store," I told Amy, who had picked up her novel and had reached the halfway point in the book. "Your father will be calling me. Please take care of your younger siblings. I shan't be long."

She gave me a nod and a smile. "Tell Papa I said hello." And she returned to her book.

I grabbed my wool coat and gloves, put on my fur-lined boots, and tied a gauze mask over my lips and nose. With a final glance at Amy, I went out the door and headed to the general store, a ten-minute walk. Along the way I passed Felina Gray, her arms around a paper sack full of groceries. We nodded at each other and kept walking, just passed each other like two strangers. A few months ago, we would have stopped to chat. I would have asked if she needed anything. The poor woman's husband had died, leaving her with a five-year-old daughter to raise. But Felina had proved herself capable. Many of us married ladies helped her out by babysitting or by donating children's clothing. We shared meals with her. The men tended to her yard and made repairs on her house. I knitted sweaters for her and her daughter and delivered them with a plate of fresh-baked cookies.

This time, however, I didn't have any gifts for Felina. Nor did I have anything to say, merely grunted a greeting and hurried off. Tears came to my eyes and threatened to freeze as they started down my face and vanished within the folds of my mask.

I reached the general store five minutes ahead of schedule. The bell above the door drew David from the back. He donned his mask, then turned to look at the phone, then at the clock on the wall. Unspoken words went between us. I moved to the canned goods section and waited there while David puttered around behind the counter.

I pulled off my gloves and kept my eyes on the clock. The minutes ticked by—2:57, 2:58, 2:59. Then a loud shrill clanging came from the phone on the wall.

"You might as well answer it," David called out. "It must be your husband."

I rushed to the phone and lifted the handset to my ear. Rising on tiptoe, I spoke into the mouthpiece. "Hello?"

A crackling sound came over, then John's voice, faint and mixed with static.

"Rosie?"

"It's me."

"I miss you so much." I could hear the tears in his voice. John never could hide his emotions, not from me.

"I miss you too, John." I paused, waited to hear him say he was coming home.

"Things are really bad here," he said. "People are dying by the truckload. Horse-drawn wagons and motorized trucks have been picking up the dead all over town. They drop them off at abandoned schools and empty warehouses that have been converted into makeshift mortuaries. They pile the bodies on top of each other, like a load of cordwood." His voice broke then. "It's a tragedy, Rosie, a real tragedy."

I pictured the anguish on my husband's face. I'd seen it the day Oskar Schmidt died and again the night the Wilson baby passed away. Now he faced a more intense challenge, and he was trying to save the unsavable.

"Are you still helping out at the hospital?" I wanted him to say he'd finished and was about to leave for home.

"Yes. I'm still helping."

His answer sent a spear into my heart.

"We need you, John. Our neighbors need you."

"I'm sorry, Rosie. I can't leave yet. As soon as I walked in the door, an orderly handed me one of their physician's gowns. They have me wrapped up like a mummy. I'm wearing double masks and a cap on my head. I have only a few minutes to talk, then I have to get back to the ward."

I couldn't speak. My husband had chosen to stay in Philadelphia, one of the hardest hit cities in the country, a literal hub of the illness. I didn't want to continue at home alone, fending off our neighbors and trying to keep our children healthy and safe.

"How's Amy?" he asked.

I had to be honest. "A little better," I told him, then caught myself. I didn't want him to think he wasn't needed at home. "Could be better," I added. "She says hello."

Static broke into our conversation. I held my tongue and waited for my husband to speak again. When he did, his words troubled me even more.

"You wouldn't believe the suffering, Rosie. People cough up blood. They're dying of a rare type of pneumonia. They're choking on their own blood. The sick come in, and the dead go out the opposite door for disposal."

I gasped. "What do you mean, disposal? What about funerals? Don't they bury those poor souls?"

He grunted. "Bury them? How Rosie? They've run out of coffins. The graveyards are full. They've resorted to digging trenches and dumping the corpses in. No funerals, no wakes, no time for the memorials people usually plan when they've lost a loved one. It's inhumane. A terrible way to say goodbye to friends and relatives."

He paused then, and I could hear his gentle sobbing. When he came back, defeat saturated his voice. "If not for the lack of medical workers, I might have turned around and come home. You know that, don't you?"

I swallowed the lump in my throat. "Yes, John." How could I expect anything less of him?

"I need to go now," he said with resolve. "Keep our babies safe. Pray the war will end, and pray for us here in Philly. Without God's intervention we could lose both battles."

There was more static, and the line went dead. I stared at the phone on the wall for at least another minute. Then I hung up the handset, mumbled a thank you to David, and left the store.

My heart was breaking. John had chosen to help faceless strangers over his own family. I couldn't deny the goodness in that man. He always did what he thought was the right thing to do, at any cost. But this time, the cost could be his own wife and children. What if the townspeople stormed our house looking for medicines we didn't have? What if the flu struck us too and killed all four of us?

During my walk home, I struggled with a mix of emotions. I desperately wanted my husband with me, but at the same time I respected him for his decision to stay in Philadelphia and help. Wouldn't I have done the same if I could? I needed to remain strong, needed to keep the faith.

"Please, God, help me," I mumbled aloud. "I have three children who need me, and the people of Sawmill are turning to me for their medical care. I can't do it alone. I need to feel you helping me."

Almost immediately, my inner spirit rose up. I remembered the vow I'd made to John on our wedding day.

"Whither thou goest, I will go: and where thou lodgest, I will lodge: thy people shall be my people, and thy God my God," I had quoted from the book of Ruth in the Bible. Lots of people say those words during wedding ceremonies. But that passage of scripture was about more than a place to live. It was about a commitment, a calling, a decision for one's life.

Conviction swarmed over me. I wasn't merely John's wife. I'd been his helper from the beginning. We shared a heart for healing the unfortunate. John had continued to live that commitment. I had given it up.

I picked up my step, marched faster toward my house, determined to do whatever I could for my family *and* my neighbors. The town of Sawmill was *my* hospital ward. It was the place where I could do the most good.

I wanted to search through the medical book I'd left on my rocker and figure out what I could use. Then I needed to get to work. No more reminiscing over the past. No more whining about the present. No more worrying about the future. I had a mission before me, and with God's help I was determined to do it.

Chapter Nine

I walked through the front door of my house, tossed aside my mask and gloves, slipped out of my boots and hung up my coat. All of that took mere seconds. I was on fire, eager to do more than cook and clean and do second-grade math with my son. I had purpose now.

Johnny was still at the table flipping through another of his father's medical books. There was no sign of Lily. She was still napping, I presumed, behind the closed door to her bedroom. Amy looked up at me from her place on the sofa and smiled, then she went back to her book, nearly finished with it by now.

My heart melted with love for my children. But I'd plunged so far into motherhood I'd forgotten about my first calling, to nurse the sick, care for the hurting, feed the poor. Like many people who get distracted by personal responsibilities, I had lost my way. Olive had said we could do both. I intended to at least try.

I was about to pick up the book on my rocker, when Lily emerged from her bedroom, rubbing the sleep out of her eyes. I glanced at the book, and I breathed a sigh. My plan came to a screeching halt. Somehow I was going to have to learn to juggle my commitments.

"Cookies and milk?" I offered, and Johnny raised his head out of the medical book for the first time that afternoon.

Lily climbed onto her chair at the table. She looked up at me and grinned. I gazed into her eyes, as black as coal and sparkling with the innocence of youth. My side of the family all had dark eyes, but Lily's had a depth to them that none of ours had. She was in her own little world and was quite contented to stay there.

Johnny had taken after my husband's family—a bunch of red-haired, green-eyed leprechauns. They had captivating, whimsical smiles and a lilt to their voices that had me feeling like I'd just stepped foot in Ireland. The thought struck me that God himself chooses what color a person's eyes will be and the thickness of their hair and what will be their physical makeup. He gave young Johnny his father's short, sinewy build and made Amy and me look like broomsticks. Johnny also had inherited his dad's mannerisms. Like John, he sometimes cocked his head and winked whenever he was about to say something out of the ordinary.

Meanwhile, Amy tended more toward feminine tastes, like a cup of afternoon tea, and she went about the house humming favorite little tunes. The Scriptures said God designed each one of us. Little Lily was small for her age and had a simple way about her that sometimes worried me. Was that part of God's plan too?

I placed a plate of homemade sugar cookies and two glasses of milk on the table, then took a serving to Amy. Johnny grabbed two cookies and handed one to his sister. Lily smiled at him with childlike adoration. Johnny was her big brother, and somehow he'd become aware that she needed a protector. When they played with blocks, he helped her stack the little cubes into a tower, then stepped back and allowed her to kick it over. He read children's books to her, sang nursery songs long after I'd tucked them in and left their room. I sometimes listened at their closed door to his little voice singing, "Twinkle, Twinkle, Little Star." It was obvious my son had inherited his father's patience and his tender heart.

Lily finished her cookie and downed the glass of milk. Then she slid off her chair and went for her cloth bag of alphabet blocks. She dumped them on the table and gave me a sideways glance. Johnny had already gone back to his father's medical book.

"Do you want some help, Lily?" I said, as I cleaned away the crumbs and the empty glasses. The tome on the rocking chair was still beckoning to me, but I hovered close to my daughter.

She smiled. That meant yes.

I helped her set the blocks in order, lining them up from A to Z. Then I pointed at each block while Lily spoke the name of the letter. We'd been doing this for two years and she hadn't progressed to the next stage yet. I at least wanted her to mouth the sound of each letter. This was how I had taught Amy, and she'd mastered the complete alphabet before she was three. She was sounding out words by the time she was four. Amy breezed through the Palmer Method of writing, and she excelled with all of her multiplication and division tables. Now she was reading adult level books that I also enjoyed.

Johnny wasn't far behind his older sister. While he pored over his father's medical books, I observed with interest as his mouth formed the six-syllable words, then he sat still, like he was figuring out what they meant from the accompanying pictures and diagrams.

The two of them were way ahead of Lily academically, and

they always would be. My heart throbbed a little harder for her, for there would always be a helpless side to my little angel.

As usual, Lily soon tired of her lesson. We put away her blocks. Then she went to her little corner of the kitchen, sat on the floor, and picked up her rag doll. She cuddled the floppy toy in her arms, stroked the strands of orange yarn protruding from its head, and mumbled something personal between her and the doll. Long ago I suppressed the thought that my little girl might never mature beyond childhood. I'd come to terms with the fact that Lily, in her childlike innocence, might always be different from my other two.

Sighing, I retreated to my rocker by the fireplace, plopped the book on my lap, and stared into the flames. John's phone call remained etched in my mind. He'd made it to Philadelphia, but he hadn't been able to purchase supplies. He'd discovered that Philadelphia had one of the highest death tolls of flu victims in the nation. He could have turned around and come home. Or he could have gone somewhere else to buy what he needed.

Instead he'd responded to the Red Cross' call for doctors to help out at the city's hospitals. With little concern for his own health, my husband had done exactly what I figured he'd do. Eighteen years ago I fell in love with him because of his unselfish, merciful nature. He was still the same man, and I was the same woman. So, just like back then, I needed to give him my full support.

The truth was, try as I might I could never measure up to my husband's standards. He kept a well-organized pharmacy. He could find something in a second. My pantry, on the other hand, looked like a cyclone had gone through it. There was no order to my jarred fruits and vegetables, my sacks of potatoes, my herbs and spices. Except for an occasional date scrawled on the side of a jar or a bag, I had no idea which items were about to spoil and which still had life in them. I trusted my eyes and nose to tell me. All I had to do was pull off the lids and untie the strings.

John was different from other men in lots of ways. For one thing, he picked up after himself, wiped the flyaway hairs off the bathroom sink after he finished shaving and combing his hair. He didn't partake in many of the typical male inclinations. Didn't smoke or chew or spit or drink alcohol, except for a couple of beers once in a while. He saved his money with intense frugality but quickly gave to charities that moved his heart. And he never denied me and the children little extras, like the six rhinestone-studded combs he brought home one day after a trip to Philadelphia. The girls and I wore them to church the following Sunday.

As for me, I was like the rest of my family. I drank Papa's bathtub wine at every meal. My brothers introduced me to smoking at an early age. I had kept a pack in my personal grooming drawer, just in case I had a moment of weakness. Mama knew it was there. Though she never called my attention to it, she didn't miss an opportunity to talk about the perils of smoking loud enough for me to hear.

"I have an herb that will take away the urge," Mama often said, though none of us ever asked her for some.

I kept on smoking whenever I wanted to, until the day a six-year-old boy died while in my care. I expected the hospital officials to let me go. I had failed. The guilt stayed with me long after I left the hospital. Olive thought I'd chosen working in the ghetto as a self-appointed punishment, like I'd sentence myself to a prison of sorts. I told her she couldn't be more wrong. I did what I wanted. No amount of psychological unveiling could sway me from my chosen path.

The truth is, conscientious, respectable John had fallen in love with a free spirit, but a broken one at that. It took three children and more than a decade of studying the moods and manners of my dear husband for me to get past the worst sin I'd ever committed and find my way in life. Now I'd become so committed to caring for my family, I had neglected everyone else. How on earth was John able to do both? Like my husband, I should be reaching out to others in need. I should be helping Emma and all the neighbors who came to my door over the last couple of days.

Only a few hours ago, I had taken a journey into the past. Those sweet memories reminded me how fortunate I was to have a husband like John. For more than 20 years, he'd remained committed to his profession. He'd learned all aspects of medicine, including every specialty from anesthesiology to vascular surgery. While many of his classmates ended up in a specialized practice, John had chosen general medicine. I sensed that from the beginning he'd had his eye on his father's practice and the townsfolk he'd come to know and love while growing up in Sawmill.

Watching him I learned what it truly was to love one's neighbors. Throughout our marriage my husband had put the needs of others before his own. He didn't merely talk about goodness, he lived it.

I'd listened to a ton of sermons about loving others in church while growing up. I'd even memorized some of the verses. *"Do unto others as you would have others do unto you."* And *"Greater love hath no man than this, that a man lay down his life for another.*" But I hadn't seen them fleshed out in a human being until I met John.

The clock on the mantle was coming up on 5 p.m. John was 70 miles away, moving from one bed to the next, breathing the stench of human waste, stopping the flow of blood from victims' noses and mouths, administering drugs to numb the pain and quench the fevers. My husband would work well into the night. He'd get little sleep, rise before dawn, and continue ministering to one patient after another. He'd declare this one ready for a bowl of soup and that one ready for the morgue. He was risking his own health to save strangers he might never see again.

And here I sat, afraid to open my door to friends and neighbors, afraid to step out in the community and help whoever I could. I had to stop beating myself up over my failures; had to *do* something and make the voices shut up.

I flipped through the book, gleaned a few ideas from it, and set it aside. I rose from my rocker and filled the kettle on the stove to get the steam going again, and then I went straight to my pantry. Perhaps there was something I could use, herbs and spices and roots, items my mother put together for her folk remedies. If I could help one person—just one—my friend Emma perhaps—I might also feel better about myself.

I opened the pantry door and breathed in the aroma of spices and herbs. I stood still for a couple of minutes and took in all the clutter. How was I supposed to find any cures in that mess? I'd have to search through every box, bag, and jar. The clutter never troubled me before. I simply grabbed something that looked like it might make a decent supper. When you grow up in a family of nine, you give up trying to keep order. I could have placed something where I'd be sure to find it again and inevitably someone else came along and moved it. Eventually I gave up.

John never knew such disorder. He had one brother. One. Which meant each of them had his own bedroom, his own closet, his own dresser drawers. They didn't have to share everything they owned with six siblings. Because of that, John kept a clean room—even as a young boy. His mother told me more than once what an exemplary son she'd raised. I heard it so often I sometimes wanted to run in the bathroom and stick my head in the sink.

"He was a fine son." Her lilting voice sang out the praises. "Hung his shirts and pants in the closet. Folded his underwear and stacked it neatly in his bureau drawer. Made his bed every morning before he left the house. Never left any toys or books on the floor for me to trip over." She produced a wink and a nod. "His brother, Martin, was the same. Neither one of my boys gave me a lick o' trouble. Out of the house for school or work, home by suppertime. It was a grand life, yes it was."

I imagined a little boy picking up his room, tossing dirty clothes in the hamper and making sure everything was in its place. It was easy to picture all of that, because John still did it, every last stitch. I never had to grab dirty socks or men's underwear off the floor. Never had to hang anything up. He set everything he owned in a specific place. Even if the electricity went off, he could find whatever he needed in the dark.

John had spent plenty of time teaching our young son to pick up after himself. "It's a sad thing when a little boy leaves all the work to his mother," John told him. I felt a little sorry for my boy. My brothers may have lived like slobs, but they were happy. Still, I never interfered. If Johnny could be half as considerate as John was, he'd make a fine husband one day.

Thankfully, my husband never complained about *my* mess. He merely peered inside the pantry, *tsk-tsked*, then shook his head and shut the door. Mr. Fastidious—that's what I called him. His pharmacy cupboard looked like the Queen of England's jewelry case—every item glittering and standing in rows, like soldiers awaiting his next command.

"A place for everything and everything *in* its place," he often quoted the old proverb, not in a mocking way, but with tenderness, like a schoolteacher showing a first-grade student how to organize her flip-top desk. Even his leather medical bag was well-appointed, with little pockets inside for the finer instruments, and everything else carefully wrapped in white linen towels, which he sterilized once a week in hot water, and all of his steel knives polished to a shine with carbolic acid. When opened, the inside of his medical bag literally glowed. I could almost hear angels singing.

John didn't mess with my slapdash pantry. Sometimes I wish he had. Or that by some miracle when I married him, a little of his organizational skills would rub off on me.

But they didn't. And now I stood in the middle of a six-foot by 8-foot dilemma, and I didn't know where to start. I walked out and shut the pantry door. After all, my mother's treatments were old wives' tales weren't they? I wasn't even sure they'd work.

I checked on my children. All three had fallen asleep. Amy, with her arm flung over the side of the sofa and the book on the floor. Lily, curled up in her special corner, clutching the floppy doll to her chest. And Johnny, resting his forehead on the open medical manual and drooling on a picture of someone's pancreas.

The mess behind my pantry door was still beckoning. I had to admit, this was as good a time as any to straighten up those shelves. I returned to the nightmare behind those closed doors, cautiously stepped inside and formulated a plan. I couldn't tackle the project all at once. I needed to deal with it slowly, section by section. If I sorted through one area at a time, perhaps the task wouldn't seem so daunting. I cleared one entire shelf and wiped it clean. Starting with the jarred foods, I lifted one item after another and placed them on the shelf with their labels turned outward, like John did with his apothecary items. Next I searched the bins for herbs, roots, and cuttings my mother swore could heal a cold or the flu faster than store-bought drugs. She and John had plunged into many a friendly debate about the benefits of folk remedies over medicines that came from a laboratory. In the end, my husband agreed with Mama that many of the drugs he used were derived from some of those plants she'd mentioned.

With my mother's image hovering before me like a schoolmarm pointing me in the right direction, I cleaned and organized each shelf. Then I set a wicker basket on the top of my stepstool and began to fill it. First a few garlic bulbs, Mama's cure for a nervous stomach. I gathered the remaining bulbs that were strewn about on the shelves, and I placed them in a small wire basket someone had hung from the ceiling. I did the same with the yellow onions, placing a couple of globes in my wicker basket and the rest of them in a medium size wire receptacle dangling beside the garlic basket. As I worked, I breathed in the scent of the newly handled bulbs They brought to mind Mama's jar of onion shavings that stood on her bedside table on nights when she couldn't sleep. She insisted it worked faster than chamomile tea.

Mama did other things I never understood when I lived at home, but now they began to make sense. She burned orange peels to freshen up a room, and she spread eucalyptus leaves around our beds when we were sick.

Spurred by such memories, I grabbed more items off the shelf—coffee beans for pinkeye, chestnut shells to chew on for bouts of laryngitis, and ginger root and popcorn kernels to fight nausea. I added a jar of honey, some lemons and limes, a box of salt, and little bundles of oregano, peppermint leaves, and cloves. Mama had ideas for using all of those items and even combined some of them to fight sore throats and runny noses, discomfort during menstruation, and the throes of constipation or diarrhea, either one, it didn't matter. Though Mama's concoctions had given us kids some relief— or seemed to—when I started nurse's training I shunned the homespun remedies in favor of what my medical books taught. Now, with John away from home and his cupboard bare, I'd come back to my roots, and I said to myself, "What would Mama do?"

After I filled my basket, I swept the shelves clean of onion peels and other shavings, and I tossed moldy fruits and vegetables in a bag to be added later to the compost pile out back. Then I arranged the remaining foods in neat rows on the three shelves. I kept my canned goods at eye-level, the small bags and pouches on lower shelves, and the heavier sacks filled with sugar, flour, and cornmeal on the bottom. I found a bin for potatoes in the corner. Some of the spuds had sprouted eyes. I made a mental note to use them before they spoiled.

When I finished the job, I stepped back and surveyed my freshly appointed pantry. My shelves looked like they belonged in Cowell's general store. The entire pantry smelled minty clean with a hint of onions and garlic permeating the air. No longer did I have to hunt for what I needed. No longer did I have to settle for whatever stood out on the shelf. I threw back my shoulders and smiled. John would be proud of me.

Satisfied, I lugged the wicker basket to the kitchen and set it on the table with a loud clunk. Johnny stirred slightly. My girls didn't move.

My next stop was my bedroom where I kept my nurse's kit underneath our four-poster bed. Like I'd told John, I had a jar of Vicks VapoRub and another of Vaseline, a bottle of hydrogen peroxide and a small vial of iodine, plus different size bandages and plenty of gauze. I set everything on the table next to my basket of home remedies.

I gazed with unease at the indiscriminate collection. Now that I'd moved the scraps from my pantry to my kitchen table, what was I supposed to do with it all? Had my mother's folk medicine really cured my cold? Or had it simply run its course? Did I really get relief from goose grease slathered on my chest? Did my brother's fever drop because of that vinegar-soaked cloth on his forehead? Did Mama fall asleep easier with a jar of onion shavings next to her bed? Or had these odd practices served as psychological cures and nothing more? And what about all the bitter drinks my mother poured down our throats? Warm tea with honey goes down easy, so does hot lemonade with a shot of whiskey, but I didn't care much for the glass of vinegar sprinkled with cayenne pepper. After drinking it I felt worse.

Different concoctions started swimming around in my brain. It's been said the mind can deceive us, that the way we think can control our physical and emotional makeup, perhaps even heal us. If that were true, then we should be able to imagine sickness away, right? We could use any available medicines, whether formulated in a laboratory or made from herbs I'd found in my pantry. A sense of urgency had descended on our village and more specifically on my home. Like a thief in the night, the influenza had swept unseen into our quiet little village. And so I'd resorted to grabbing at straws, if necessary, to keep my children well.

The next time someone came to my door, I wanted to open it wide, listen to the complaint, and then do what my mother always did—offer a handful of herbs with confidence and a smile. I could share a remedy from my wicker basket. Or perhaps all they'll need is a listening ear and a little tender loving care. That's what my nursing supervisor, Mary Prichard, always emphasized. Yes, she taught us the names of different medicines and their uses. She stood nearby as we wrapped and rewrapped each other's arms and legs in an effort to learn how to set a broken bone. She hovered behind us while we delivered babies. All the while she insisted that a well-trained nurse should maintain a sweet, nurturing spirit. Otherwise whatever we did to ease the pain wouldn't be enough.

"And keep confident," Mary said. "Very little can be done under the spirit of fear," she added, quoting Florence Nightingale. "The most important part of your job is to give comfort and kindness. Be a true Florence Nightingale nurse. You'll soon discover that complete healing comes when you can treat your patients as if they are members of your own family. Chances are, *you* might be the one lying on a sickbed one day. *You* might be the one who has to depend on doctors and nurses to get you back to good health. So treat your patients like you want to be treated."

As Mary's words came tumbling back to me, they stirred up another idea. It wasn't enough to simply place a basket of potential remedies on my table and wait for someone to come to my door. I knew who was sick. I had kept a list. It was ready for John when he decided to come home.

I released a long sigh, stepped away from the table and went to my sewing pile. I sorted through fabric remnants and pieces I'd cut from burlap sacks, grabbed my scissors and several skeins of colored yarn, and returned to the table. I cut the cloths into 10-inch squares and arranged them in a pile. Then I selected one and laid some of the herbs and roots on top. I folded up the sides and bound them with a piece of yarn. Then I picked up the next square of cloth and did the same.

One by one, I repeated the process. I lined up the plump little pouches across the top of my table. They could fill a temporary need until John returned with the badly needed medicines.

I was tying up my eleventh pouch when a weak moan came from the sofa. I dropped the yarn and hurried to Amy's side. The sight of her tore my breath away. Her face had turned a sallow yellow. Her eyes were open, but a film had clouded their color. I placed my hand on her cheek, then on her forehead. Her fever had returned and it was raging.

I ran to the table, pulled a thermometer from my nursing kit, and took my daughter's temperature—104 degrees. With a sense of urgency I went through the routine John and I had used earlier. Cool compresses, chips of ice from the freezer, more steam in the room. I checked her temperature again. This time it read 103. Still not enough of a change.

Desperate, I went to John's pharmacy cupboard. Perhaps he'd overlooked something. Anything that might help to bring Amy's fever down. From where I stood two feet below the top shelf, the entire cupboard appeared to be empty. I slid my kitchen stepstool in front of the cupboard, climbed up on it and stood on tiptoe. I swept my hand across the surface of the top shelf. Nothing, not even a fluff of dust. Then my fingertips touched something small and round, way back at the farthest point of the shelf. I eased it forward, rolled it to the edge of the shelf, then grabbed it and held it in front of me. In my hand was a tiny pill bottle with no markings. I shook it and heard a clattering of little pellets. I unscrewed the top and peered inside. A few small white tablets stared back at me. I had no idea what they were. Several new medicines had hit the market since I quit my nursing career. I hadn't bothered to keep track. I'd trusted John to know what they were and when to use them.

I poured the tablets in my palm. There were five. Then I looked at Amy. I hadn't forgotten the rules of medicine. Never administer anything to anyone without knowing exactly what it is and what it's for.

Amy stirred. "Mama, my head hurts," she whimpered. "So do my arms and legs."

I chewed my bottom lip and looked at the white spheres in my palm. Some drugs, if used incorrectly, could poison a child. With slow, purposeful movements I stepped off the stool. Amy let out another frail cry.

Impelled by a mother's heart, I squeezed the warning to the back of my mind and hurried toward my ailing child.

Chapter Ten

I stood before the sofa still clutching the little white tablets. They could be aspirin or quinine. Something to bring Amy's fever down and stop the aches. But why had the bottle been rolling around up there on the top shelf? And how old was it? The label was blank. It could be anything. Sure it was medicine, but what? And how lethal was it? If it was on the top shelf it had to be something powerful.

I wanted to help my daughter, but I didn't want to kill her.

I took a deep breath and walked over to the table. Among the herbs and cuttings in one of the pouches were slivers of willow bark. I could steep them in boiling water, like my mother used to do for fever. The salicin inside the bark worked like aspirin. The hot herbal tea might also help to soothe Amy's body aches.

I returned the tablets to the bottle and set it on the table. Then I started a pot of water on the stove. While I waited for it to boil, I dug through my basket for the willow bark, took a paring knife and cut shavings into the pot of water. I hovered beside the stove and watched the liquid begin to darken to light gray, then tan. When it reached a golden color, I removed the pot and strained the steamy liquid into a cup. I went to the freezer, chipped some slivers off the block of ice and added them to the hot broth to cool it slightly. Then

I returned to the sofa and found Amy struggling to sit up. I held the cup in front of her and urged her to take a sip. She lifted her head off the pillow, took the cup in both hands, and sipped the bitter tea.

She wrinkled her nose and shoved the cup at me.

"Come on, dear, drink. You'll feel a lot better."

"It tastes horrible." She pouted for a moment but sipped a little more, then she tried to give me the cup again.

"Amy, you need to drink all of it. We have to bring your fever down. Please, honey, drink."

She shook her head in stubborn refusal. I hurried to the pantry for a jar of honey and spooned a healthy dose into Amy's tea. She sampled the liquid, managed a weak smile, then finished the cup. A few dregs remained on the bottom. I took the cup from her hand and helped her settle back against the pillow. Then I stood holding my breath, waiting to see if the color might return to her face. She shut her eyes, but the wrinkle on her forehead told me she was in great distress.

John had spoken about the deceptive nature of the influenza, how it swept into crowded military training centers, infecting thousands and killing hundreds. How it moved from one soldier to another, from one bunk to another, from one barracks to another, from one fort to another, and ultimately from one country to another. He spoke of the brief lull when it looked as though the disease might have run its course, and then its surprising return with more intensity.

In the beginning, the people of Sawmill went about their daily routines with little concern about flu bugs and viruses. Being in the country we had access to homegrown food and farm products. Then, with World War I raging in Europe the U.S. government introduced ration cards in the bigger cities. We still remained in our own little world. Many of us had stockpiled cured meats and we'd canned our own fruits and vegetables. We visited the farmer's market to buy produce, and we went to the dairy farm for milk and butter. Everything went on as usual.

Then the second wave came through in October, and our friends and neighbors started getting sick. The germs spread quickly. It was like an avalanche had fallen on our sleepy little village.

Earl Prescott was the first to die. He was only 19. Shortly after, two young women became ill. One of them died. The other survived, but afterward she suffered with heart palpitations. People passed the germs from one to another, oblivious to the mandates being promoted in the bigger cities where stores and schools and churches were shutting their doors, and people of all walks of life were wearing masks, including the police, the street cleaners, and the baseball players.

We became aware of the intensity when entire families contracted the disease. Most of them recovered. Then little Robby Wilson died, and we knew it wasn't over yet. Like so many families had done, Emma hung a strip of gauze to her front door, a white one that let people know a child had died there. Some doors bore darker strips of gauze, a sign an older adult had passed away. As people locked themselves inside their homes, Sawmill began to look like a ghost town.

Over the last few weeks John had trekked from one house to another, trying to help as many as he could. Once a week he drove his buggy out to the farms and discovered that even they, isolated as they were, had not been able to avoid the disease. It wasn't long before my husband used up his store of medicines that should have lasted through the winter months.

Neither of us had adequately judged the virility of that disease. Now John was in Philadelphia, and I was still at home. For the first time in our married life, we were separated.

Again I felt Amy's forehead and then took her temperature. Her fever had remained.

I flew about the house. More towels doused with cold water and this time I added a drizzle of vinegar, like Mama would have done. More offers of herbal tea which she heartily drank. More prayers for God's healing miracle.

Discouraged, I trudged back to the table and looked through my collection of home remedies, searching for something—anything that might help my daughter. I dug back in my memories. What would my mother do? Which herb would she use? Which dried flower? Which leaf? Which root?

Johnny raised his head from the book. He'd been sitting at the table napping for an hour. He rubbed his eyes and looked at the array of home remedies strewn across the table.

"What's going on, Mama? What's all this stuff?" He swept his little hand toward my basket and the pouches I'd put together. I didn't want to alarm him. Tied up with pieces of colored yarn they looked like birthday presents.

"They're gifts, honey. For our neighbors. And maybe something to help Amy feel better."

He slid off his chair and came around the side of the table, wrapped his arms around my waist and gave me a squeeze. "When I get big, I'll be a doctor like Papa. Then I'll be able to take care of Amy and Lily and even you."

I patted his head, mussed his hair, then I bent over and planted a kiss on his forehead.

"You're going to make a fine doctor, son."

He turned his freckled face up at me and grinned. His shiny green eyes sparkled with mirth, much like his father's did when he was about to suggest a picnic in the park or a canoe ride on the river.

"Can we play a game, Mama?"

I knew what that meant. Marbles or Old Maid or perhaps a game of checkers.

I forced a smile. "Maybe after supper. Like always."

Supper tonight meant runny potato-and-leek soup and pumpernickel bread. I could whip something together and still keep an eye on Amy. Perhaps the potato soup might do her some good.

Lily was still asleep in the corner, her arms and legs wrapped protectively around her little rag doll with the button eyes.

I gave Johnny a gentle pat on his arm. "Wake your little sister, and I'll get supper going."

While he went over to the corner to rouse Lily, I went to the pantry and gathered an apron full of bug-eyed potatoes, dumped them in the sink and began to pare them for soup. I got a kettle of water started, dropped in the diced potatoes and the chopped leaks, and allowed the mix to simmer on the stove for a while. In almost no time, a pungent aroma filled the air and stirred my appetite.

All the while, I kept glancing at Amy. She lay very still, her mouth open as though gasping for air. This troubled me. I had thought she'd gotten past the worst of it. I repeated the question I'd been asking myself for two days: *was it influenza or something else?* My daughter had displayed a few of the symptoms—fever and achy arms and legs. But she hadn't coughed or sneezed, not even once.

While I waited for the soup to finish cooking, I went back to the table and sorted through my basket. Surely, I had something that might help Amy. I fingered the roots and the herbs, set aside the willow bark.

The next moment my eyes drifted to the spot on the table where I had left the strange pill bottle I'd found at the top of John's pharmacy cupboard. It was gone. In a panic I searched the table. No pill bottle. I looked on the floor. Checked my apron pockets.

The next thing, I heard Johnny's voice from the corner where Lily had been napping. "Come on, open your mouth, Lily. This'll make you feel better."

My face went cold. I turned toward the corner. Johnny was kneeling in front of Lily, his hand outstretched, and he was holding three little white tablets.

"No!" I squeezed the word from the bottom of my throat. "Don't!"

I tried to rush toward my children, but it was as if someone had grabbed onto my skirt and was holding me back, forcing me to run in slow motion. Somehow, I had to get those pills out of my son's hand before Lily opened her mouth and swallowed them. Suddenly, my legs felt like cinderblocks. I tripped on the leg of a chair, stumbled over my own feet, then fell face down on the hard, wooden floor.

A sharp pain seized my left elbow and took my breath away. My forehead throbbed like someone had hit it with a hammer. I lifted my head. Both of my children were staring at me, their eyes wide. But what I saw next sent me reeling. Johnny's hand was empty.

I tried to push myself off the floor. My left arm hurt so much I couldn't put weight on it. I pressed my right hand against the hard wood and drew my knees up to my chest, then I struggled to a kneeling position. I felt my left arm and determined it wasn't broken but badly bruised. Then I turned my attention on Lily and I froze. She was holding the little white tablets against her doll's mouth, a single row of black needlepoint stitches.

I didn't want to startle her, so I took a breath and softened my voice. "Lily, let me have those." I reached out with an open hand.

She stared at me, confusion washing over her young face.

"It's okay, honey. You're not in trouble. Just give me the medicine."

She smiled mischievously.

"Please, Lily. You have to give it to me. They're not good for your doll."

She darted her round, dark eyes toward Johnny and then back at me.

"Your brother's not in trouble either. But I need you to give me those. They're not for little dolls and they're not for little children."

Tears flooded into her eyes. She balled up her little fist, hiding the tiny ovals within her grasp.

Still on my knees, I crept toward her. She slipped her hand behind her back.

"The thing in your hand, Lily, it's not good. It tastes terrible and it could harm you."

She gave a little smile then, like she thought we were playing a game.

I furrowed my brow and stared with intensity at her, letting her know I meant business.

"This isn't a game, Lily. Give me the pill."

Suddenly, Johnny lunged at his sister, pulled her hand from behind her back and wrenched the tablets from her tiny fingers. Lily burst out crying. Johnny handed me the pills, grinning smugly, like he expected me to reward him.

Relieved, I grasped the tablets and released a sigh.

"Never," I told him. "Never, never, never, put your hands on something if you're not sure what it is." I opened my hand and showed both of them the tablets. "These could be very dangerous. I found them on the top shelf of your papa's cupboard, and you know what that means. That's the no-no shelf where he keeps medicines that are too strong for young children. Medicines that have to be given out carefully."

I made it to my feet and towered over the two of them. Their faces cringed with apprehension, their smiles had disappeared. Tears gushed from Lily's eyes and ran down her cheeks. Johnny scooted away from me, his face flushed in a mix of shame and fear.

"It's all right, children." I softened my voice in an attempt to ease their anxiety. "I love you both. I didn't want you to hurt yourselves. Mama was concerned, that's all."

I dropped the tablets into the bottle, then counted to make sure there were five. Satisfied, I hid the bottle on the top shelf of the closet in my bedroom, safely away from curious little hands.

Johnny rose to his feet. Lily did the same, dropping her doll to the floor. I rushed back to them, bent low and gathered them into my arms. They pressed their faces against my skirt. I held them there, cooing to them, for as long as they needed. Then, noticeably soothed, the children gradually pulled away from me.

I stroked their faces, ran my fingers through their hair.

"You're not in any trouble," I said. "I love you both so much, and I didn't want you to be in danger."

Johnny nodded his understanding. Lily continued to look up at me, her watery brown eyes wide with bewilderment.

"How about some potato soup?" I offered. They both managed to smile. Johnny let out a "Yeah!" It seemed to me that everything had gone back to normal again. Yet, I knew until the flu left Sawmill, nothing would be normal or even close to it.

I went to the stove and stirred the soup, found it ready to serve, and ladled the chunks of potatoes and leeks into three bowls reserving only the broth for Amy.

I found my oldest child had fallen asleep again. A check of her forehead revealed that her fever had not subsided. Gently, I shook her shoulder to awaken her. She opened her eyes slightly and coughed a couple of times. I pulled a handkerchief from my pocket and wiped her chin. Blood was mixed with her sputum. My heart nearly stopped.

Amy moaned, then opened her eyes a little more and stared at me, her eyes filled with confusion. I struggled to revive my training of 20 years ago. On the verge of panic, I glanced at Johnny and Lily. They were slurping up their soup like starved orphans. My own serving was growing cold. It didn't matter. Amy needed me. I had to do something to bring down her fever.

I hurried to the bookshelf against the wall by the fireplace. It held my old nurse's textbooks along with my collection of novels. I located what I wanted, a battered medical manual.

I sat in my rocker and turned to the section on fever and headaches. Several pages covered the etiology and symptoms and how to treat them. If I'd had any of those medicines I would have used them. The next page covered the complications, including encephalitis and meningitis, the mention of which got my heart racing.

If only John were home. He could have done a more thorough examination, maybe diagnosed Amy's condition without having to check a manual. He had the information in his head, had memorized much of the book in my hands, had sat in lectures given by some of the top physicians in Philadelphia, and he'd seen case after case of people infected with various diseases. *He* was the medical expert in our family. Not I. He had stayed with the work. I'd quit. He had kept up on the latest medicines and treatments. He received medical journals in the mail and he talked on Cowell's telephone to different experts in other parts of the country.

I had done none of those things. It was as if when I packed away my nurse's uniform I'd also packed away my brains.

In his absence John had left me with a huge responsibility. If Amy were to survive, I had to do the right thing, had to choose the right herbs or powders. I had to think like John. Had to set aside my anxiety and make rational decisions. In effect, I needed to act like a nurse again.

The manual pointed out that sometimes a fever, if it's high enough, will cause a headache. Once the person's temperature goes back to normal, the headache also should subside. Perhaps such a situation could also work the other way. Maybe if I healed Amy's aches and pains, the fever might also diminish.

I closed the book and raised my eyes toward heaven. "Please, God, show me what to do. Help me save my daughter. Grant me wisdom, Lord. This burden is too much for me to bear alone. Please, don't abandon me now."

Out of nowhere, I thought of something we nurses did to

Plague

help patients recover in the hospital. Some had intense fevers
that didn't respond to the usual treatment of cool towels
and aspirin. We ended up placing the patient in a bath of
lukewarm water, then got them into clean, dry clothes.

I tossed the book aside, hurried to the bathroom, where I
ran warm water into our cast iron bathtub, it's porcelain inte-
rior warming with the flow. I threw in a handful of lavender
bath salts. Then I guided Amy to her bath, helped her slip
out of her clothes, and braced her arm as she stepped into
the aromatic water. As she lowered her body into the pool,
she released a sigh, a sound that momentarily comforted me.

Aware that her hair, if it got wet, could cause a chill, I drew
her curls to the top of her head and pinned them there, away
from the moisture. My daughter shut her eyes and leaned
back against a rolled up towel I had placed behind her neck.

I was determined to do everything in my power to rescue
my daughter from sickness. If she did have the influenza, I
was facing a major battle. Already the monster had taken the
lives of a half-dozen people in Sawmill. Those who survived
suffered with other complications. Some coughed incessantly.
Others lost their appetite. And almost all of the victims
struggled to take a deep breath.

But my Amy had been born with that same fighting spirit
I possessed. With two brothers picking on me I learned to
fight back at a young age. I'd seen the same spunk in Amy,
who stood up to a playground bully when she was only five.
The girl was twice her size and was determined to take the
swing away from her. But Amy didn't falter. She pushed
off the swing, stuck out her pointy-toed shoes, and clipped
the bully in the left shoulder. The girl never bothered my
daughter again.

But here was Amy, weakened by a different bully, one so powerful she might not be able to defeat it. I stood close to the tub, ready to grab her arm if she should slip beneath the froth.

"Fight, Amy, fight," I said beneath my breath.

Amy's skin coloring had remained a sallow yellow. I checked her extremities, grateful to see they hadn't darkened. Some of those who had died had succumbed to pneumonia, and the lack of oxygen had disrupted their blood circulation. Dark hands and feet were a sure sign that death was closing in.

Amy appeared to be relaxing in the lavender-scented bath. A smile tugged at her lips, and, though her eyes were closed, she was humming a faint tune that I couldn't make out. Nevertheless, it brought me a reasonable amount of comfort.

I kept Amy's bath brief, dried her thoroughly, and helped her into a fresh nightdress. A hint of pink had returned to her cheeks. I pressed my hand against her forehead. The fever had dropped a little.

I put a fresh pillowcase and a crisp bed sheet on the sofa and helped Amy settle in again. This time, she sat upright and gratefully accepted a bowl of potato broth. I ladled out a fresh bowl of soup for myself. Then I pulled a chair up to the sofa, and Amy and I ate together.

The other two children had finished their meal and were playing tiddlywinks on the floor in Lily's corner. She'd sat her doll against the wall to watch their game. Thankfully, the children had kept their distance from Amy and hadn't shown any signs of illness. I escaped from my troubles temporarily, amused by their play. Johnny pressed the squidger and sent a wink soaring. Lily squealed with delight. For the moment, life was good. My children were safe. I could go about my business as usual. While I still hadn't determined the cause for Amy's distress, I was determined to fight the symptoms as best I could. And I would keep watching for other signs and do whatever I could to heal her.

As the current head of the home I had one job, to keep my children safe and well. Still, the charitable pouches beckoned to me from the table. I spent the next hour filling more bags. In the end I'd put together two dozen gift bags of home remedies for our friends and neighbors. If they stopped coming to my door, I could go out in the street and deliver them.

Though I could do with a breath of fresh air, until dear Amy surfaced from her affliction I wasn't about to leave the house. My responsibility to my children took precedence over everything else. For their sake I would tolerate the claustrophobic atmosphere of being locked up in a small cottage for weeks. I tried to ignore the four walls that seemed to be closing in on me. My resistance was waning, but there was nothing I could do.

The truth was, I'd become a prisoner in my own home. It struck me then that I not only needed to take care of my children. I needed to take care of myself. I had to stay well, had to remain alert to any changes in Amy's condition. I'd kept the little ones away from her, but I'd been hovering by her side like a mother hen. I may have already picked up her germs. Panic set in. I struggled to take a deep breath. My heart was pounding, my hands were shaking.

The realization struck me like a bolt of lightning. *What will become of the three of them if I get sick? With John in Philadelphia, who will protect them?*

Chapter Eleven

Amy finished eating her broth and was already falling asleep again. It seemed she'd been sleeping a lot. I wasn't sure if that was a good thing, but I decided to let her rest. I removed the bowl from her fingers, then checked her forehead. The fever had subsided a little more. A hint of color had returned to her cheeks.

I gathered up the little gift pouches, put the rest of the paraphernalia in the wicker basket and placed everything on the hearth by the fireplace. I picked up the medical books Johnny had been looking at and returned them to the shelf in John's cupboard. Then I set about washing our supper dishes.

When I finished, Johnny and I played a game of checkers. He beat me two out of three games. I may have cheated a little—in his favor.

Afterward, I got the two little ones ready for bed. Once they'd snuggled under their quilts I told them the story of the *Three Bears*. Lily fell asleep before I got to the part about the bears coming home. She had the sweetest smile on her lips. I kissed both of my children on the forehead, tiptoed out of their room, and quietly shut the door behind me. My last glimpse of Johnny was seeing him wide awake and staring out the window at the stars. The fairy tale must have bored him to tears after he'd had his nose in his father's medical books, but he didn't complain. It was as if he didn't mind coming down to Lily's level once in a while.

The hardest part of this isolation had been keeping the children away from their friends. Johnny told me more than once that he missed playing with the Wilcox boys. Their dad, Frank Wilcox, was part-owner of the sawmill along with his brother, Ed. They made a substantial income and had purchased a couple of army tents so the boys could camp out on their property. They also took the kids fishing at the lake and held cookouts on the front lawn at Frank's house, or *castle*, as Johnny liked to call it. Our entire cottage could have fit inside the Frank Wilcox' front room.

Johnny spent most summer afternoons and winter breaks with the Wilcox boys. The flu had changed all that. For one thing, there'd be no more playing outside, not as long as germs continued to hover in the air. No more Saturday afternoon parties. No more trips to the village park. My son must have thought he was being punished for something. I made sure I reminded him now and then that he'd done nothing wrong. The isolation was all due to the flu. He looked up at me with those curious green eyes and a confused half-smile on his lips.

I made a mental note to remind Johnny once again in the morning that once the influenza was gone, we could go outside again and celebrate like we'd always done before.

I checked on Amy and found her sleeping comfortably. I added a log to the fire, sending up a spray of sparks. Then I brewed myself a cup of chamomile tea. While it steeped, I picked up the medical manual I'd been looking at earlier and flipped through the pages. The diagrams and my hand-written notations took me back to a healthier time when I cared for the sick without worrying about catching what they had.

All I wanted back then was to learn everything there was to know about medicine and to become one of Philadelphia's most efficient nurses. Everyone, especially Mama and Papa, were surprised when I chose the streets as my workplace.

When the tea was ready, I went to the dining hutch and pulled out one of my good tea cups that I reserved for special occasions. Like the rest of the set it had blue birds and pansies hand-painted on its side. I returned to the rocker, and with the manual opened on my lap, I coddled the tea cup in both hands. Setting the rocker in motion, I breathed deeply of the herbal vapor as it blended with the scent of charred oak in the fireplace. Nighttime was settling on our little berg. The streets were quiet. Except for the rattle of the undertaker's wagon passing by once a day, the streets of Sawmill had been nearly empty for several weeks. At the present, there was only the sound of tree branches clicking together, jostled by the rise of a northerly wind.

Momentarily soothed, I glanced at the open page in the manual and allowed my mind to drift back to my college days. I took a sip of the hot tea and began to relax. Suddenly I was walking the stark white halls of the hospital, a stethoscope in my pocket, and in one hand a paper cup of pills for the old woman in Room 2-A. She'd come into the emergency department struggling to breathe. The staff had provided an oxygen mask and a quinine pill to get her fever down. Then they shipped her to the second floor, north wing, under my care.

I paused in the doorway, listened to her raspy breathing, watched for any sign of awareness—an opening of her eyes or the twitching of her fingers. Except for a slight up-and-down movement of her chest, the poor, frail thing lay motionless.

She was so thin the bed sheet formed a sheer outline of her bony arms and legs. She had to be at least 85, maybe 90. People didn't live that long back then. She'd already been on the earth twice as long as the average woman.

I walked in, my rubber-soled nursing shoes gliding soundlessly across the tiled floor. As I drew close to the bed, the woman's eyes opened as if she'd sensed my arrival. I stepped back, startled by the intensity of those pale blue eyes.

I took a breath and quickly recovered. "How are you today, Mrs. Dougherty?"

Her oxygen mask moved slightly and smile lines appeared near her temples.

"I've brought your meds."

She nodded and tried to lift her head, then she went limp and fell back against the pillow.

I turned the crank at the foot of the bed and manually raised the top portion. Now that she was sitting upright, I gently removed her mask and hand-fed her the little pills along with a cup of water from her bedside table.

She gulped them down loudly, and I couldn't help but think that someday I could be lying there and some young nurse would have to take care of me.

Similar thoughts had crowded into my mind now and then, prompting me to give the best care I could. Like nurse Pritchard had said, it was a do-unto-others kind of job, no question about it.

With her mask back in place, Mrs. Dougherty's muffled voice grabbed my attention. "My son," she said. "Has he come to see me yet?"

I caught my breath. Her chart said her only child had preceded her in death by twenty years. This woman lived alone. If it hadn't been for an alert neighbor who'd taken her to the hospital, she might have died at home and wouldn't have been found until days later.

I thought it better to ignore her question. What good would it do to remind her that her son was gone?

"Why don't we get you bathed and ready for a nice breakfast?" I offered.

Another crinkled smile told me I had successfully distracted her from asking again about her son. I got started with preparations for her bed bath. A pan of warm water, a soap-filled washcloth, and a soft towel, all arranged within easy reach. After bathing her, I changed the sheets with her still lying in the bed, a part of the training I'd found difficult in the beginning but now carried out effortlessly. Having a patient who weighed less than most children probably helped.

I no sooner cleared away the bath items when an aide came to the door with a breakfast tray. Curious, I lifted the lid. There was a plate of scrambled eggs, a slice of toast with jam, and a cup of English tea, hardly enough for a sparrow, but plenty for this wisp of a woman.

I left Room 2-A and started down the hall toward Room 2-D, when someone spoke my name from behind me.

Turning, I caught sight of my friend Olive, her short-cropped blond bob peeking out from under her nurse's cap. She picked up her pace and drew up beside me.

"Rosie," she said in a half-whisper. "Do you have a minute?"

Did I have a minute? For Olive? Of course I did. She and I had bonded early in our training. We'd met in the lecture room on the first day, had giggled through the instructor's butchering of medical terms, and had formed an instant friendship. We'd supported each other through the initial bookwork, quizzed each other on anatomical terms, and memorized together the various medicines, their uses and their dangers. Then there were our clandestine smokes out back of the hospital, where we consoled one another after being reprimanded by an impatient doctor. The threat of being kicked out and sent home hovered over our heads more than we cared to admit.

But we made it through those initial days, survived the first time we witnessed blood and guts in the operating room, and wept together when one of our patients died. It's a helpless feeling when you think you know the right thing to do but nothing works. I even caught a doctor brushing tears from his eyes, something I never expected to see. I came away with a different view of those men in white who had succeeded in hiding their hearts from the rest of us.

This time, when she caught up with me in the hallway, Olive's face was aglow. I knew what that meant. She'd gone out with Jerry again.

She drew close and giggled softly. "I don't care what anybody says. I love him, Rosie. There's no reason why I can't be a nurse and get married too."

I looked behind me. "Shhh. Olive, be careful. Someone might hear."

She shrugged. "I'm not worried. It's a silly rule, don't you agree?"

"I suppose so, but don't you want to graduate? Don't you want to be a nurse?"

"Of course I do. But I don't want them running my personal life. If I want to have a smoke, I can grab a cigarette and go outside where no one can see me. And if I want to marry Jerry, by golly, I'll do it. I'm going to do whatever I want. No more rules."

She was so happy I didn't want to spoil it for her. I offered a sweet, accepting smile.

Then I rested a comforting hand on her shoulder. "Really? Marriage, Olive? Are you planning to give up your career?"

"I don't have to give it up. I found a doctor who doesn't put that kind of demand on his staff of nurses. They're antiquated rules, anyway. I can have my job and my life too."

I reminded Olive of the spiel the supervisors had drummed into our heads. "How are you going to care for a family and your patients at the same time? In the end, you're going to have to choose. Marriage or career. You can't have both."

She glared at me.

"You're wrong, Rosie. They've brainwashed you. I can be a nurse-midwife. I'll only deliver babies. No more operating rooms, no wrapping of wounds, no meds or beds or deadheads."

She started laughing. I gazed at her, amazed at her confidence. At the time, nursing had so consumed me I couldn't imagine doing anything else. Once we graduated, the hospital would send us out into the world. We'd work in doctors' offices or in private homes. The hospital would then fill our vacancies with a fresh batch of nursing recruits, and their training would begin, like ours had, and their heads would be filled with the same rules and stipulations we'd absorbed from the first day we entered that hospital until we left.

As for my own future, I could take a job as a private duty nurse like so many of my classmates wanted to do. Such a position meant a steady income, but it also meant following patients wherever they chose to go, or, in some cases, straight back to the hospital to comfort and nurse them until they were healed—or died. Of course, the moment a patient died, the private duty nurse was out of work and had to find employment elsewhere.

I wasn't sure where I wanted to work. I just knew I couldn't wait to get out on my own. Midwifery sounded possible. So did the work of a visiting nurse. Patients did far better when a nurse came to call. In fact they sometimes requested a nurse instead of a doctor. It wasn't until after I left the hospital and met John that Olive's argument started to make sense. Gradually, I was able to peel away the rigid rules that had kept me from having a social life. After all, we weren't nuns. We were vital, healthy, baby-bearing young women.

Meeting John had made all the difference for me. Almost overnight my heart took over and my inner spirit began to kick aside all the rules. I began to think Olive was right. I figured I could marry John and still keep on nursing.

Little did I suspect that when Amy was born I wouldn't want to do anything except raise my little girl. I couldn't leave my child in the care of anyone else. I wanted to stay home with her. I wanted to hear her first word, see her take her first step, enjoy all of her milestones.

While Olive adeptly juggled her midwifery with her home life, I discovered that I couldn't do both. I began to realize how taxing it would be when I reached my eighth month of pregnancy. I'd been keeping long hours at John's side. He was like a runaway train, working from dawn to dusk, limping up and down the streets in south Philly. I was tagging along, handling whatever task I could, and tiring long before John did. Blame it on my one-inch heels. Blame it on my strangling garter belt. Blame it on the tightening of my uniform during my pregnancy. And don't forget my swollen feet and my aching back.

We started out early in the morning and worked until nightfall. While I kept the pace quite well as a single woman, I now found it increasingly difficult trekking up and down the streets, carrying my medical bag, and struggling to stay focused on those final patients of the day.

Getting pregnant had opened up a whole other door for me, one that I walked through willingly. I thought John might object when I told him it was time for me to stay at home. He never complained about my decision. In fact, he'd smiled sweetly and his emerald eyes sparkled like those of an expectant father.

"It's what I'd want you to do, Rosie," was all he said.

So, I packed up my nurse's uniform, slid my medical bag under our bed, and put the little pin John had given me in my jewelry box. Then I began to prepare for the birth of our first child. I never regretted that decision. I spent 16 years nursing my children through diaper rash, croup, and the usual colds and stomach aches. Now this flu had struck and it wasn't just about my children anymore. The disease reminded me of my first calling, that I was a nurse, and I'd been neglecting those who needed me.

There was a whole world out there of people suffering with a deadly flu, and I was living like a recluse. Just me and my children, waiting for the horrible thing to pass, but knowing it wasn't going to go away overnight. This flu was entirely different from the every-day infections I'd treated on the streets of Philly. Amy's sickness was a stark reminder of how quickly a few minor signs can turn into a life-threatening illness. When a patient's condition changes from one day to the next, you can't predict the outcome. You can only treat the symptoms and hope for the best.

With my daughter sleeping soundly, I pictured her the way she once was, a helpless baby asleep in her crib without a care in the world. When Amy started walking, she kept me running all over the house to find out where she'd gone off to. By that time John had taken over his father's practice, and we'd moved to a simpler life in Sawmill. The residents of the quiet little village didn't need a whole lot of medical care. These were people who lived off the fruit of the land. With several farms providing fresh produce and animal products, their mode of living surpassed what was offered in the big cities. The country folk breathed fresh air and basked in sunshine, while those living in the city inhaled the stench of factory smoke. They drank chlorinated water and dined on rich foods, often coming away from the table uncomfortably stuffed.

Once John was accepted as the sole physician in Sawmill, he worked from home, tending to people who came to our door and doling out medicines from his ever-expanding pharmacy cupboard. Occasionally, he headed out with his horse and buggy to answer a call at one of the farms a few miles outside of town.

It was a comfortable life. I had my children at home, and John had his work. And if he wished to discuss anything with me, he knew I'd understand most of the medical terms and names of diseases. I also accepted that his job wasn't like the normal 9 to 5 operation. I didn't complain when someone knocked on our door at 3 a.m. or when a frantic neighbor interrupted our supper. I'd been groomed. I'd been trained. I was content to simply care for my husband and our children.

Then the plague hit, and I didn't know what to do. The problem was I'd forgotten so many details of my profession. Back then we brought babies into the world, we treated common colds, mended broken bones, soothed first and second-degree burns. Anything worse and either a doctor took over or we sent the patient to the hospital.

When I started having children, I left all of that behind me and transferred the knowledge I'd acquired in nurse's training to the care of my family. My children rarely became ill, and they had never suffered a broken bone or a serious burn. Over the years I forgot much of what I'd practiced at the hospital. I also forgot what it was like to take care of a complete stranger, to have a dying woman look at me with eyes pleading, to have a strange man grasp my hand while in the throes of death, to have other people's children beg me to cuddle them. I had no excuse except that I'd moved on to a different life.

Somehow, in the midst of changing diapers and finding new ways to cook chicken, the elements of nursing had seeped from my mind. Now with the influenza full upon us, memories began to surface and I recalled the exhilaration of bringing a patient out of an illness and back to good health.

Like the young man who'd torn up his leg in a farm accident and had to learn how to walk all over again. I spent hours with him, bracing his arm, slowly and painstakingly guiding him along the hospital hallway. Then there was the young cancer patient who'd been told she couldn't have children. She simply needed a shoulder to cry on. More patients came before me, like a parade of pleading faces, and I remembered why I'd chosen the nursing profession in the first place. I had learned how to heal a wound, how to soothe a broken heart, how to raise someone's spirits.

My younger sister, Annie, once asked me why I had chosen nursing. We were sitting on the edge of her bed looking at family photos at the time. At 15 years of age, Annie had begun to consider different careers for her own life. In a couple years she'd be graduating from high school. She'd either get married, like our older sisters had, and bear lots of children, or she'd go on to higher education, like I did. By this time I was already married to John and was working alongside him in the ghetto.

"It wasn't an easy decision," I told her. "It meant I might never be able to get married. Nurses are expected to marry their careers. It also meant I might have to live at home forever. Papa would have liked that. He doesn't think women should leave home until they get married. He's old-fashioned, don't you think?"

Annie giggled and pointed at a picture of Papa in a stodgy, high- collared suit and a bowler hat. With his face of stone he looked as unemotional as the leafless tree in the photo's background. No smile, not even a glimmer in his eye. Looking back now it's hard to believe I could ever let anyone control me. Not the hospital supervisors, not the other nurses who'd bought into their rules, not even my own father.

"If you hadn't gone into nursing, what else would you have done?" Annie innocently asked me.

I shrugged. "I don't know. Waitressing, I guess. Or I could have taken a job as a receptionist at one of the factories in town. Boring jobs. I had made up my mind to be a nurse the day I delivered Annette's baby. You were only six at the time, and they wouldn't let you in the room. The midwife stood nearby. And afterward Mama smothered me with praises. It was Mama who urged me to go to nursing school."

"So it was Mama's idea?"

"Let's just say she supported my dream."

"What about all her home remedies? She always thought she knew more than the doctors did."

I laughed. "That's true, but it was her home remedies that convinced me to go. Some of them failed and some worked. I figured the same thing might be true of manmade medicines. Some will work and some won't." I breathed a long sigh. "Anyway, I knew there had to be more to medicine than plunging a person's feet in vinegar to bring down a fever or cracking an egg in a basin over someone's head to ease a headache."

We laughed together. Both of us had suffered through Mama's homespun quackery on numerous occasions, and we had survived.

Annie folded her hands and gave me her full attention. "So what's it like? Nursing, I mean."

I sensed the budding of another angel of mercy in the making. She needed to hear the good and bad aspects of nursing and what such a commitment might require of her.

I gazed lovingly into my little sister's eager face, her dark eyes shining with anticipation.

I gave her the same spiel the instructors at the hospital told us on my first day of training. I told her how we must take our time and evaluate a person's condition, adding that the doctor determined the diagnosis and prescribed the medicines.

"A good physician will ask your opinion," I said, then I paused and watched her eyes, blinking quizzically, then staring out the window, then a flicker of understanding.

"You can expect a lot of hectic days," I went on. "Sometimes the doctors are busy, and you're the first one to see a patient who's been wheeled into the ward. You just have to slow down and try to use all your senses. Ask questions. Find out where it hurts. Determine the symptoms. Take the patient's blood pressure and pulse. Take his temperature. Listen to his heart. You might even have to smell his breath."

"What?!" Annie lurched back, a pile of forgotten photos on her lap. "Smell his breath?"

I nodded and chuckled. "What if he's drunk? Or a diabetic? You can tell those things just by using your nose."

"Did you ever get in a panic situation?"

"I always try to take my time," I told her. "But there are moments when, in order to save a life, you have to move fast. The main thing is, be certain before you act. Using good sense can make the difference between life and death."

My own statement halted me for a second. Like many times before, the boy with the ruptured appendix slipped into my mind. I'd made a bad decision, and I was still beating myself up over it. I forced my mind back to the present, but a hint of guilt remained and promised to resurface again one day. It was like trying to bury a dead corpse over and over again.

Annie's forehead wrinkled, and she released a long breath. I patted her hand and smiled with compassion.

"Believe me, Annie. If I can do this, so can you. Most of the time, nursing simply means doing whatever you can to make the patient comfortable. You have to check on the person's condition from time to time, keep them hydrated and well fed. It's no different from what you'd do if Mama became ill."

"What if the patient gets worse? More creases gathered on her forehead.

"You call for a doctor. You've done everything you can and

the rest is up to the doctors. And, of course, you can always call on the great Physician to help you."

Annie lost her worry lines and she laughed. "You sound like Mama now."

I chuckled with her as I realized how much Mama's home-grown medical care had impacted me.

"Do you ever get attached to one of your patients?" Annie's question sent a stab of pain into my heart.

"Too often," I admitted.

I could think of dozens of patients who'd plucked at my heartstrings, most of them little children. That's what had made quitting so difficult.

Such memories brought tears to my eyes. My mind came back to the present. I finished my tea and set the cup aside. Staring into the fire I was struck with one main thought. All those Nightingale techniques I learned 20 years before were still useful. Hadn't I made my daughter comfortable? Hadn't I bathed her in lavender water, kept her hydrated and fed, checked her temperature, felt her pulse, sat by her side, and immersed her in loving care, like any good nurse—or mother—might do?

I looked at my daughter, my heart throbbing with love for her. She was still sleeping like a baby, a peaceful smile on her lips. I had mentioned the great Physician to Amy. Now I prayed that he would heal my daughter.

With John 70 miles away and giving no promise when he might return, the entire burden of caring for Amy had fallen on me. The word helpless came to mind. If my daughter went the way of the barber's son, straight to the grave, I would feel responsible.

I rose from the comfort of the fire and went to check on

my children, starting with Amy. Her fever had risen with nightfall. The home remedies had stemmed the flow but the disease was still winning.

I could repeat what I'd done that afternoon. Lavender bath, clean clothes, a hearty broth. But Amy was sleeping so soundly, I hesitated to disturb her. My heart was breaking. Like most mothers, I would have preferred that God take me instead of my daughter.

There's something about a firstborn that stays with you for the rest of your life. It's like a first love or the first of anything. John and I had been married less than a year when I discovered I was expecting. My initial thoughts strayed to the many childbirths I had witnessed. After I left my training at the hospital, at least 75 percent of my work involved the care of pregnant women and the delivery of their babies. Like my friend Olive I had assumed the role of nurse-midwife most of the time.

Olive and I often met in town for coffee and a chance to catch up. Our conversations always strayed to the joy of bringing a newborn into the world. We celebrated with the happy parents, gave the news to the waiting grandparents, even counseled perplexed siblings. We also shared horror stories about having to make a little slit to help an oversized baby escape. And there were a few occasions when we had to turn an infant head down while taking care not to break an arm or a leg. Then there were times when we had to call in a doctor in to perform a Caesarean section. Most difficult of all were the still births, though rare. I wept along with the mother. All the loving care in the world did little to ease the pain of such a moment.

With all those different scenarios on my mind, as Amy's

birth date drew closer I became more and more anxious. While I longed to hold my baby in my arms, I had seen far too much to believe I might not face one of those traumas of a difficult childbirth. Everything from stillbirth to unforeseen deformities went through my mind. Of course, I'd made up my mind I would accept whatever came.

The truth is, we don't know what God will hand us tomorrow. We raised Lily the same way we raised Amy and Johnny, but she hadn't matured like they had. I soon discovered I needed to exercise a little more patience with Lily.

Not all situations work out the way we want them to. Not all my prayers were answered the way I wanted. I still prayed, but each time the wrong answer came I lost a little more of my faith. I once read somewhere that God blesses us most of all when he rejects our prayers.

Though hard for me to accept, I have to agree. I've seen good things come from painful situations. Like when the hospital let me go, and one thing led to another, and then I met John.

Now I was waiting for Amy to show some sign she might be getting better. I had prayed, knowing God might reject that prayer, that he might say no, or not now, or so many other ways that he answers. Somehow I had to keep the faith, had to believe Amy would recover.

Chapter Twelve

I slept fitfully that night, got out of bed several times to check on my children. Nothing had changed. Amy still had a slight fever. The other two had plunged into dreamland, content in their comfortable beds, untouched by the beast for the moment.

When the sun came up I dragged myself out of bed and glanced at John's side—still empty. We'd rarely spent a night apart. Where had my husband slept? On a cold, hard cot in a back room of the hospital? Had he gone to stay with his brother, Martin? I shook my head. He'd never travel that far from where he was needed. Not John.

I could picture him moving from one sickbed to another, with hardly enough time to take a patient's temperature or blood pressure before another one called to him from across the room. I imagined his sadness as he pulled a sheet over a patient's head and called for aides to carry the dead into the hall. I could almost hear his voice, commanding nurses to clean up the soiled bedding and the blood-stained sheets. And in the absence of any help, I could see him doing it all himself.

On a brighter side, I imagined his patients rising from near death and walking away, cured. John might have a smile on his lips, maybe tears in his eyes, or both. I knew my husband well enough to picture him in a variety of situations. I could predict how he'd respond.

From the moment we teamed up in the tenement community John proved his loyalty as a doctor. He never faltered, never backed down from even the dirtiest job. He spoke softly to his patients, yet he possessed a professional ethic that didn't waver no matter what challenges came before him. He mourned the losses and praised God for the successes. He could pull a tooth, wrap a wound, saw a limb, and a host of other medical procedures, without having to carry a manual around with him. His mind was like a filing cabinet where he stored medical terms and procedures, always ready when he needed them.

One particular day came to my mind as I busied myself about the kitchen. As I opened a fresh bar of lye soap, the kind we used for the toughest jobs, its biting scent triggered an unpleasant memory.

John and I had been navigating the narrow inner city alleys surrounded on both sides by poorly constructed apartments. In one particular dwelling we tended to a woman and five children who were suffering with scabies. My husband threw around words like *Sarcoptes scabiei* and *infectious epidermis*, terms from my training days that I had long ago forgotten.

He explained the same thing in lay terms to the mother. He told her the children's rash was caused by a tiny, ugly mite that lived in their bedding. He told her to wash all their clothes, also the bed linens and quilts in lye soap. Then he gave her a jar containing a topical cream to spread daily on their rash. We had seen several similar cases in the neighborhood, a tragic affliction of those who lived in overcrowded dwellings with poor sanitation.

As we left that humble home, John grew very quiet. Perhaps he needed to think, or maybe he was praying silently. Most likely he was trying to figure out how he could prevent such diseases that targeted the indigent. I waited until his demeanor changed from a deep frown to a brightening of his face.

Then he opened his heart to me. "I'm troubled, Rosie. I doubt I could have endured that visit if not for you standing beside me. You're my rock. My strength." His green eyes flashed with admiration. I was speechless. This happened long before we went on our first date. I'd been working with him for only a few weeks. I was just getting to know the man.

"I lead a lonely life, Rosie," he went on. " Until you came along, I hired one nurse after another. They didn't last, didn't like what they witnessed in the slums." He shrugged. "Who does? It's not a pleasant place, especially when you're there for one purpose—to treat illnesses you also could catch. Every one of my nurses left to either work in the immaculate private homes of the rich, or they quit the nursing profession altogether, got married or whatever. They got as far away from the miserably sick as possible. I sensed their revulsion. Deliver a baby on a soiled mattress? Unheard of. Spoon-feed medicine to a toothless old man with lip sores? Never."

He stopped walking and turned to look at me. "I'm no saint, Rosie. There were times when I also questioned my reasons for being in this place. I could have kept a nice clean position in the hospital. But a small voice nagged at me and tugged at me, and I couldn't stop thinking about the people who had no way to get to the hospital, people who might die of easily curable diseases unless someone came to help."

We both grew very quiet then. I walked beside John, tried

to keep my attention on the path ahead, but I couldn't ignore his inner strength.

"I know why *I've* chosen to help these people," I told him, breaking the silence.

He looked at me, and his impish eyebrows went up with interest.

"I grew up in one of these neighborhoods," I confessed. "Still live there."

He looked surprised.

"Oh, it isn't as terrible as what we just witnessed with that family." I waved my hand at the run-down tenement. "We live in the Italian section, closer to the city. The buildings are better constructed, and Mama keeps our place spotless." I chuckled. "May God help my brothers if they don't take their shoes off before entering the house when they come home from work." I shook my head slowly. "I wouldn't call us poor. But we've learned to live without the luxuries. Everybody in the family pitches in a portion of his or her pay, except for my younger sister Annie. She's still in school. We don't have much, but we're better off than some. And I've always been aware of the really poor people who have to share a two-bedroom flat with another family, like the ones we just left."

John stared straight ahead and kept walking. "I spent my entire youth in the village of Sawmill. I didn't know such poverty existed until I came here to attend medical school."

I shrugged. "Sawmill? Never heard of it."

A peacefulness illuminated his face. "It's a small community in the country about 70 miles west of Philadelphia. Must be close to 1,400 people there now, many of them farmers. Except for the sawmill and the quarry, there aren't many opportunities for work. Most of the folks either have jobs at the sawmill or they own their own shops. A few families settled there after retiring. It's a serene and friendly village, an ideal location to get some much needed relaxation."

"Sounds quaint."

He spread his hands, palms up. "What can I say, Rosie? I enjoyed my life in that little town. Swimming in the creek, running barefoot through the woods, grabbing an apple or an orange off the vendor's cart and slipping away without getting caught."

I couldn't help but laugh at the image of John as a little scamp.

"It sounds wonderful. If you liked it so much, why did you leave?"

"My father is the town physician. I left there so I could go to college and medical school."

"That must have made your father happy. Most men wish their son will follow in their footsteps."

He nodded. "That's true. My father had two sons. We both pursued careers in medicine. Marty chose the high road. He works at one of the hospitals in the city. More lucrative, I suppose."

He stared past me down a dark alley. It was littered with garbage and wet newspapers. Dirty-faced children sat in the muck, playing games they'd created out of sticks and stones. I wanted to weep for them.

"I chose to come here," he said with an air of determination. "I didn't know how dejecting it was going to be, but I decided to come, and now I've decided to stay."

I understood. Though such an assignment had proven overwhelming at times, I had no desire to leave it.

"I suppose I disappointed my father," John said, with a

shrug. "He always dreamed that one of us might take over his practice in Sawmill. He'd gone there pretty much for the same reason I chose the ghetto. He wanted to serve people who couldn't get to a hospital."

He stopped walking and faced me. "I followed a different calling, Rosie, one that led me into the slums to people who could only dream of lying on a crisp, clean mattress. Even small-town life is far better than what you see here." He waved a hand at the walls dripping of moisture and smelling of rotted food and urine, and overhead the lines of laundry strung across the alley between walls that closed in on either side of us. The thick air was severed by the shrill cries of babies and the harsh scream of a mother scolding her children.

"My friend Olive said I was crazy to come here," I told John. "She works as a midwife to rich people who want to deliver their babies at home. She keeps her own work schedule, smokes whenever she wants to—"

John shook his head and chuckled.

"She's married now," I went on. "To a financial accountant who works for a big firm in the city. They live in an apartment in the heart of the downtown district where she can shop to her heart's content. They dine in fine restaurants almost every night of the week, and they don't answer to anyone. Olive doesn't want any children. She wants to keep things just as they are. No ties, no restrictions, no diapers."

I must have sounded a little envious, and maybe I was. I looked at the man beside me and smiled to myself. I'd made the right choice.

By the time John and I married I'd already made peace about not having a lot of the frills Olive enjoyed. Like my mother always told me, "You made your bed, now you can lie in it."

My particular *bed* after we married was in a pleasant studio apartment on the outskirts of the city where I could shop for groceries, and John could put in a couple days a week at the hospital. Together we continued to serve the lower class people, often without being paid, but I could think of no greater reward than the round eyes of children gazing up at me in gratitude and the praises that poured from their mother's lips.

Thinking back over those days brought a mix of memories. Sure, it wasn't all roses and sunshine. Sometimes I dragged myself home, weary from trudging from one tenement to another, tired of the anxious pleas and the dirty fingers grabbing at my cloak. The cries of anguish lingered at the back of my mind for several hours after I'd left. The first thing I did when I got home was shed my uniform. I dropped it in the laundry basket and then took a long, leisurely bath, washed my hair with a medicated soap, and donned a flannel nightgown. John also freshened up while I put together our supper. Then we'd sit at our little table by an open window, breathe in the aroma rising from the Italian restaurant below us and listen to the squeal of carriages and trolleys as they navigated the streets.

It was during just such an evening meal as we dined on potato soup and raisin bread when John hit me with his new plan. By this time I'd found out I was pregnant with our first baby.

"How would you feel if I take over my father's practice and we move to Sawmill?" John said.

I stared at him. I'd never envisioned leaving the city.

"I think it's time, Rosie. My mother's gone, and my father wants to give up his practice. He said he wants to retire and move in with Marty." He reached across the table and grabbed my hands. "Sawmill has a hometown feel. It would be a wonderful place to raise a little one."

I blinked in shock. "What about our patients in the slums? The people who depend on us?"

"They don't need us anymore. Several new hospitals and clinics have gone up. Some of them are closer to the section where we've been working. There's no reason why those people can't get health care. We've done all we can, Rosie. We've helped these people through the worst of times." He gave my hands a gentle squeeze. "I'd like to honor my father's wish. And I'm tired, Rosie. All the walking has taken its toll on my injured leg. And with a baby coming, I think Sawmill is the answer." He paused and gazed into my eyes. "What do you say?"

John's limp had grown more pronounced over the last few months. There was a tiredness in his speech that hadn't been there before. But as he spoke about his hometown and his desire to take over his father's practice, a lilt returned to his voice. I slipped one hand out of his grasp and pressed my palm against my abdomen. Though I hadn't felt any movement yet, life had begun to stir within me. A protective spirit came over me and for the first time I pictured a different life for us. We'd visited John's folks in Sawmill when his mother was still alive. The little house his parents lived in stood like a refuge in the center of town. People came to the door at random. Martin Sr. often interrupted our conversations to dole out medicines and to lend an ear to various complaints. The cobbled streets rang out under the clip-clop of horses' hooves. The general store provided nearly everything a family needed. The police department had two constables and a mayor who oversaw everything, which wasn't much. Quaint houses were situated along tree-lined streets, their flowerbeds adding flecks of color to the brown and green landscape. And the church bells chimed every Sunday morning, summoning the residents to services in the two churches in town. Such a place promised a normal life. An Eden-like dream began to formulate in my mind.

I smiled at John and nodded. Then I placed my free hand over the top of his. "We need to raise our child in Sawmill. But could we wait just a little while longer? I'd like to deliver our baby at one of the hospitals in the city. This is my first child, John. I want to make sure everything goes well. Also, my father hasn't been well. I don't want to leave the city just yet, not while he needs me."

My husband agreed. Amy came into the world, healthy and bright-eyed. My delivery went smoothly. After my father passed away of a stomach ailment, we started making plans to move to Sawmill. John's dad proudly handed his practice over to John, and he went to live with Marty and his wife. Now here we were, nearly 15 years later, and a terrible flu bug also had come to stay.

I went to the front window and stared out at the empty street. When we first moved in, the town buzzed with activity. Horse-drawn carriages rumbled past, people walked on both sides of the street, kids played stickball and kick the can. There were Friday night dances, Saturday picnics, holiday parades, church socials, sewing bees, and men's club meetings—all the trappings that give a small town a nostalgic air.

But in October of 1918, after the flu scared everyone indoors, the streets went dead. I peered through the front window at our lone elm tree, it's tangle of branches looked like long fingers clinging to a remnant of stubborn leaves. Our world was dying amidst autumn's lingering chill. I let my gaze drift to the houses across the street. Yellow lights in the windows assured me that life continued inside those dwellings. The couple across the street had hung a black crepe on their door, a sign that Caroline's mother had passed.

My friends and neighbors in Sawmill were different from the people in the slums. Not only were their homes a lot nicer, but the residents wore clean clothes and new shoes, and their cupboards were full. They didn't have to worry about where their next meal might came from or whether their rooms would stay warm in the winter. They were less likely to get scabies and typhus. One thing was certain, it didn't matter where a person lived, whether in Sawmill, or the slums, or the heart of Philadelphia. The influenza would find them. We were all vulnerable.

In John's absence I had to do something. Had to help in any way I could. I turned from the window and went for my home remedies. I placed the little pouches on the table.

Chewing my bottom lip, I went to my catch-all drawer and withdrew a notepad and pen. Then, back at the table I started writing out instructions on how to use some of the ingredients in the bags. I copied the same message on 24 notes and added a verse of scripture to the bottom. *"A merry heart does good like a medicine."* Then I placed a note inside each of the tiny bundles and retied the yarn.

I was determined that when Amy returned to good health— and I prayed she would— I would deliver the pouches to the people who'd come to our door over the last couple of days. I hadn't been able to help them, except for some meager words of advice. Small as this was, it was something tangible. If

John could go to Philadelphia with no concern for his own wellbeing in order to save others, how could I do any less?

Chapter Thirteen

I placed the pouches on a shelf in the kitchen, two rows of little soldiers ready to do battle. They would have to stay there until I was satisfied that Amy had passed the danger and was going to stay well.

Another day and night passed. I continued with our routine, took care of the children, cooked meals, washed dishes and laundry, helped Johnny with his schoolwork, entertained Lily, and I continued to nurse Amy back to health. If I could get her well, the rest of us might also be safe. Fortunately, her temperature was normal now.

It was the fourth day since John left. I hadn't heard from him. I needed the assurance that he was all right. Waiting was the hardest thing I've ever had to do. I had to wait for Amy to get well, and I was waiting for John to telephone again. Better yet, I needed him to come home.

To my relief, Amy roused from sleep that morning, eager for a helping of oatmeal. She went to the bathroom on her own. While I prepared breakfast, my daughter spent a half-hour in the tub. She washed her hair and came out of the bathroom humming a tune. It was like we'd been to a healing service at a tent revival. I praised God for the amazing transformation in my daughter.

"Can we have lamb stew and boiled potatoes for supper

tonight, Mama?" Her request both startled and amazed me. It had been almost a week since she first took ill. Apart from a few sips of water and tea, she'd eaten nothing but oatmeal and broth every day. Now her appetite had returned, a positive sign she was on the road to recovery.

For the first time in days we laughed and talked over breakfast. Johnny wanted to know when their father was coming home. I soothed his mind by explaining a little about the work John was doing. My son listened with obvious fascination. I could almost see the wheels in his head turning, like he was imagining himself treating the sick and perhaps coming up with a cure that would save everyone.

"Will he go to see Uncle Martin?" Amy wanted to know.

"Perhaps," I said, though I doubted he would make time for such a visit.

With breakfast over, Amy helped me clear the table. Having her back to good health, I assumed she'd be able to take care of her younger siblings so I could leave the house for a couple of hours and deliver my gift pouches to our neighbors.

I lined up my care packages on the table, 24 little sacks of home remedies, one for every family that had come to my door over the past few days. Then I stood back and eyed my creations with satisfaction. They weren't miracle cures, but they were better than nothing. At least they would show our friends I cared.

The children gathered around the table. Lily's eyes grew wide with curiosity.

Johnny crinkled his nose. "What are *those?*"

"They're tiny medicine bags," I announced proudly. "For our neighbors."

Amy smiled with approval. Her two best friends, the

Prentice twins, lived a block away. Their mother had come to my door two days ago.

"Will you deliver one to Jenny and Jan?" Amy asked, raising her eyebrows. "Their little brother was sick last week."

"Their house will be one of my first," I promised.

The sun was at high noon, a good time for me to go outdoors. The sun had taken the chill off the air, and I only needed to wear a light coat and a pair of walking boots. No scarf or knitted hat, no mittens to interfere with my handling of the bags. Of course, I hadn't made enough for the whole town, but I could at least visit the people who'd already asked for help.

The little ones were engrossed in their own activities. Johnny shoved aside his schoolwork and pulled another one of his father's medical books off the shelf. I didn't interfere, but marveled at his persistence. Truly, he was a medicine man in the making.

He turned the pages slowly and mouthed out words not even *I* could pronounce. Lily had settled in her corner of the kitchen, her rag doll and a cardboard children's book on her lap. She glanced at Johnny now and then. When he turned a page, so did she.

Convinced the children would be fine in my absence, I donned my coat and went out back to the shed, took hold of John's wheelbarrow and brought it around to the front porch. I went inside, grabbed a handful of pouches and stacked them in the wheelbarrow. After loading a dozen pouches, I decided I had enough. I needed to keep the wheelbarrow light so I could maneuver it down the street.

Johnny was at the door. "Can we come?"

"No, son. Not this time." I had to keep the children home,

safely isolated from the illness that had settled like a dark cloud on our village. Except for those doorways that bore the crepe of death, I had no idea which homes were contaminated and which weren't.

I turned my attention to Amy. "Will you take care of your sister and brother while I'm gone?"

She nodded. "Don't worry, Mama. We'll play some games."

That was Amy. She often played games with the little ones, and she helped them with their schoolwork. I had visions of her becoming a schoolteacher one day. She had a special way with children. Eight years had elapsed from the day she came into the world until Johnny was born. Eight years and two miscarriages. I had given up hope on ever having any more children. Then Johnny surprised us, and Lily followed four years later. Amy immediately turned into a mother's helper. She doted on her siblings, often entertained them with games that escaped me.

I layered two masks over my nose and mouth and bound them behind my head.

"See you in a little while children. Stay warm." Though my voice was muffled by the layers of gauze, they heard me well enough. The three of them backed into the house. Amy offered a smile and a wave, then she shut the door.

My heart burst with love for them. My friends and neighbors must have felt the same way about their little ones. We were all concerned that the flu might take them from us. I headed out in the street to perform the kindness I should have done days ago. Perhaps a few of the deceased might have had a chance if I'd responded sooner. The little Wilson boy most of all. I couldn't let another day go by without doing *something* for my friends.

A cloudless, blue sky spread like a bold canopy overhead. The sun scattered its warmth on the pavement where icy patches had begun to melt. Redbirds chirped in the trees, then flitted from branch to branch. All of nature was telling me everything was going to be all right.

Though it was difficult to take a deep breath through those layers of gauze, it was good to be outdoors again. For the first time in my life I understood the meaning of the words, *cabin fever*. I had needed a diversion, something that could get me out of the house. Delivering those little bags of home remedies had served as an excuse to go outdoors for a while. If I could bless my neighbors at the same time, that would be an extra bonus.

As I had promised Amy, I pushed the wheelbarrow to the next block and stopped at the Prentice home first, shocked speechless by the white crepe hanging on the door. I knew what it meant. The twins had lost their little brother. How was I going to break the news to Amy?

I blinked against the sting of tears and placed a pouch on the porch anyway. I didn't knock, just quickly left. It wasn't too late to save the others, assuming any of my concoctions even worked. Still, I kept reminding myself I had to try. No more hunkering down within the safety of my four walls. If nothing else, I could do this small act of charity. Once John came home, he could take over. For now, perhaps I could spread a little ray of hope in the village.

Bent over with sadness I left the Prentice household and moved on down the street. I walked along the path pushing the wheelbarrow ahead of me. Crisp leaves rustled under my step. I plowed through them. The little pouches jostled against one another emitting a crackling sound, a reminder of the herbs and roots that lay within them. A flicker of doubt settled on my heart. These people expected real medicine from John. But couldn't they create medicine from some of the herbs and pieces of bark in those bags? During some of our coldest winters my mother had boldly handed out home remedies to her friends and neighbors. She even made a list of the people she'd reached out to and prayed over that list. Most of those people got well. Was it because of Mama's folk medicine? I never knew for sure. My nursing instructor would have called such methods quackery.

My next stop was at the home of Emma Wilson. Though my dear friend had lost her youngest, she still had two other sons who needed help. I held onto her pouch and knocked loudly, then waited with anticipation for her to answer the door.

There was the shuffle of slippered feet. Then the door opened only a crack, the way I had done when Emma came to *my* door. I offered her the little pouch. She stared at it, furrowed her brow, and started to shut the door. An instant later, she opened it wide and covered her mouth and nose with a handkerchief.

"Emma—" I said hopefully and lifted the pouch. "Please take this. It isn't much, but you might find something in here that will help your boys."

Tears flooded into her eyes. The skin beneath then was puffy, like she'd been weeping for days. "You're too late, Rosie. Both my kids are bed-ridden. My husband is sick, too."

I grabbed another pouch. "Then take two. Do whatever you can to keep them going until John returns."

"You said you expected him home four days ago." A bitter tone had filtered into her voice. In all the years I'd known her, she'd never spoken harshly to me.

"I thought he was coming home," I moaned. "The Red Cross convinced him to stay in Philadelphia and help out. The situation is much worse in the big city. There's a shortage of nurses and doctors."

"What's that to us? We had a doctor, and now he's left us."

"You're right, Emma. We're on our own for now. We have to do what we can with the resources we have, which is why I want you to have this. It's not much, but it might help your boys."

Emma sighed and lowered the handkerchief. Her chin quivered and her mouth grew shapeless as she spewed out her anger.

"What's in these little bags? Worthless home remedies? Like your mother used to do? What are they, scrapings from your pantry? What about medicine? What about a miracle drug? You've let me down, Rosie. Our situation has grown worse. I doubt even John can help us now. He couldn't save Robbie. He might as well stay in Philadelphia. And you might as well have stayed home."

She started to close the door. I grabbed the edge of it.

"Don't do this, Emma. I never stopped being your friend. I just couldn't think of what to do until now. Yes, these are scrapings from my pantry. It's all I had. The medicines are gone." I gazed at my friend, a terrible sadness building in my heart. "Amy was sick too. I had to take care of her without medicines, just like everyone else. Now she's better, and I'm doing what I can." Then I added hopefully, "Don't turn me away, Emma. Please."

Emma raised the handkerchief and dabbed at the tears flooding from her eyes, then she pressed it over her nose and mouth. Her forehead relaxed slightly, and a spark of understanding flashed in her eyes.

"I don't blame you, Rosie. This terrible plague has put a

curse on our village. It's divided neighbors and friends, even people within the same household. My husband lost his job at the sawmill. We have no income. Like I said, I don't blame you, but our relationship can never again be like it was."

"Don't say that, Emma. You'll feel differently when all this passes."

She shook her head and started to close the door again.

"Do you need food?" I hurried to ask. "I have smoked meat—plenty of cuts from the deer John shot in September. I have chops and hams, plus sausages and scrapple, all from the hog we bought from Tom Duprey. I did a lot of canning this summer. Fruits and vegetables and chicken. I have enough to share. Please, Emma, let me help."

She shook her head with a hopelessness that pierced my heart. "I don't want your provisions, Rosie. If you had wanted to help me, you should have done something four days ago. Now it's too late. You aren't the friend I thought you were. Please, just leave us alone."

She stepped back and slammed the door.

I stood very still for a minute, just staring at the closed door, a symbol of the barrier that had risen between two friends. With mounting sadness I left two pouches on Emma's porch and reluctantly moved on.

My heart was breaking. I'd lost my best friend. Emma and I had developed the kind of friendship few people enjoy. We could talk to each other about anything, even secrets we'd long-ago buried in our hearts. We could admit our faults to one another without fear of criticism or disapproval. We shared our deepest anxieties, our past mistakes, our failures, and our private thoughts. She knew about the boy who died while I was away from his bedside smoking a cigarette. She knew I couldn't let it go, that I'd been carrying the guilt around with me these many years.

"You need to give that over to God, Rosie," she'd said whenever the subject came up. "You need to lay that burden at the cross of Christ."

Knowing something and doing it are two different things. I was like Christian in John Bunyan's book, *Pilgrim's Progress*, traveling an unpredictable road to the Celestial City while carrying a weight on my back the whole time. Somewhere along the way Christian found the cross. He laid his burden down. Why couldn't I?

As I got farther away from Emma's house, I forced my attention on the next house on my list. I went from door to door, like one of those Fuller Brush salesmen, plying their wares to receptive housewives, except I wasn't selling anything, I was giving something away. And though I didn't know if my remedies would work, perhaps they'd offer something for them to try until John returned.

He'd said he couldn't purchase anything, but I knew my husband. He'd taken every last bit of cash we had in the house—even cleaned out the coins I'd saved in the cookie jar. If there was anything to be bought, John would buy it. With no medicine in the house and very little else to give people, I hoped my neighbors might at least try to make use of the herbs.

I still had the mysterious bottle I'd found on the top shelf of John's cupboard. But until I knew exactly what was in it and whether those tablets were lethal, I couldn't give them to anyone.

John hadn't phoned in several days. This was the longest we'd been apart with no contact. We were once inseparable.

The two of us worked side-by-side for long hours without a single interruption. We didn't have to discuss how to handle each case. Once John made the diagnosis, we went into action, our hands moving simultaneously like members of an orchestra, blending our different talents together in a grand symphony of healing.

Like a seasoned orchestra conductor, John rarely needed to direct my next move, for I anticipated what he needed.

I stopped accompanying him during my eighth month of pregnancy with Amy. He came home every night exhausted from a long day on the road. We followed the same routine. He took a bath and freshened up while I cooked dinner. He talked about his day while we ate. After Amy came along, I divided my attention between John and the needs of our daughter. And as years passed and we had Johnny and Lily, John's share of my attention shrank considerably. Fortunately, I had married a self-assured man who didn't demand my undivided attention.

While I became more involved with my role as a mother, John accumulated more medical information through physician's journals and hospital reports. Little by little I lost interest in the medical field. My life was consumed by feedings and diapers and midnight bouts with croup and later getting the older ones off to school and putting my efforts toward housework, canning, sewing projects, and games with the children. Lily had needs the other two didn't have. I worked with her daily to get her to sit upright, and she didn't take her first step until she was almost two. Eventually, she didn't require as much of my attention, and she drifted off into her own little world. In the end, she turned out to be the easiest to care for of all three of them.

Lily had an inner clock that told her when to wake up—8 a.m. every morning—and when to get ready for bed—9 p.m. on the dot. She often beat everyone to the table for breakfast, lunch, and dinner, perhaps anticipating the time by the aromas wafting from the kitchen. She enjoyed an occasional snack of cookies or sliced carrots. Except for a story at bedtime, she had few demands and was content to play with her blocks and her favorite doll. Try as I might, I couldn't get her past the simpler lessons of life. Instead of Lily adjusting to our routine, we adjusted to hers.

Now as I trudged through the deserted streets, my mind was on John and what he might be doing at that very moment. He was 70 miles away but he could have been on the moon. One thing was certain, my husband wasn't handing out home remedies. Most likely he was handling prescription medicines, perhaps using up a vital supply of drugs that he could have brought home with him. I sighed with discouragement.

Those scientists should have come up with a serum by now. What were they doing behind the closed doors of their laboratories? Why couldn't they put their heads together and come up with an effective treatment? It had been almost eight months since the first signs of a worldwide epidemic. Surely by now they should have had a breakthrough.

I picked up my step and pushed the wheelbarrow through clumps of leaves and over ruts in the street. I gave each door a gentle knock and left a pouch on the porch, then I hurried off before someone opened the door.

After I delivered the last pouch, I went back to my house, and I loaded up the wheelbarrow with the remaining bags. I followed a different route this time. The blue sky had disappeared behind gray clouds which also hid the sun. The temperature took a sudden dip. I shuddered, partly from the cold and partly from the task that still lay before me. Though my legs had begun to ache, and I was tired of pushing that old wheelbarrow, I'd made up my mind to keep at it until all the bags had been delivered.

For the most part, people had barricaded themselves behind closed doors. I passed a couple of masked strangers on the streets, but I didn't see anyone I recognized. A man in a trench coat came toward me. He crossed over to the other side. The clip-clop of a horse's hoofs drew my attention to the next street where a wagon bearing the Sawmill logo rumbled by with a load of boards for Jack Morgan, the undertaker. I spotted another wagon farther down the same street. It was empty, heading back to the sawmill for another load.

The images got me thinking. How many people had we lost? Surely, Jack didn't have to build that many coffins. The deserted streets, the darkening sky, the crisp wind that swept leaves about my feet and bent the tops of the trees created an immediate sense of doom. My heart beat in time with my footsteps. I could feel it pounding in my chest, in my neck, in my ears.

I turned a corner and headed away from the undertaker's shop, afraid I might catch a glimpse of the dead piling up on his front porch. Was this a reality or just something I'd conjured up in my mind from newspaper reports and from what John had said on the phone?

I moved through the downtown section—past storefronts with darkened windows, along empty streets where shoppers once strolled. Nobody bought clothes or jewelry or perfume these days. Nobody bought hardware or garden supplies. The only building with a neon OPEN sign was Cowell's

Grocery Store. A couple farmers had continued to supply David with meat and produce, and if not for the continuing need for canned goods and frozen products, he might have shut his doors long ago along with all the others. I left a bag for David and rang his bell. He lived in a back room, alone, since his wife passed away a few years ago. As I walked by the shop's plate glass window I peered inside at the telephone hanging on the far wall. It was deathly silent. I paused and willed it to ring, willed John to call while I was standing right there outside the store. Wouldn't it be nice to hear his voice again, to ask him questions, to tell him Amy had improved? He, in turn, could ease my mind by telling me his plans for coming home.

A flood of concerns filled my head. What if John had come down with the flu? What if he had died? A conversation, no matter how brief, would be better than not knowing. After all, not knowing is worse than hearing the truth no matter how dreadful. I needed assurance, needed to hear my husband's voice again.

I passed from the downtown streets into another section where the working class lived in a tapestry of magnificent structures, their windows shuttered, their chimneys spouting gray clouds of smoke. Inside were more of my friends and neighbors, hunkered down with their families. The specter of death had struck one here and another there, as indicated by the black and white crepes hanging from different doors.

Except for my friend Emma I didn't wait for anyone to answer my knock. I just left the bags on their porches and hurried off down the street. I spent the entire afternoon delivering bags. By the time I reached my street, the sun had begun its descent, and the sky had darkened even more.

I distributed the remaining packs and held onto one for the widow Schmidt.

At 82 years of age, Greta was our oldest living villager. Having her right next door to us was both a blessing and a curse. The woman who once treated Amy like her own granddaughter had now shut herself off from us. For months after Oskar died I'd been trying to make peace with her, tried to help her understand my husband had done all he could to save him. She refused my explanations, spent all her days inside with her three cats, and rarely left her house. My efforts had little effect. It was like trying to bring a burned out building back to life. Still, I had to keep trying.

Heaving a sigh, I grabbed the last pouch, mounted Greta's front steps, and knocked on her door. I listened for the swish, swish of her fuzzy slippers crossing the wooden floor. Listened for the click of the latch. I was surprised when the door opened. Greta didn't wear a mask. She didn't believe in them.

"Zey don't verk," she'd been known to say. And perhaps she was right, for a few years later some the top scientists agreed the masks did little more than give people peace of mind.

I offered the pouch. She hesitated at first, stared at the little bag, then at me. Her arthritic fingers grabbed onto it, and a spark of acceptance entered her pale blue eyes, but maybe it was a flicker of recognition and nothing more. There was no expression of thanks, no smile, not even a nod of the old woman's head.

I turned away and I left her standing in her doorway. When I reached my front walk, I looked back and was saddened by the image of a lonely soul, trapped within her own stubbornness. Defeated and spent, I stored the wheelbarrow in the shed. My legs ached from all the walking I'd done. My fingers were stiff from not wearing gloves in the descending cold. My cheeks and nose stung from the bite of the icy air. And I had an appetite for the first time since breakfast.

Then I entered the house to the warmth of a freshly stoked fire and the aroma of lamb stew. A loaf of date bread was warming on the hearth. Amy was pouring apple cider into four mugs, and the other two children emerged from the bathroom showing off their washed hands.

I forgot about the widow Schmidt. A surge of pride erupted within me as I looked at my three children. Not pride in myself, for I didn't deserve any accolades. All I'd done was give birth to those three. But I was in awe of them, especially my oldest who had taken charge of the family while I was out on the street delivering my little packages. Amy had kept the house warm, and she'd made supper.

I slipped out of my overcoat and helped bring the food to the table. Moments later, with all of us seated, we held hands during a giving of thanks.

I took that moment to say a prayer for the Prentice family. I reached for Amy's hand. "Your friends lost their little brother." My words sounded weak. "They've hung a white crepe on their door."

She slid her hand from mine and began to weep. Right then I felt John's absence more than ever. He should have been there to soothe our daughter's heart. He should have been the one to say the prayer. I missed him so much I thought my heart would burst from my body.

I needed him to help me adjust to all the changes the influenza had brought about, not only to our town but to our household. It was as if the disease controlled our lives now. It had taken my husband away, and it had locked us, and everyone else, in prison cells we once called our homes. I had no idea if I'd ever see my husband again. Word was that some of the doctors and nurses had succumbed to the disease. One newspaper article had reported that the nurses were "dropping like nine-pins." Doctors were collapsing on the job. John could be one of them. After all, I hadn't heard from him in three days. Not a phone call. Not even a message through David.

He was probably working day and night. From what he'd said on the phone, the hospitals needed volunteers—doctors and nurses and other helpers who could carry the burden of healing the sick. Another seed began to germinate in my mind. I was a trained nurse. I hadn't joined the fight. I looked at each of my three children. A sense of urgency flowed through me. My children wouldn't be completely safe until the pandemic was defeated. Perhaps it was time I also went to help.

Chapter Fourteen

W e weren't only fighting an epidemic. We were at war. When the United States entered World War I in 1917, the influenza had already begun to spread. The Council of National Defense became concerned about this invisible enemy that was killing off our American troops. The government created a volunteer medical service to bring doctors and nurses to the battlefield. Numerous health care workers and volunteers enlisted to work at receiving hospitals where they could care for the sick and injured military personnel. This action resulted in a shortage of doctors and nurses on the home front.

Meanwhile, the U.S. hospitals were overcrowded with flu patients. Philadelphia had the second highest number of flu casualties in the the country, second only to Pittsburgh, with Pennsylvania having the most deaths of any state in the union. With many of the staff physicians serving in wartime battlegrounds, doctors like John had responded to the Red Cross petition for volunteers to fill in the gap. He'd been there for four days. And I was sitting at home, safe. Our greatest concerns in Sawmill included how long before we could visit friends again and go to church again and get the children back in school again. Less than two months ago we walked around without having to wear a mask. We hugged friends and shook people's hands. We socialized with neighbors without the fear of picking up germs.

Life had literally come to a standstill in Sawmill and in many other small communities in the country. I sat at the table with my children and mulled over this ongoing dilemma. I ate some of the lamb stew Amy had made. It was better than mine.

"What did you season this with?" I asked her.

"Don't you like it?"

"I love it. You did something different."

She smiled coyly. "I added a couple shakes of cinnamon."

Johnny and Lily also were cleaning their bowls as if they hadn't eaten in weeks.

"Thank you, Amy, for doing all of this." I waved my hand over the table. "And for taking care of the children."

Her dark eyes sparkled with pleasure. It was good to see her looking healthy again. I glanced at the other two and whispered a prayer for all three of them.

Then I thought about John. He and I had always worked as a team. Now he was miles away. It didn't seem right.

Amy caught me frowning. "Is everything okay, Mama?"

I forced a smile. "Yes, dear. I was just thinking about something." I took a drink of cider.

"Missing Papa?" she said.

I nodded. "I'm worried about him, that's all. We'll simply have to—"

A soft rapping drew me out of my chair. I hurried to the front door, hoping to see John standing there, or maybe David with another handwritten message. Instead it was the widow Schmidt, her blue eyes streaked with red lines, as if she'd been crying.

I stood frozen, unable to move or speak. She was the last person I expected to see on my doorstep.

"Danke, for your little gift." Her clipped German accent assured me it really was Greta. "I put it in a safe place in da kitchen, to be used later if I shud need it."

Somehow I found my voice. "Greta, I'm so glad you came." In that instant I threw caution to the wind and opened the door wider. "Have you had supper? We have plen—"

She raised her hand. Her eyes crinkled at the corners. "I did not come here to ask. I come to gif."

Puzzled, I stepped aside and offered her a chair in the living room. The children had stopped eating and were staring at us from the table. I pulled up another chair and sat across from Greta. Then, still unsure of the reason for her visit, I waited, my hands folded on my lap.

"Your little gift bag," she began. "I pulled off zie string and opened it, and vat a surprise! Ven I vas a little girl, mein Mutter brewed herbs for a remedy for head colds. Zey verked. I vas cured overnight."

Greta beamed as she traveled back in time. For the next few minutes she talked about her early years on the German countryside when life was simpler and more peaceful. I let her ramble on, thrilled that she'd finally taken down the wall between us.

"Ve didn't talk about var back zen," she said, a sadness flooding into her eyes. She froze then, and the lines on her forehead gathered. "I don't like vat zie German army is doing, taking country after country. My people vant peace, not var. Now I live here, I am an American. I have citizenship papers. I use American dollars. I buy American food."

I reached across the space between us and grasped her

hand. "I never looked at you as the enemy, Greta. You're my friend. You're my neighbor. We don't have to think about nationalities. Not here. Not in this house. Or in this town, for that matter."

She nodded. "I have vatched you, Rose Gallagher."

I'd known this woman for 15 years. In the beginning she was a substitute grandmother to my daughter Amy. Then her husband died, and she blamed John. Then America entered the war, and she shut herself off from the rest of the town. How could I have known that a simple gesture of giving her a pouch of herbs might break down the barrier that had grown between us?

Perplexed, I furrowed my brow; just stared at this stranger in my living room.

Greta's angry creases vanished. "I understood about your miscarriages," she said, her blue eyes swimming in moisture. "I had several myself, enough to feel zie kind of pain when part of a Mutter dies. Enough to make me feel a little less like a vomen because I couldn't have children of my own."

We both glanced at my three. They'd gone back to eating their dinner, but I knew my kids. Their eyes were on their plates, but their ears were on us.

Greta leaned toward me. "Ven Oskar died, I needed to blame someone. Anyone but myself." She straightened. "And so, I blamed your husband." She shook her head of white curls. "I vas mistaken. I should have helped my Oskar change, and maybe add years to his life. But he vas a stubborn man. I had given up long before you and John moved to Sawmill."

All I could do was sit there, stunned. This woman was opening her heart to me, and for the first time in my life I was speechless.

Prompted by my silence, Greta went on. "You stood by your husband. You offered kindness to me. I refused it." She shook her head and her smile faded. "I apologize."

"No, Greta. No apology is necessary."

She gave a little. "Zis illness—it has kept us locked in our homes. Ve are lifing like strangers in zis town. But today you came out of your safe place, and you reached out to me vis a little gift. It vas a small gesture, but it touched mein heart."

Tears burned my eyes. "I'm glad you're here, Greta. Your kindness means a lot to me."

"Now, I vant to gif you a present too. I vant to help you."

An angel had come out of the darkness of night, praising me and telling me she had something to give. For several days, I'd been scrubbing and cleaning and feeding and worrying and praying, and I'd just finished trekking all over town pushing a wheelbarrow full of herbs, and now someone had come to *my* door with the promise of a gift.

Curiosity flowed through my entire being. I perched on the edge of my seat and listened closely to what Greta Schmidt had come to say.

The older woman tilted her head to one side. "I know vat it feels like to have the love of your life slip away from you. It's like your heart has departed mit him."

I could only nod. When John drove off in that rickety truck, I wanted to run after him. I sensed he might not return for a long time. My premonition turned out to be right. And like Greta had said, it felt like a big chunk of my heart had gone off with him.

"John followed his calling, Greta. When he arrived in Philadelphia he became aware of a need, and he chose to fill it."

"I know." Greta patted my hand. "I vas outside on my porch

ven Emma Vilson left your house a few days ago. She told me John had gone to buy medicines."

I nodded. "We're out of everything. He *had* to go. I had nothing left to give Emma, or anyone, not a single pill for my own family." I sighed. "But I should have at least let Emma inside my house. If nothing else, she needed comfort."

My visitor shook her head. "No, you should *not* have let her in. You did the right ting, Rose. Emma's children are very ill. You had to protect your own." She took a deep breath. "Ve all have regrets. Oskar and I ver married 50 years. He didn't take gut care of himself. He smoked those awful cigars even ven I begged him not to. He ate too much, vas a good 50 pounds over. He had a heart attack years ago, and he kept right on eating and drinking and smoking, right up to zie end."

Her pale blue eyes were shimmering. I hurried to get her a handkerchief. Between dabs at her cheeks and an occasional blowing of her nose, she continued to speak. I listened quietly, my dinner already cold but no longer a concern of mine. Greta had mentioned a gift. I looked her over, my curiosity mounting. She had carried nothing in with her.

"I'm all alone," she went on. "I couldn't have children. I envied vomen like Emma mit her boys, and Margaret Duprey and her eight children, and zen you living right next door. Your beautiful children reminded me of my losses every day. I resented all of you. Zen came the var, and I had to hide myself."

I leaned toward her and shook my head. "It didn't have to be that way, Greta."

She shut her eyes and squeezed out a stream of tears. "I know dat now." She wiped her face with the handkerchief which was now damp and wrinkled. "But let me speak of the reason I came here tonight." She smiled at me, kindness flickering in her cool blue eyes. An unexplained peace fell upon our little corner of the room.

"I've been praying about the epidemic," she confided. " Praying for you and John."

Her admission set me back. "Praying? For us?"

"I know, it's a surprise, isn't it?" She released a little chuckle. "Zie widow Schmidt gets on her knees and prays."

I gave an uncomfortable shrug. The poor woman had bared her heart to me. What she said next disarmed me even more.

"You need to be mit your husband."

I frowned in puzzlement. "Greta, I told you, he's—"

She waved her hand and cut me off. "I know. He's in Philadelphia. And that's ver you need to be—at his side."

"I can't. My children—"

I turned around. The three had finished eating. My two youngest had squeezed into my rocker by the fireplace. Johnny opened a children's book—*Peter Rabbit*—and read the text to his little sister. Amy had cleared the table and was at the sink washing the supper dishes. She'd set my bowl on the warming shelf and had placed a towel over it.

"Your children vill be fine," Greta insisted. "Bitte, allow me to be der Grandmutter and look after zem." She held my gaze. "Your place is mit your husband. You are a nurse. You need to use your skills to help others. Look here—" She pulled a portion of a newspaper from her pocket and unfolded it. "My friend mailed zis to me from the city. I received it today."

The headline read, *Philadelphia hit hardest in the nation with 3 million dead and climbing.* The subhead was even more distressing. *Red Cross begging for more doctors and nurses.*

"Do you see zis?" Greta pointed at the subhead. "You are

needed. You go to Philadelphia, help your husband do his verk und zen come home togedder."

I shook my head. "What about the people right here in Sawmill? They're sick too."

"And vat vill you do with no medicines? Give more herbs from your garden? Ve have enough. Philadelphia has medicine but no one to give it out, no one to care for the sick. You can do zat. You can verk by your husband's side. Your children vill be fine. I can come by every day. Ve can go a little time outside. Your Amy vill be here, und so vill I."

The idea appealed to me. I'd already been fretting about my lack of usefulness, and I'd been missing John. Only a few minutes ago I'd been thinking about how I should be using my nurse's training. More than ever I needed to be at my husband's side, working together like we used to do. Was Greta's visit an answer to prayer?

"I'll think about it, Greta."

She rose to her feet and placed the newspaper clipping in my hand.

I walked with her to the front door. As she shuffled off to her own house, I watched after her until she was inside. An imaginary hand squeezed my heart. A broken relationship had healed. Was God telling me through Greta that he wanted me to go to Philly? If so, then I also could trust him to care for my children during my absence. I shut the door and leaned against it. I mulled over Greta's words. Her humble offer solved all of the issues that had been swirling around in my head for four days.

Amy turned away from the sink and approached me with a towel in her hand. "I overheard," she said. "The widow Schmidt is right."

I shook my head. "I don't know, Amy. What if you became ill again?"

"Mama, I feel fine. I can take care of Johnny and Lily. I'll catch up with my school work and help them with theirs. If I need anything, I'll go next door and get Mrs. Schmidt."

I looked around the kitchen. The table was clean. The dishes were done. My sewing projects were piled in a corner of the room. Amy knew our routine. She could keep things going for a few days while I answered the call for help. Philadelphia was 70 miles away. I could be home the same day if needed.

Johnny had lowered the *Peter Rabbit* book to his lap, and both children gazed at me wide-eyed. I was certain there were tears in Lily's eyes, although it could have been a reflection from the flames in the fireplace. Johnny looked puzzled, but he said nothing.

"I'll let you know what I decide," I told Amy.

She smiled and brought me a bowl of stew she'd reheated on the stove. I savored the rich flavors.

"Cinnamon, huh?" I looked at Amy.

She nodded and danced away from me back to the sink where she cleaned the empty pot.

I slept little that night, still pondering the widow Schmidt's suggestion. I imagined all sorts of scenarios. What if I got to Philadelphia but couldn't find my husband? Would it help to contact his brother? Had John even taken the time to call him? My husband had said a number of clinics had opened up. Should I drive up and down the streets and look for Thompson's truck? What did it even look like? I couldn't remember.

I was still mulling over my options the next morning. I rose from bed to the aroma of fresh-brewed coffee and bacon frying in a pan. Amy was flitting about the kitchen. She'd already gotten the children to the table and was scrambling eggs in a bowl.

At the sound of my footsteps she turned toward me and smiled. She appeared to have fully recovered. Her face had flushed a healthy pink, and her brown eyes had taken on a golden sparkle.

"I wanted to send you off with a good, hardy breakfast." There was a lilt in her voice.

She poured my coffee and set the cup before my place at the table. Then she hurried to the stove with the bowl of eggs. She flew about the kitchen like she was happy to be in charge of the cooking. Was she even aware of the horror that awaited me in Philadelphia?

Overwhelmed with uncertainty, I could do nothing but drop into a chair and sip the steaming liquid. It felt good going down. Its warmth revived me from what had been a fitful night. I hadn't yet made up my mind about going to Philadelphia.

I took my coffee to the sink and peered out the kitchen window. Flossie was grazing on a patch of weeds in the far corner of our yard. She might be able to get me to Philly. The buggy was standing by the shack, its rear wheel slightly bent. John had pounded it almost round during a trip to farmer Brice's place, about ten miles outside of Sawmill. That was two weeks ago, and he hadn't used it since.

My eyes then strayed to the clapboard house next door. The widow Schmidt was gazing back at me from a side window. Did the old woman ever sleep? She gave me an encouraging nod. I lifted a hand to wave.

Swallowing the lump in my throat, I went to my bedroom,

and as though propelled by invisible hands, I pulled my tapestry bag from underneath the bed. Someone else must have been moving my arms, because the next thing, I was tossing in a change of underwear, my hair brush and combs, my toothbrush, a bar of soap, and a towel and washcloth. Then I rolled up a flannel nightgown and tucked it inside. I pulled my nurse's uniform and cap out of the storage trunk and added several gauze masks to the pile. I strained at the zipper, jerked it several times in an effort to close the overstuffed bag. Lastly, I opened my little jewelry box and lifted out the nursing pin John had given me years ago. I slipped it in my pocket for the time being.

When I entered the kitchen Amy was placing platters of bacon and eggs on the table. We gathered for the blessing, with Amy quickly taking charge of it. The children and I ate in silence. I could feel the tension. Amy kept smiling at me, a reassuring sparkle in her eyes. Lily was shoveling eggs in her mouth, oblivious to the conversations we'd been having.

Johnny was another story. He ate quietly. In fact, he was exceptionally still for a rambunctious little boy. He didn't appear to share Amy's enthusiasm. He even shot resentful glances in her direction, as if he didn't approve of her sending me away.

But the wheels were already turning. Between the widow Schmidt and my precocious eldest child, my trip was moving forward.

Amy had finished eating and was running around the kitchen putting together a bag of food much like the one I had provided for her father several days ago.

"I'll take care of the dishes, Mama. You go and find Papa. It's the right thing."

Heaving a sigh, I rose from the table and moved like one of those rag dolls Lily liked to play with. No brain. No control over my own actions. Just doing what I'm told. Someone else had taken over and was making the decisions for me.

I donned my coat and went outside, pulled our buggy from behind the shack, then went through the double doors and poured enough oats in a bag to keep Flossie happy while we were in Philadelphia. I had no idea if a livery was available or if I'd have to tie our old nag somewhere outside the city. I hoisted in two sizeable jugs of water, then gathered up the harness and went for the horse.

A bitter cold north wind had settled on Sawmill during the night turning blades of grass to frostbitten shards. Though second thoughts scrambled through my brain, I suppressed them and walked along the path to the pasture beyond the wire fence where I caught up with Flossie. She was just standing there, shivering, her graying face flecked with bits of ice. Trickles of moisture oozed from her tired eyes. She didn't even flick her tail—not that there were any flies around to flick at. But I expected at the sound of my footsteps there'd be some sign of life in her. I doubted the old nag could make it to Philly and back. If she could at least get me there I could ride home with John in Thompson's truck.

I stared at the broken down mare and saw my own future, tired and useless and depending on others to keep me going. Her head drooped like she was half-asleep or maybe just waiting to die. That would be me one day, if the influenza didn't get me first.

I reached for Flossie's mane. It was brittle from the cold. She dug her hoofs in the hard ground. I fit the reins on her and pulled and tugged until I got her out to the buggy, then I harnessed her up and went back inside the house for my bag.

I spent a few minutes explaining the situation to Johnny and Lily. I was wiping away their tears when the grating sound of an engine and the squeal of brakes sounded at the front curb. Next came the thump of footsteps on the porch. I stopped talking mid-sentence and held my breath. The latch lifted. The door swung open, and in walked John.

Chapter Fifteen

Our two youngest children reached their father first. They lunged at him and caused him to stagger backward. Their happy shrieks pierced the air. Amy got to him next, spreading her arms and squealing with delight. I held back for a while and took in the joyous reunion. Then awed beyond belief, I stepped closer and snuggled into the huddle.

Moisture blurred my vision. My throat tightened with a mix of relief and elation. My husband had come home. I didn't have to leave, after all. We could be a family again. Our protector was back. I didn't have to do this alone anymore. A huge weight had been lifted from my shoulders.

I leaned back and looked him over. Tears spilled from his tired eyes and ran down his cheeks. Weary lines creased his forehead. A chin of stubble had blossomed into a short beard, red with streaks of brown running through the hairs. His entire frame sagged under the weight of secrets he had yet to reveal. It was obvious John had been through something horrible. I had never seen him so troubled, so utterly exhausted.

Gradually, we each released our grasp on him. He hadn't said a word yet, merely wept quiet tears of relief. He looked from one of us to the other, patted the little ones' heads, gently brushed a knuckle against Amy's chin.

"So glad to see you're well again, princess," he said to our daughter, his voice breaking.

Then he turned his attention to me. "I missed you, darlin'."

"I missed you too, John." I reached for his hand and held it fast. "It's good to have you home." I gestured toward my tapestry bag. "You didn't arrive a minute too late, dear. I was about to come to Philadelphia. I'm all packed, and I've even hitched old Flossie to the buggy."

"What? Why on earth would you do such a thing?"

"Lots of reasons. Mostly because I missed you, but also because I felt as though I might be needed there. I saw the reports, how they've been crying for medical workers."

He shook his head and gazed into my eyes with such intensity, a ripple of relief ran through me. "You wouldn't have wanted to see the suffering and the horror of what this disease can do to its poor victims. No, Rosie. Count yourself lucky to have stayed at home."

I slipped my hand through his arm and started to guide him to the table. "Come and sit. I'll fix you something to eat."

He nodded. "God knows I could use a good, home-cooked meal." He hesitated then. "I didn't come home alone, Rosie."

Puzzled, I gave him my full attention.

"I brought someone with me. He's waiting in the truck."

Had I heard him right? "You brought someone with you? Who?"

"The Duncans' nephew. You remember Daniel, don't you?"

"Daniel Duncan? Of course. He used to visit Tom and Grace when he was a boy. Grace has mentioned him many times. Didn't he join the army?"

"Yes, he did. He's on medical leave. He came to the hospital in Philadelphia yesterday complaining of trench foot. I've been treating him and trying to keep him separated from the flu victims. He had nowhere else to go, couldn't go back to his base. His parents are missionaries, you know, still in Africa or some other god-forsaken place. I didn't know what to do except bring him with me to Sawmill."

I looked around our tiny home. We barely had enough room for our three youngsters, and now John had brought Daniel home?

I was incredulous. "Where will we put him?"

John snickered. "No worries, Rosie. He'll stay with his aunt and uncle. But can we at least clean him up and give him something to eat before I take him there?"

My relief must have been evident because John rested a comforting hand on my shoulder. He looked me in the eye, his own eyes twinkling with mirth. "It's just breakfast, Rosie."

I nodded. "Of course, ask him to come in."

John went back out to the truck. He returned carrying his medical bag. Behind him entered a strapping young man I hardly recognized. What had become of the little blond-haired youngster who used to run barefoot through our front yard? He wasn't running now. He was limping on bandaged feet. He came into our house, wincing and dragging one foot behind the other. Daniel wore a soiled olive green uniform that fit his muscular frame like a glove. In one hand he carried a battered pith helmet, in the other he had a burlap sack, most likely filled with all his worldly belongings. He dropped it to the floor with a clunk and placed the helmet on top.

John set his medical kit on the floor near his pharmacy cupboard along with the burlap sack he had taken with him. Both the kit and the bag bulged until the seams looked as though they were about to pop open. I tried to imagine what was inside. I looked inquisitively at John.

"Medicines," he said, giving a sheepish smile and a wink of his leprechaun eye. "I've brought precious medicines."

I shook my head in amazement. My husband had accomplished what he'd set out to do. From the looks of those two bags, he'd made out quite well with the little bit of cash he'd taken along.

He kissed my cheek. "I should freshen up before we eat. I'm certain I look a sight, and I must smell like a herd of pigs."

"I don't care," I told him, linking my arm in his. "My husband has come home."

While John went into the bathroom to bathe, I offered Daniel a chair. The poor young man hobbled to it and sat down with a sigh. Pain was etched on his face. He slumped over a little. Then he caught sight of Amy, who'd been standing by the sink. He straightened his back, his face brightened, and it looked like the pupils had dilated in those clear blue eyes of his.

Amy stood very still, but her face was aglow. She had the slightest hint of a smile on her lips. She smoothed her gingham dress, then clasped her hands in front of her. All the while she kept her eyes on Daniel. I looked at him and then at her. It wasn't difficult to spot the first signs of a budding romance right there in my own kitchen. The thought both surprised and troubled me.

Those two used to play together whenever Daniel spent his summer breaks in town. They took off every morning for a day of fun by the river. Amy rarely returned home wearing clean clothes. Her hair hung in wet ringlets and she definitely needed a bath. I could tell they'd been swimming in the creek, climbing trees, hunting for snakes in the woods, and doing all sorts of boyish activities. Gazing at her now I couldn't picture her doing those things anymore. She'd blossomed into a beautiful young woman. And from what I could gather, Daniel had seen the change in her too. He sat there with his mouth open.

"Amy, will you go outside and unload the buggy, and put Flossie back in the field?"

"Huh?"

I repeated my request.

"Oh, yes, Mother."

Mother? My daughter always called me Mama, like the little ones did. Mother sounded much more—grownup.

She grabbed her coat off the hook and left the house, gliding like she'd entered a beauty contest at the state fair. I shook my head, aware of what was happening before my very eyes, and unable—or unwilling—to accept it. I wasn't so old that I'd forgotten how my whole demeanor changed whenever John came near me. But I was 20 years old when I met my future husband. Amy was only 16.

While my daughter was out of the house, I cleared away our dirty breakfast dishes and started a fresh batch of bacon and eggs, plus a couple of boiled potatoes, which John always liked with his breakfast.

I sent Johnny and Lily to their room to play, then, as I worked I chatted with Daniel about incidentals. The weather. His trip from Philadelphia. His long, uncomfortable ride in the Thompson's clattering truck.

John emerged from the bathroom, his face shaved clean and his body smelling like Amy's bath salts. Daniel shuffled inside and shut the door. I frowned with concern. I'd heard horror stories about the young men who stood for days in ankle-high water in the trenches on European battlefields. The longer their boots remained waterlogged the more serious the infection. After a few days, the skin begins to tear and painful blisters start to form.

"Will you have to amputate?" I asked, hesitantly.

John released a sigh. "I hope not. The boy's a stubborn lad. He put up with this problem far too long, should have complained to his sergeant weeks ago." He shrugged. "But, that's the way the young folks are these days. Resilient. Stubborn. When the lad came to the hospital last night he could barely walk. I got him into a clean bed, pulled off his socks, and applied ointments right away. Every few hours I broke away from the patients in the main room, came to him and replaced his bandages. I knew I needed to get him out of that hospital and away from the contagion. He could have gone home to his grandparents' place in Massachusetts, I suppose, but I insisted he come along with me. It was time I left the hospital."

I placed a plate of bacon on the center of the table and went back to the stove to scramble eggs. "I'm glad you left, John. Things are getting pretty intense here."

"I wanted to get home to you and the children, darlin', and I kept thinking about this town full of people who depend on me. Word was out that the flu was spreading like wildfire into civilian communities." A sadness filled his eyes. "I knew if I told the other doctors I was leaving, they would have tried to convince me to stay. I got a hold of Daniel, and we left before the sun came up. I'm ashamed to say I wouldn't have survived another day in that hell."

He blinked and his shoulders sagged, like he was about to crumble. I rushed to his aid.

"The Duncans will be happy to see Daniel," I said in an attempt to divert his thoughts.

He nodded, though a terrible sadness remained in his eyes. "They're a fine couple. I know Tom well. Used to see him at the town council meetings. And you're in that sewing club with his wife, aren't you?"

He grabbed a chair at the table and settled into it with a sigh.

"Yes, but we haven't met in a while, not since this whole flu business hit us." I stirred the eggs. "Grace is a fine woman. The two of them never had any children of their own. A visit from Daniel will bring a little joy into their home, especially at a time like this."

"We'll eat breakfast, and then I'll take Daniel to their place. I can check on his condition every day while he's staying there."

Amy returned to the house and joined me in the kitchen. Seconds later Daniel emerged from the bathroom smelling a whole lot better than when he went in. He dropped back into the chair at the table. His breathing was labored like that of an injured animal. It was obvious that gunfire and bayonets were not the only threat on the battlefield. The soldiers suffered with everything from typhus to festering sores and attacks by rats and flies. And trench foot. In the past few months the troops also had to contend with the influenza.

As I looked Daniel over, I tried to see past the mud-stained uniform, past the heavy wrappings on his feet, past the manly beard on his jaw. Gone was the little rascal who used to scamper into my kitchen begging for a cookie and a glass of lemonade. Gone was the suntanned mischief-maker who broke Mrs. Schmidt's window, who trampled my petunias, and who cocked his head in a whimsical manner, like he was attempting to divert my attention from some misbehavior of his. Now sitting here in my kitchen was a grown man, and to my dismay he'd had his eye on my daughter from the moment he stepped through our front door.

I glanced at my Amy. Did she even remember him? Did she recall how they spent hot summer days down by the river, swimming and throwing rocks in the water, and playing games in our living room? Did she remember the blond-haired, blue-eyed boy who came to our door every morning, with the same request, "Can Amy come out and play?"

The thought of these two as a grown man and woman had sent me into a state of shock. Somehow Amy had matured right before my eyes, and I hadn't seen it coming. All of my instruction—the training in the kitchen, our needlepoint projects, my lectures about marriage and family—all of it was coming to the fore, but far too soon in my mind.

Suddenly, I felt old. In a few years, my daughter would marry someone—maybe Daniel. She would have children of her own. I'd be a *grandmother*. I was getting older by the minute. None of those realities of life had troubled me in the past. It was as if they didn't exist. All of a sudden they not only existed, they were coming far too fast to suit me.

I pulled a few loose strands of hair back inside the bun at the nape of my neck and fastened them there. I'd found a couple gray hairs the other day and I'd quickly yanked them out. After what happened today, I was certain more of them were growing.

These two were making an old woman out of me.

I had to admit, though, Daniel was a nice young man and probably a good catch. As the Duncans' only nephew and them having no children of their own, he stood to inherit a small fortune one day. His parents were missionaries, which said something about his spiritual walk. Still, I had a problem with him sitting at our table, eating our food and all the while flirting with my daughter.

I gave John one of my penetrating stares, the kind that could bore a hole in his brain. He picked up my message immediately.

"We have a lot to talk about," he admitted, casting a glance at Daniel and then at Amy. "But right now, I'm hungry as a bear. Do I smell coffee?"

Amy grabbed the coffee pot and poured two cups. She set one in front of John and the other in front of Daniel, lingering by his side a little longer than was necessary. Daniel turned his face up at her and smiled. He didn't say a word. Neither did she. Yet they spoke volumes to each other.

While trying to ignore the interaction between those two, I busied myself in the kitchen. I fixed two plates of eggs and toast, set them before the men, then added a bowl of boiled potatoes to the center of the table. I stepped back in amusement as the two men plunged in like hungry wolves.

My heart began to soften toward Daniel. Perhaps he'd given John a reason to come home when he did. My husband couldn't stay in Philadelphia if he wanted to get Daniel out of there.

They ate heartily. "Sure beats the hard bread and beef jerky they fed us at the hospital," John quipped.

Daniel perked up. "Really? Sounds as unappetizing as the ground turnips, canned sardines, and horsemeat we ate on the battlefield."

John laughed. "I drank the worst coffee I've ever had— tasted like burnt rubber."

A little friendly competition had erupted at the breakfast table.

"How do you know what burnt rubber tastes like?" Daniel chided, his eyes sparkling.

John shrugged. "I've smelled burnt rubber before, so I can guess what it *might* taste like. Just use your imagination, Daniel. What do *you* think burnt rubber tastes like?"

The young man tipped the coffee cup to his lips and grinned. "It ain't as good as this, that's for sure." He flashed a smile at Amy. "This brew brings back memories of home."

Amy giggled shyly. She hadn't taken her eyes off of Daniel. Then she settled into a chair and leaned toward him. "What was it like, Daniel?"

He frowned in puzzlement. "Huh?"

"The war," she pressed. "What was it like on the battlefield?"

Daniel set down his cup and leaned back. His youthful brow furrowed like he was remembering something he'd been trying to forget.

He spoke slowly and with a hint of tension in his voice. "It's not like any of us wanted to go to war. It was our duty." He swallowed, looked from Amy to me and then to John. "When the Germans torpedoed the Lusitania they killed hundreds of American civilians." He shook his head. "Those people were minding their own business, traveling from New York to Liverpool—innocent souls on a work trip or a vacation. We needed to avenge them."

Daniel stabbed a boiled potato with such force I wondered if he'd seen the face of Kaiser Wilhelm II on it. He took a large bite, chewed it to bits, and swallowed.

"President Wilson had been insisting the United States would remain neutral, but many of us trainees agreed that the attack was a definite act of war." Daniel continued with a seriousness that denied his youth. He glanced around the table. "Then Congress passed a $250-million arms bill. We figured we were going to be sent overseas. We just didn't know when."

Daniel finished off the last piece of bacon. "Germany forced us into the war."

I thought about the widow Schmidt, holed up in her house like a self-committed prisoner of war. A wave of pity swept over me. The poor woman thought the people of Sawmill had blamed her for Germany's attacks. How ridiculous. Yet there were some who couldn't ignore her clipped accent or the German flag plastered to her living room window. But blame her? Ridiculous. Though she loved her fatherland, Greta was ashamed and hurt by what was happening.

Daniel had stopped talking long enough to clean his plate. He lifted his head and his face tensed up with more bitter memories. It looked to me that he'd traveled back to the battlefield in his mind.

"I was part of the 3rd infantry division," he reminisced with an air of pride. "We landed in Brest, France, with orders to cross the Marne River into Mezy. We constructed a large raft from logs cut out of the forest. It took a while, but it was a sturdy raft, big enough for at least a dozen of us. A bunch of us piled onto it and made it to the other side. Others followed. American troops disembarked at other locations, and within a few days more than 85,000 of us went to the aid of the Allied Powers. The Germans suffered huge casualties, and they lost most of the territory they had gained in France and Belgium."

His intensity subsided and he smiled. "Me and my buddies

celebrated that night around a campfire with a case of beer a couple of the guys had swiped from a German bivouac." He cocked his head in that whimsical way he'd always done as a boy. "We had escaped death," he said with confidence. "The problem was, some of us were already suffering from trench foot and dysentery." He glanced with embarrassment at Amy. "It's all part of the war, I guess," he said with a shrug. "Anyway, those of us who couldn't go on were sent back to the good ol' U.S.A."

"Didn't the military care for your wounds while you were still there?" I said.

He smirked. "A little. The medics had greater concerns. The cots in their makeshift hospitals were filled with men in far worse shape than I was. Head injuries, bullet wounds, and way too many limbs scheduled for amputation. They did what they could for the rest of us and put us aboard a ship heading for America. We disembarked three days ago at the Navy shipyard. Those of us who could walk—or limp," he said wincing—"went to a hospital. That's when I met up with John."

My husband gave Daniel's shoulder a fatherly nudge. "I recognized Daniel right away. In spite of the dirty face and rumpled uniform, I knew Tom Duncan's nephew was standing in front of me. I guess it was those striking blue eyes. Then when I saw his badly infected feet, my heart went out to him."

Daniel chuckled. "People think artillery and hand-to-hand combat are the biggest threat in wartime. Sure, we didn't like getting shot at, but we kind of expected it. What we didn't expect was spending many a night hunkered down in water-filled trenches and coming away with sores on our feet."

"Were you ever in any danger?" Amy asked, her face flushed with interest.

Daniel nodded. "We had one major confrontation. I think it was about midnight when the attack came. Me and my buddies found ourselves face-to-face with a contingent of Germans. They didn't stop to say, *Hello*. Just charged at us with their weapons drawn. Almost too late we grabbed our rifles. Some of the guys fired. I couldn't bring myself to shoot one of 'em, so I clubbed a guy in the face with the butt end of my rifle. He went down like a sack of potatoes. Didn't get up. I stepped closer and gagged at the sight of his face. It was covered with blood."

Without taking his eyes off of Amy, he held up his coffee cup for a refill. She ran for the pot and quickly served him. Then, obviously transfixed by his story, she settled back into her chair.

Daniel took his time and sipped the dark liquid. Like a good storyteller, he was holding us captive. He blinked a few times, then, trembling slightly, he went on.

"I had flattened the kid's nose, and I'd knocked one eye out of its socket. I didn't mean to kill him, didn't ever want to take a human life, but my training had kicked in, and I'd reacted fast." A sadness crept into his voice. "The poor guy looked about my age, had to be no more than 18 or 19. My buddies had taken care of the other attackers. We lost one soldier, a kid we'd nicknamed Mouse because he was so small. Guess he didn't have a chance against those hulky Germans."

He drained his coffee cup and set it aside. He gazed at Amy like he was offering her a bouquet of flowers. My imagination went wild as they flirted with each other over the stack of toast that still sat, untouched, in the center of the table.

"I'd never killed anyone before, and I never want to do it again." Daniel's young face distorted with the memory.

"It's something you carry with you for the rest of your life." He gave a little shrug. "At least we never got sprayed with mustard gas. But there were other problems, mostly psychological. Things got so bad some of the guys were looking for a way out. They cut themselves or shot a bullet into their foot, just so they could go home. I didn't do any of that. After hunkerin' down in the trenches for another week and getting my boots soaked with dirty water, I had found my way out, though it wasn't on purpose. My feet got so infected I couldn't even walk back to our base camp. I had to be carried there on a stretcher. My commanding officer took one look at my feet and said, 'You're goin' home, boy.' First thing, I had to go through a delousing, and they gave me a tetanus shot. They kept wrapping and rewrapping both of my feet with heated towels. I was ashamed that a little thing like trench foot had taken me away from fulfilling my duty."

I reached across the table and patted Daniel's wrist. "You're a hero, Daniel. You served your country well and came home to talk about it. You could have been shot or bludgeoned to death. You could have ended up a prisoner of war. You escaped a lot of traumatic situations that you knew you'd have to face when you signed up, but you went anyway."

His deep blue eyes filled with moisture, like he was remembering something else, something heartbreaking. "The thing is, I lost a couple of good buddies. They didn't get to go home." He blinked, and the tears spilled onto his cheeks. "The rest of us came down with all kinds of illnesses. I got trench foot, but other guys ended up with pneumonia, dysentery, and then the flu. We knew how to shield ourselves from the Germans. It was the filth and the mosquitoes and the human waste that got us."

"You're here now, Daniel," John said, his voice low and calming. "You can leave the war behind you and get on with your life."

The young soldier ran a hand down his leg, shuffled his feet, and winced from the pain. "Maybe I'll forget someday," he said, a hint of sadness in his voice. "I've got a long road ahead of me. But I was one of the lucky ones. The medics decided not to amputate."

He looked down at his feet, noticeably swollen beneath the layers of cloth.

"You agree with them, don't you Doctor Gallagher?"

"I'll do my best to heal those feet of yours, son," John said kindly. "Already I've seen improvement. You have to believe you're going to walk again and run again and do everything you once did before leaving to fight in that blasted war."

I stood up and started clearing the dirty dishes off the table. I glanced at Amy, didn't say a word, but she caught the look in my eyes and rose up to help me.

John pushed his chair away from the table. "I'll take Daniel home now," he said.

Amy was at the sink. She turned around and sent Daniel a smile.

"Bye, Amy," he said. "I'll se ya' in a day or two."

"Okay, Daniel."

So casual, so unassuming. They were stepping into uncharted waters, each of them edging closer to the deep, unaware of the dangers that lay beneath the surface. They'd already set sail, and I could do nothing to stop the journey.

Would it be so bad? Amy married to a war hero? An heir of the Duncans? Tom and Grace were one of the wealthiest couples in Sawmill. They lived in a huge, Victorian mansion that stood out from the rest of our modestly built cottages of stone and mortar. It rested on the top of a gentle rise at the edge of town, where it could be seen from anywhere in the village. Springtime was lovely on that property. The well-landscaped acre had a border of holly bushes and cherry trees. Pink flowering azaleas ran along the walk. And clusters of rhododendrons and forsythia added an array of pink, purple, and bright yellow to the front lawn. Of course, everything went dormant during the winter months, but hidden beneath the mounds of snow rested the promise of new life. At the first sign of spring, many of us took a walk out that way just to admire the emerging floral artwork.

Grace had hosted our sewing group many times. I'd marveled at the high ceilings, the heavy brocade furniture, and the china and crystal Grace had ordered from France. Now Daniel was going to get his rest and rehabilitation in that place. The Duncans' surrogate son had come home.

As the two men left our house, I gazed at my daughter. She was wiping dishes with a towel and was humming a familiar tune, one that stirred up memories of my own. Softly I began to sing the lyrics. *"I love you truly, truly dear. Life with its sorrow, life with its tear. Fades into dreams when I feel you near."* Suddenly it wasn't about Amy and Daniel anymore. It was about me and John. *"For I love you truly, truly dear."* There was another stanza, but it slipped away along with my tears dropping into the dishwater.

In recent years, after John and I settled into a husband-and-wife routine, I realized we'd somehow lost the romance along the way. These days I looked at him as our faithful breadwinner, the father of my children, the town doctor who belonged to everyone else as much as he belonged to me.

And what did he see when he looked at me? A frumpy housewife? A baby-maker? A mother hen rounding up her chicks? I raised my eyes to the window and caught my reflection in the pane of glass. My hair stuck out at all angles. Dark circles rimmed my eyes. I looked tired. Old. Like Flossie. If only—

"Is something wrong, Mother?" Amy had stopped drying dishes and was staring at me with sympathy in her innocent eyes.

I gave her a comforting smile. "No, Amy, just remembering."

At that moment, John returned from taking Daniel to the Duncans' place. He stopped inside the doorway and sniffed the air.

"Smells like home," he mused. "I can still taste the fried bacon and the freshly brewed coffee. No burnt rubber there," he chuckled.

I turned and faced him. He was standing beside the bulging sack next to his cupboard.

"Those medicines, John, I thought you said you couldn't buy any."

He nudged the bag with his foot. Then he shrugged and a flash of shame colored his face.

"I didn't buy them, Rosie. I stole them."

Chapter Sixteen

"You what?!" I almost dropped the dish I'd been holding. John produced an embarrassed smile. Had my near-perfect husband just told me he'd robbed the hospital supply room?

Thankfully, our two youngest children were still in their bedroom playing. But Amy had been listening.

"Good work, Father." She beamed with approval.

I stared at my daughter in disbelief. What had become of the responsible girl who'd claimed she could take over the household during my absence? What kind of house was I living in where the head of the home broke God's commandment against stealing, and my eldest child not only supported him but was thrilled about it?

I grabbed the back of a chair to keep from falling over. My husband had stolen medicine. I was still sorting through it in my mind. *I* would be more likely to do something like that. Not *him*. Not perfect John. Whatever happened to my husband from the time he left home until he arrived in Philadelphia? What had changed him from an upright man of integrity into a thief?

"John," I said, cautiously. "We need to talk."

"Oh, leave him alone, Mother. Be glad he's come home." Amy gave a little shrug and went over to the bags.

"Don't open them," I snapped.

Her hand halted inches from the strap that bound the burlap sack.

She straightened. "All right," she said, jutting out her chin. "I'll wait for Father and help him put everything away." She brushed her hands together as if she'd already accomplished what she'd set out to do. She looked at John. "Whenever you're ready, Father."

"Amy," I began, striving to control the tone of my voice. "We should talk about this."

"What do we need to talk about, Mother?"

Her nonchalance disturbed me. I waved my hand toward John's haul. "The bags—the medicine—the way your father acquired it. It's—well—it's wrong."

She shook her head and her curls bounced a little. "Father's simply trying to help our own people. How can that be wrong?"

I stood firm. "Amy, stealing is wrong, no matter what is the reason."

She tilted her head to one side, a bewildered wrinkle crossing her forehead.

"You've read the Bible, dear. The eighth commandment warns against stealing. Your father has broken God's law."

John was standing there looking back and forth at us like a spectator at a cricket match. He had an amused smile on his lips, and his eyes glistened.

Amy stepped closer to me and narrowed her eyes. "Why don't we hear what Father has to say about it? He must have a reasonable explanation."

Something told me I was going to lose this argument. I held my tongue, aware that my daughter had, without my realizing it, moved into a place of authority in our home. She'd spoken with such control I didn't know how to respond.

I'd been nurturing that girl for 16 years, and now she was defying me. No longer was I her voice of authority. She was making up her own mind about things. I could only hope that John would be able to explain what he'd done to the satisfaction of both of us.

A sudden terrible sadness came over me. For years, my husband had breezed in and out of our home, tending to his patients in town while I took care of the children. He'd reserved a small part of himself for family outings. Now he'd come back from Philadelphia, and he'd charmed our daughter into thinking he could do no wrong. She'd actually praised him for stealing those medicines.

I ignored Amy and turned my attack on John. "I need an answer."

I pinched my lips together and clenched my teeth.

"All right, Rosie. If it will make you feel better, I paid for the medicine by donating my time. All those hours I put in had to be worth something. The city promised $50 a week to any doctors who volunteered. I let them keep my share."

"You didn't stay a full week."

"No, I didn't. And I never collected any pay."

I raised an eyebrow. "Are you telling me you bought all that with less than $50?

"I also donated every last dime I carried with me."

I continued to eye him with suspicion.

He shrugged like a little boy who'd been caught lying. "Okay, darlin', maybe it wasn't nearly enough."

My husband had somehow convinced himself that taking the medicines was for a good cause, that he hadn't done anything wrong. I shook my head.

He caught my disappointment. "I know you don't approve

of how I acquired these things," he said. "But I had to do it, had to take what we needed."

Without another word, he turned away and left through the front door. I listened for the rumble of his truck. It never sounded. The scraping of the rocker on our front porch filled the crisp autumn air. Whenever he'd needed to think, he'd made a habit of going out on the porch, no matter what the weather. And he always went there alone.

I turned toward the sink and went back to my dishwashing. As far as I was concerned, the subject was not dead, only asleep for now.

Amy joined me at the sink and picked up a towel. I turned to look at her. She was staring out the window, her face aglow. She was thinking about that boy. I was certain of it. She ran the towel over the dishes in a slap-dash manner, leaving beads of water behind.

"Do a better job, Amy." I nodded toward the plate in her hand.

She gave it another swipe. She was smiling, like she had a secret.

"What is it, Amy?"

She grabbed another plate, but paused.

"You do approve of Daniel, don't you, Mother?"

"Of course. He's a fine young man. It's just that—well—I think you should slow down. You're awfully young to be consid—"

"Mother, I'll be 17 in a few months, and then 18 before you know it. Weren't you 18 when you entered nursing school?"

"Yes, but—"

She blinked against a sudden rise of tears. The tiny beads clung to her lashes.

"I've loved Daniel all my life," she whimpered. "From the time we were little we promised that we'd get married one day and that we'd always be together."

"You were kids, Amy, just two impetuous children. Marriage is serious. It's hard work. It's–it's—" I stopped myself then, instantly aware of how ridiculous that sounded, not only to Amy but also to me.

Yes, marriage took work. But *hard* work? Like pounding rocks on a rock pile? Or the kind of work a husband and wife engage in because they love each other? That kind of work should be easy if love is there.

I thought of John sitting out on the front porch, rocking and thinking. I looked at my reflection in the window. The worried lines remained on my forehead, aging me. Had I been too harsh with John? Why didn't I trust the man, let him be, and take care of my own business? Was that so hard?

Then I looked again at my daughter. She was so vulnerable, yet she was on the verge of making her own way. She returned my gaze, the innocence returning to her face.

I placed a soapy hand on the towel she was holding. "Forget what I just said, Amy. I want you to follow your heart, but go slow and allow your good sense to guide you. I trust you to make the right decision."

With a rush of emotion, Amy flung her arms around me. "Thank you, Mother."

"Take it slow," I cautioned her again. "Give Daniel a chance to settle in with his relatives. He's been through a lot and might need time to deal with the effects of the war."

"I know, Mother."

Mother? There it was again. One more sign my little girl had left behind her adolescence and was grappling with womanhood. It wasn't very long ago when I, too, had emerged from childhood and began to envision a future with someone. When I met John I knew without a doubt he was the only man for me. Maybe that's what had happened with Amy too.

"I'll be right back," I said. I dried my hands and hurried out to the front porch.

"It's good to have you back with us, John."

He stopped rocking. I wrapped my arms around his shoulders and pressed my cheek against his forehead.

"Forgive me?" I said.

He nodded and smiled with acceptance. "I could use a little sleep," he mumbled.

He rose from the rocker, and we entered the house together.

"Papa's tired," I told Amy. "He's going to take an afternoon nap."

She tossed aside the dish towel. "I'll turn down your bed for you, Father. And after your nap I'll help you put the medicines in your cupboard."

John gave me one of his impish smiles. "Is that really Amy or someone else?" He shook his head. "When I left a few days ago, she was a sick little girl, unable to lift her head from the pillow. Now she's not only well, she's been transformed."

"She's growing up right before our eyes, John." I linked my arm in his and we followed Amy into our bedroom.

"What do you think about Amy and Daniel?" I whispered in his ear.

"It's happening way too fast for me," he murmured. He turned toward me and winked. "They remind me of us."

His comment surprised me.

"Really?"

He nodded. "It's a wee bit early to say for sure, darlin', but something was brewing in the kitchen today, and it wasn't just coffee."

I looked into his eyes, found them filled with love. He didn't have to say a word. Silently he was telling me how much my loyalty had meant to him, that he'd married the right woman, and that we were a team and always would be.

Through a flood of tears I blinked back my answer. *I'll always stand by you, John, no matter what.*

Amy turned down the bed covers. She smiled at us, then she left the room and shut the door.

John collapsed, fully clothed, on the bed. I removed his shoes, then I sat on the edge of the bed. He was staring at the ceiling, hadn't yet fallen asleep as I'd expected he might.

"Let's talk a bit," he said, and he slid an arm around me and pulled me to his side.

I snuggled closer. "What do you want to talk about?"

"My time in Philadelphia." He craned his neck to look at me. "That is, if you think you can handle it."

"I can. What's more, I *want* to know. Tell me, John, did you find the city terribly different?"

"Different? Extremely. You wouldn't recognize Philadelphia, Rosie. All the storefronts were boarded up. The windows were dark. Every shop and restaurant—including McGillin's—had closed their doors. None of the department stores were open. Some buildings had been deserted and were being used as morgues."

He paused and took a deep breath.

"I drove through the city in shock. The few people on the streets were the undertakers and volunteers who'd come out to drive the sick to the hospitals and to transport the dead for burial. They used the same wagons for both purposes.

My heart was warmed by the number of volunteers who came to help. Nuns worked alongside the doctors in the hospital, though many had no nursing experience at all. Men and women left the safety of their homes to take food and clothing to the shelters. Then they used the same vehicles to haul away more of the dead. With only one city morgue, they piled corpses in abandoned buildings, cold storage plants, and empty schools. Wagons went through the poor sections and picked up more bodies that had been left at the curb."

He took a deep breath. "Embalmers came from the military to help with the overflow of the dead. Seminary students volunteered as grave-diggers. Prisoners were temporarily released from jail to help with the digging. Ultimately, the number of corpses was so great, they brought out steam shovels and dug trenches. Priests helped prepare the bodies for burial. So did the local police. Ministers said prayers over the dead as they were lowered into a common grave." He shook his head. "Church bells rang a death toll all day long. We could hear them inside the hospital, a gentle reminder to us to whisper another prayer."

Living in Sawmill I was nowhere near that nightmare, but my relatives still lived there. When the influenza first hit, I'd used the phone at Cowell's store to call my sisters a couple of times. Though a few of my siblings had gotten sick, Mama was still holding on. Now I wondered if they'd survived the pandemic.

"Were you able to check on my family?" I dared to ask him.

"No, Rosie, I'm sorry. Entrances to the tenements were blocked. Those streets where the different ethnic groups used to hold block parties are serving as outdoor funeral parlors now. The people who live there are conducting their own services. Then they pick up a shovel and find a decent plot of ground to bury their loved ones."

"Did you see your brother?"

"There wasn't time. Besides, he was at a different hospital. This wasn't the time to try to connect with family. The moment I entered those hospital doors I was inundated with medical workers asking for help. When they learned I was a doctor, they handed me a list of duties and ushered me into the main room." A tear oozed from his eye and dribbled to the pillow. "Every bed was filled. It was overwhelming, Rosie."

"Is there no hope, John? Is there an end in sight?"

"I wish I could say there is. But the entire city lies in the grip of the flu. It's like a constant parade of the dead from the hospital to any one of a dozen morgues and then to a common grave."

"All day?"

"All day and all night."

"Even in the dark?"

He nodded. "After sundown they use kerosene lanterns to light the way. The constant flow of mortuary wagons gives off a strange aura. Their swinging lanterns cast an eerie glow against empty sidewalks and boarded up storefronts. Instead of a festival, they're conducting a procession of the dead."

Noticeably drained, John pulled a handkerchief from his pocket and mopped his brow. "That's what's happened to Philadelphia." He choked out the name of his beloved city and succumbed to sobbing.

My heart sank. Philadelphia. The place where I was born and raised had turned into a ghost town, or worse. No ghost town held parades for the dead.

He drew his arm out from under me and turned toward

the wall, a sign he was ready to fall asleep. I reluctantly left his side. We'd have plenty of time to talk later. I had lots of questions.

John was already snoring. I took one last lingering look at him, left the room and quietly shut the door.

While my husband slept, I tried to forget the images he'd described and busied myself with the children. We had let far too much time pass between their studies. Amy went off to the sofa with her classic literature book, and I got young Johnny and baby girl Lily seated at the table with their lessons. I quizzed Johnny on his spelling words, then I helped Lily trace the dotted letters in her penmanship primer. She gripped the pencil in her little fist. If I removed my guiding hand she strayed off the line. I eyed her with a mix of sadness and affection. She was my baby, always would be, I conceded.

My husband slept through lunchtime and joined us in the middle of the afternoon, refreshed and ready to get to work organizing his cupboard. Amy had just begun working in her math book. She tossed it aside and went to her father's cupboard.

"Why don't I hand you the medicines, and you can place them on the shelves?" My daughter said, taking charge.

Her father appeared stunned at first. Then he grinned and nodded with acceptance.

"All right," he said. "That's a good plan, Amy."

I left them to their task. As I walked away I thought I heard Amy singing, "Danny Boy," but I could have imagined it.

I went to the kitchen and made John a sandwich of sliced ham and pickles on pumpernickel bread. A slather of mustard, and it was ready to go.

"Here you are, John," I called and set his plate on the table.

He paused from sorting bottles long enough to devour the sandwich and a glass of milk. While waiting, Amy perched on the arm of the living room sofa and stared out the front window. I assumed from her starry-eyed countenance that she'd mentally left our house and had traveled up the street to the Duncans' home.

I shook my head with resolve. There was no stopping this runaway train.

John gulped the last of his milk, then he set aside the mug. "Let's go, Amy."

Our daughter awoke from her trance, and the two of them went back to work. I pulled a half-knitted quilt I'd been neglecting out of my sewing basket and picked up my needles. I sat on my rocker and kept an eye on my husband and daughter from a safe distance. They didn't need any words of advice from me. They already knew me as the keeper of a disorganized pantry. I chuckled to myself. I couldn't wait for John to stick his head in there and see what I'd accomplished.

Amy dug into the bags and handed her father the medicines. He carefully arranged the little bottles like the big city pharmacies did, with all the labels facing out and everything lined up in a row—alphabetically, I presumed.

As he always had done, John placed the more lethal drugs on the top shelf. The lower shelves held a supply of gauze, ointments, salves, and bandages of all shapes and sizes. His instruments and other tools remained on the bottom behind a locked door, away from inquisitive eyes.

When they finished, John stepped back, looked everything over, then he walked up and made a few changes. He shifted items around to his liking, then stepped back again and crossed his arms.

"These medicines will keep us going through the rest of the winter." He turned to look at me. "No more trips to the big city," he said.

"Dream on," I warned him. "You can't imagine how many people came to our door that first day you were gone. Things have gotten really bad around here, John. Our neighbors are passing the germs from one family member to another. But you'll see for yourself once you start visiting them."

He smiled with confidence. "I can help them all, Rosie. I have more than enough medicines."

I shook my head. "I hope so."

I glanced at Amy. The glow on her face told me she didn't think her father could do anything wrong. She would defend him all the way to the courthouse, if necessary. I, however, still had doubts. I set aside my knitting and walked over to them. The three of us stood looking at the display of drugs.

I waved my hand at the shelves. "How were you able to take all of this and not get caught?"

He gave an awkward shrug. "I just did it. Every day I slipped medicines into my pockets. When I took a break, I went outside for a breath of air and dumped them in the burlap sack on the floor of my truck. Then I went back to work inside that miserable place and tried to heal as many patients as I could. Those who died, I sent off to the undertaker. It was the same thing, day after day. The odors were unbearable—fresh blood, dried blood, urine, vomit—the orderlies couldn't clean it up fast enough. A man can go insane after a while."

I took a deep breath and attempted to hold my tongue. I didn't want to pressure him again. He'd lived through a nightmare. Now that he'd come home, I wanted to make him feel welcome. Yet, I couldn't shake the thought of what he'd done.

I scanned the shelves again, overwhelmed by the amount of medicines John had fit inside those two bags. It was obvious he'd acted spontaneously. One bottle of pills must have led to another and then another. I looked again at the rows of life-saving medicines.

"Well, you didn't come home empty-handed, that's certain."

He chuckled. "All the while I was remembering our friends and neighbors. And I thought of Amy." He gave her arm a friendly nudge. "Our daughter was sick when I left. I had to do something to help her."

I released a sigh. "Of course, John. But all of this?" I gestured again toward the cupboard, now filled to overflowing.

He glanced at Amy, his brow wrinkled with indecision. Then he turned to our daughter. "Amy, dear, I'd like you to go and check on your brother and sister."

She gave a little pout, but nodded and reluctantly left the room.

He stepped in front of me, gently grasped both of my arms, and held my attention. His voice turned deadly serious. "Think about Emma and her boys. If I'd had the pills a week ago I might have saved Robbie. And what about all the other people in town? What about their children? I didn't merely take such a risk for our friends and neighbors. I did it for everyone, even strangers who might pass this way and fall ill. And, Rosie, believe it or not, I did it for you."

"For me?" My jaw dropped.

"Yes, for you, darlin', so you can whisk that nurse's uniform out of the old trunk and get to work. You're a nurse. I want you out there by my side like we used to do. You do want to help me again, don't you, Rosie?"

Chapter Seventeen

John's words confirmed what I'd already been thinking about. Of course I wanted to help him. I'd been dreaming about renewing my commitments as a nurse. A stirring of excitement went through me. Go out there with John? Visit our neighbors? Bring healing to our community? Nothing would please me more.

"I have a big responsibility to the citizens of Sawmill," John pressed. "They have depended on me for 15 years. And if the flu continues to spread as it's already done in the big cities, we're in for a terrible time."

I couldn't agree more.

"But don't give me your answer yet," he said, holding up his hand. "I need to prepare you for what to expect."

He went to the stove and poured two cups of coffee. Then we sat across from each other at the table. John's smile faded to a look of dire concern. I froze, aware that he was about to tell me things I might not want to hear.

"If we don't do something—together—the situation in Sawmill might deteriorate the same way it has in Philadelphia and in other parts of the country. This second wave is more deadly than the first."

He paused and allowed me to absorb the weight of what he'd just said.

I took a deep breath and tried to appear calm. He'd asked me to join him in this battle. I didn't want him to give him any reason to change his mind.

John sipped his coffee, then he folded his hands on the top of the table and leaned toward me.

"This influenza is unlike any other epidemic in the history of the world," he began, pensively. "What's amazing is the newborns and the elderly get sick for a little while and then fully recover. Meanwhile, the disease takes a terrible toll on the young and healthy, particularly the soldiers and medics who stepped up to serve our country—most of them between the ages of 15 and 44. They stepped up to serve, and they're dying."

I immediately thought of Amy. She was in that age group and she'd been seriously ill. I glanced at John's pharmacy cupboard. What he'd done made sense to me now. What if Amy hadn't gotten better? I should fall at John's feet for taking such a risk. Instead of reprimanding him for stealing the medicines, I should be praising him. What's more, when he left four days ago his cupboard was bare. He had to fill those shelves again. Now he could help our friends and neighbors, and us too if we got sick.

While I was pondering all of that, John had continued talking. I picked up what he was saying somewhere in the middle "—problem with any flu is that it spreads from one person to another, sometimes before the sick show any symptoms. Some of our patients in Philadelphia responded to treatment and recovered within a few days. Quinine was our main choice. Though it's a malaria drug, the doctors said it would treat the symptoms. We needed to bring their fevers down. We needed to relieve the intense muscle aches. Though some appeared to get well, their recovery was short-lived and they declined rapidly. Seemingly healthy individuals collapsed and died, sometimes before we could figure out what to do for them. Some had left the hospital and were on the street when it happened. This thing was out of control or, to be more accurate, it had *taken* control."

By this time, my nurse's inquisitiveness had taken hold and more questions surfaced. "What was killing them, John? What were the complications?"

He sat back and moistened his lips. "Pneumonia, mostly. They couldn't breathe. Their lungs filled up with blood and puss. With no oxygen available, cyanosis set in. Many a day I came away wearing a hospital robe covered with someone's blood. People were drowning, Rosie, drowning in their own blood, and we couldn't stop it."

He shuddered then from the memory. He pulled out a handkerchief, brushed tears from his cheeks and blew his nose.

I was speechless, still trying to absorb the images he had described.

He shook his head with sadness. "The dying turned blue from lack of oxygen. Then the blue turned purple, and the purple turned black, so dark, in fact, we couldn't tell if they were Caucasian or Negro. A couple of the doctors gave the condition a name. They called it *the Black Death*."

By this time, I was weeping along with John. I knew things were bad in the bigger cities, but until that moment I didn't know how bad.

"Once a person's skin turned black we knew it was hopeless," he continued. "The patient was going to die, and there was nothing we could do to stop it."

I wondered why we weren't better prepared. Hints of a

worldwide epidemic had originated in April. That was more than six months before. But the news reports were either sketchy or nonexistent. It wasn't until recently that we were aware of the danger, and by that time the pandemic was out of control.

I looked at my husband, confusion swimming around in my head. "The influenza has been around for months. After all this time, hasn't anyone found a cure? A vaccine? Anything?"

"It's a been a terrible challenge," John said with shrug. "The scientists have been working on vaccines and serums from the very beginning. Nothing has worked. They've never encountered anything this diabolical before. It isn't that they haven't tried. The top scientists are working day and night in their private labs. Then they come together and share what they've discovered. Even with all those brilliant heads working we've gotten no closer to a cure."

"So the responsibility fell on you and the other doctors and nurses to tackle the symptoms and hope for the best?"

He nodded. "All we could do was keep the patients separated—the deathly ill ones from those who had fewer symptoms. We hung sheets between the beds, and we laid the sick in opposite directions, with one patient facing north and the next one facing south. The extra effort helped reduce the spread of germs."

I thought about the hospital where I had worked during my training. If I were still there I'd be dealing with the same horror John had encountered. Back then we had even fewer medicines.

"Times have changed since I was in training, haven't they?" I said.

John's eyes lit up. "You'd be amazed at how the hospitals

have advanced since we began our careers. They do chest x-rays now. Blood tests are more advanced. They use more powerful microscopes. One new test, the Wassermann reaction, looks for antibodies that may help in the creation of an effective serum. The doctors at the hospital where I volunteered were relying a great deal on that test, but so far with no results. In any case, it's amazing what they've been able to accomplish. Some of the best scientists in the country have been experimenting with the blood and sputum cultures of influenza survivors. They hope to isolate the type of agent that may be responsible for this disease. They've even started using sick patients' body secretions in hopes of creating a vaccine."

I caught my breath. The scientists had gone way beyond anything I'd ever encountered during my nursing career. Yet the disease continued to stump them.

"Still, there's no cure," I said with unfeigned disappointment.

"No, darlin'. Not yet. They still haven't determined whether the initial cause was a bacteria, a virus, or a new type of microbe. Several theories have arisen. One physician insisted it was a type B influenzae, a highly contagious form that is spread from human to human. Another argued that it was caused by a filter-passing virus like those that migrate from animals to humans and vice-versa."

He drained his coffee and went to the stove for another. Then he settled in the chair across from me looking much like a defeated man. The image unnerved me. How was my husband going to save anyone if his confidence had diminished?

"Don't worry, Rosie," he said as though reading my thoughts. "I'm not going to quit. I'm going to use the methods we practiced in Philadelphia. I can make an impact right here in Sawmill."

I snickered. "With what, John? If the scientists in Philly don't have a cure, what will you use?" I raised my eyebrows. "Are you going to conjure up some miracle drug out of thin air?"

He cocked his head and eyed me with amusement. Blushing, I looked with innocence into his sparkling green eyes.

"No, darlin'," he said, softly. "You and I are going to use what I brought home with me. We'll treat the symptoms. For secondary pneumonia, digitalis and epinephrine. For headache and fever, aspirin. For intense aches and pains, quinine. And so on."

"You said nothing worked, that the drugs gave only temporary relief."

"We had a constant flow of patients," he said, shaking his head. "The sick came in one door, and the dead went out the other. We wrapped the deceased in blankets, bags, whatever was available. Orderlies carried away the corpses. The memory is embedded in my brain, Rosie. Horrible images, and the stench was something awful. Sometimes I think I can still smell death."

I glanced at the children's door, grateful to find it closed. Never in my wildest dreams had I imagined such a curse would fall upon the entire world. One day people were going about their daily activities—work, school, meetings—and the next day they were sick and dying or already dead.

"Be honest with me, John. When you saw how bad it was in Philadelphia, why did you choose to stay?"

Lines of remorse gathered on his face. "They had such a need, Rosie. I *had* to stay." The lines softened a little and determination filled his eyes. "It was overwhelming, but it was also an honor to be able to join those dedicated doctors in their fight to save lives. By the end of my time there, the number of fatalities had diminished. More than 90 percent of our patients were able to leave the hospital cured, though they faced a long, uphill road to full recovery."

My heart surged with love and respect for my husband. I had been pressuring him with my anxieties, and he had proven himself a hero. I bowed my head and grieved for the victims and for the courageous doctors and nurses who, like John, had remained. Many of them lost their lives while trying to help complete strangers. I lifted my head to find John staring at me with compassion in his eyes.

"If you had been there—"

I shook my head. "But I *wasn't* there. I was here with the children. Safe."

"You would have come with me if you could have."

I chuckled then. "I almost did. Then you came home. Only by the grace of God did you arrive moments before I was about to leave."

I chewed my bottom lip. "I'm not sure I could have stayed there. I would have been thinking about the children the whole time. I would have left long before you did."

He shook his head. "You never know what you might do until you're in the midst of a situation." His cheeks flushed pink, which they always did when he was about to make a confession.

"I didn't put in near the hours some of the nurses and doctors worked. Most of them had joined the team long before I arrived. Some of them were working 20 hours a day without a break."

He puffed out a shaky breath. "Several died. Every time another doctor or nurse collapsed, I thought about leaving."

I shuddered. Medical workers who had been decorated for their military service now had fallen prey to an invisible enemy.

John succumbed then to a wave of emotion. "They gave their lives, Rosie. Overnight doctors and nurses became patients. Some recovered. Some passed. No one could predict who the next victims would be or how they might fare. They just kept on working, determined to beat the disease or die in the attempt."

I wept with him then, painfully aware of the horror he had escaped. He was home now and he'd brought with him medicines and the experience of having dealt with the worst stages of the disease. But one question had been roiling around in my mind. I released it now.

"Is it possible you might have brought the germs home with you?"

John's sharp green eyes pierced my own. "Listen to me, Rosie. I took every precaution. I wore a full medical gown and cap. I covered my nose and mouth with five layers of gauze, sometimes six. And I either disinfected my masks every night or I swapped them out for fresh ones in the morning. I wore surgical gloves, and still I washed my hands repeatedly in strong soap."

His voice broke as he continued to open his heart to me. "I knew it was time to leave. I had gathered enough medicines to help our people. Then I turned my back on the sick and the dying. I had to leave quickly. I knew if I looked back I'd return every last bottle of medicine. I forced myself to keep going, Rosie, always with thoughts of you and the children spurring me on. I climbed in my truck beside Daniel, and I drove out of the city with the cries of the dying lingering in my heart."

He slumped forward and buried his face in his hands. "The things I stole—I knew it was wrong, but I took them anyway."

I rose from my chair and went around to his side of the table. I wrapped my arms around him and pulled his head to my breast. "Oh, John, my dear husband." I sensed the weight of his guilt. My husband had spent his entire life serving others. He'd lived with integrity. Now he'd made a terrible mistake, and he didn't know how to deal with it. I stroked his hair, shut my eyes and enjoyed the silky feel of those red strands.

He raised his head, and I saw his face was streaked with tears. He choked out his remorse. "If I could go back and change everything, I would leave Philadelphia empty-handed. But I was selfish, Rosie. I kept thinking of our children, especially Amy lying here sick, and I thought of you, and the people of Sawmill, and how much they needed me. So I stole those medicines. Medicines that could have been used to heal more people in the hospital. I've committed a terrible sin against them and against God."

I backed away from him and put my fists on my hips. "The problem with you, John Gallagher, is that you've been trying too hard. You're a good man. You've helped a lot of people. But instead of trusting God to guide you, you've been doing it all under your own strength. Now you feel like a failure. Yes, stealing is a sin. You need to confess it to God and be done with it."

A surge of awareness washed through me. Strange how I knew the right words to say to someone else, but I'd been carrying my own burden of guilt for 20 years. I was still pining away over the six-year-old boy who died while under my care.

I recalled what Emma had said, how I needed to lay that burden at the cross of Christ. Over the years I'd confessed my sin multiple times, but I'd never released it.

From out of nowhere, a still small voice grabbed my attention. *How many times must I die for the same sin, Rose? It's time to let it go.*

Stunned, I realized God had forgiven me the first time I asked him to. But I'd been nailing the same mistake to the cross over and over again. What did the Savior say just before he died? *It is finished.*

Tears spilled from my eyes. I fell on my knees and I wept with unimaginable relief.

John wrapped his arms around me and mumbled a simple prayer of repentance. I stood to my feet and slid onto his lap. We clung to each other and cried together for several minutes. Then John looked into my face and smiled sweetly.

"I have one question," he said.

I tilted my head with interest.

"How can I make restitution to the hospital for the things I stole?"

I thought for a minute and came up with what seemed to be a reasonable solution.

"You said you gave them your time and your money. If you don't feel like it was enough you can write them a letter of apology. Admit the wrong you did and let them decide what to do about it."

He chewed his bottom lip. "I might go to prison."

"Maybe. Maybe not. Whatever happens, I'll stand by you, John. I'll never leave your side. As for your invitation to work with you here in Sawmill, of course I'll go with you. We're a team. We may not be able to beat that monster, but we can try. The main thing is, we'll be doing it together."

Chapter Eighteen

John spent the rest of the day looking through his supply of medicines. He wanted to be ready at a moment's notice in case someone came to our door seeking his help. I marveled at his organization, every bottle labeled, every label turned outward so he could grab them on the run. If nothing else those four days in Philadelphia had instilled a sense of urgency in my husband. He'd left there knowing how much we also needed him. Now he was ready to pick up where he'd left off. He was Sawmill's only doctor. Every second wasted could mean life or death for someone.

I surveyed the shelves closer. There were dozens of bottles of quinine, two different kinds of cough syrup, laxatives, iodine, jars of chloroform and nitrous oxide, digitalis, epinephrine, plus syringes, sacks of catgut and multiple rolls of gauze and other dressings. The upper shelf held small pouches of different powders, with heroin and opium scrawled on their sides in black ink. Several bottles were labeled laudanum, morphine, and cocaine—powerful painkillers hospitals used regularly, but we rarely found a need for them in our quiet, little village. It occurred to me that John was preparing for the worse, which sent a wave of apprehension through me.

There was an entire row of small bottles bearing the name *aspirin* and the dose, *5 gr.* They looked an awful lot like the wayward bottle I'd found on the top shelf. I ran to our bedroom and returned with it in my hand. "Look." I showed John the bottle.

He eyed it with a puzzled raising of his eyebrows.

"I found this on the top shelf of your cupboard after you left. It has no markings. I didn't know if it was safe, so I hid it away."

He took the bottle and opened the lid, dropped a tablet in his palm and tasted it with the tip of his tongue. He smiled. "Aspirin, Rosie. Nothing more."

I laughed with relief. "Johnny had these pills in his hands for a few terrorizing seconds. I stopped him just before he could feed them to Lily."

John smiled. "Playing doctor again?"

I nodded. "That's your son."

He recapped the bottle and put it in his pocket. "I'll dispose of this. It's likely too old to do any good, could even be poisonous by now. With no markings it had to be something my father left behind." He chuckled and shook his head. "That man didn't organize his supplies well. There's no telling how long it was rolling around up there."

Once again, John stood back to enjoy his pharmaceutical display.

"Tomorrow, we'll visit our neighbors," he announced.

I went to get the list of 24 families who expected John to call on them, to save them from the disease that was creeping through our village. I'd given most of them a pouch of homegrown remedies. Now my husband had brought formulated medicines, and I prayed they might make a difference. From what he had told me, they'd used every one of them in Philadelphia, but some of the patients had died anyway.

I handed the list to John. He frowned with concern, and I could almost read his mind. Which house should come first?

He turned to me. "Help me out, Rosie. You must have talked to these neighbors. Who needs us most?"

Without hesitation I pointed at Emma Wilson's name, not the least bit ashamed of choosing my best friend above the others.

"Her other two boys are sick, like Robbie was. So is her husband, and he's lost his job."

John nodded pensively. "In the morning, as soon the sun comes up, we'll go straight to Emma Wilson's house." He cocked his head. "Will the children be all right without us for a few hours."

"They will. Amy's feeling better and she's already shown me how responsible she can be. I feel comfortable leaving the children in her care. Besides, Greta Schmidt has offered to help out if needed."

John lurched backward. "What?"

I giggled and explained the astonishing transformation that had taken place in our neighbor.

John shook his head, amusement etched on his face. "That woman blamed me for years for her husband's death. When did she come to her senses?"

I shrugged. "I'm not sure. I think it was the home remedies I gave her the other day. She said they reminded her of her mother's *miracle cures* when she was a little girl back in Germany."

"Home remedies?" John's eyebrows went up.

I nodded. I hadn't yet told my husband about my little project. To my relief, he didn't press for information. He chatted with Amy over dinner that evening, and later he played games with our two little ones.

After getting the children into bed, we went to our own room and shut the door. That night I gave myself to my husband, overjoyed at having him home again. We lay for a long time, holding each other. I wasn't ready to fall asleep. A multitude of images were rolling around in my mind. Tomorrow I planned to step out of the house on a real mission, beside my husband, and I could hardly wait.

John also lay there, staring at the ceiling. I assumed he was still mulling over his time in Philadelphia. Such a trauma must have left a terrible ache in his heart. Poor John had escaped a place of uncommon suffering only to come home and face more of the same. If the flu took hold like it had in the bigger cities, the people of Sawmill were in for a terrible period of suffering. And much of the responsibility had fallen on John. This time he wouldn't be taking orders from other doctors. He'd be in charge. He'd be able to claim the successes, but he'd also suffer the losses. My husband took every situation to heart.

I shifted onto my side so I could get a better look at him. A ripple of moonlight oozed through a split in the curtain and fell on his boyish face. A pink glow had returned to his cheeks, and his chin jutted out with the confidence of a man who'd already prepared for battle. I hated to spoil the moment, but he needed to know how many people we'd lost in Sawmill. Better to tell him now while he had time to assimilate the information.

"We've lost a few more of our neighbors," I began.

He turned to look at me, the green of his eyes darkening. "How many?"

I hesitated and mentally counted the crepes I'd seen on the front doors.

"How many, Rosie?" he insisted.

I let out a sigh. "Eleven as of yesterday. There could be more by now."

He returned his gaze to the ceiling. A tear slid from his eye and down his cheek.

"We're living in a different world, darlin'," he said, a certain sadness in his voice. "Do you remember our first date? It seems eons ago."

"I do. Those were wonderful days. I wish we could relive them."

"Remember how we walked the streets of Philadelphia and looked in all the shop windows, the lunch we ate at McGillin's Tavern, how we drove down by the water and enjoyed the sailboats and the couples in their canoes?" He didn't wait for me to answer. He was opening his heart to me, and I wasn't about to stop the flow.

"Remember how pristine everything was?" he went on. "The streets had been swept clean of debris, the storefronts were whitewashed, the windows sparkling clean. Remember our jaunt through the suburbs, the homes of the wealthy with their verdant lawns and flowering gardens, their stone walls and white picket fences? Remember the azalea bushes in full bloom, the cherry blossoms, the willows and elm trees and oaks lining the streets, their branches filled with greenery?"

He paused then and gave me a wink, like he was taking me on a journey of sorts. Then he released a shaky breath, and his smile faded. Lines of distress gathered on his face.

"You wouldn't recognize the city now, Rosie. A specter of death has settled there. It looks like a ghost town and smells like a sewer. Wet newspapers and garbage litter the streets. People have locked themselves in their houses, or they've lined up in front of the hospitals and makeshift clinics, begging for medicine. Looters have broken some of the windows in town. They sweep in during the night and disappear before dawn, never to be caught. This second wave has decimated the city.

"Then there's the death toll. The number of dead keeps rising every day. Nearly every household has hung a crepe on their front door, particularly in the old neighborhood where you and I used to work. Those people aren't able to keep the healthy members of their families away from the sick. They're crowded together in one or two rooms. And so the numbers soar. Many parents have died, leaving their children to wander the streets as orphans. It's a terrible tragedy, Rosie.

"Shortly before I left, the authorities released the city's latest death toll—12,000 and still climbing. The sad thing is, the government leaders should have seen it coming. Months before it struck Philadelphia, the authorities knew about the overcrowded military camps. New York, Boston, and Philadelphia were all breeding grounds for the flu. To make the situation worse, the city's public health director made a grave mistake by allowing a Liberty Loan Parade to take place in downtown Philadelphia. It happened a month before I arrived, on September 28. They wanted to raise millions of dollars in war bonds. The event drew more than 200,000 people to Broad Street. By that time the flu was in full swing. Keeping people in isolation would have helped curb the spread of the disease, yet they plunged ahead with that ridiculous plan. Now the downtown area is empty, the stores have closed their doors, and no one is cleaning the city's streets. It's as if the City of Brotherly Love has also died."

My throat tightened. It was hard for me to imagine the devastation of the place where I was born and raised and where John and I both started our careers. Tears ran down my face. John gently brushed them away.

"What about you, John? How did you know which hospital to go to?"

"When I entered the city, I connected with the Philadelphia Council of National Defense. They had set up an information center in the Strawbridge & Clothier Department Store. A volunteer there pointed me to the nearest medical facility. It turned out to be the one where I'd received my training."

"And they wouldn't sell you what you needed?"

"Not one pill. Their situation was disheartening. Every bed was filled, and as soon as one person died, the orderlies brought in another, sometimes without taking the time to change the sheets."

"Were the symptoms anything like what happened to Amy?" I asked, fearing his answer.

"Not really. Patients spoke of sudden dizziness, the first sign something was wrong. They complained of unbearable muscle pain and headaches, sore throats, and, in the more advanced cases, difficulty breathing. When I learned they had a shortage of doctors, I had to jump right in and help."

"I can picture you doing that," I said, not as an accusation but with a sense of pride.

"It was a hit-and-miss operation, Rosie. Each case was different. If someone became ill with secondary pneumonia, we injected epinephrine. If they had trouble breathing, we applied an oxygen mask. One of the doctors suggested we try boosting their immune systems by injecting antibodies. Nothing we did worked. This particular disease was stronger than anything we'd ever encountered. It was as if we were searching for a way out of this dilemma but never finding the right door."

"Then what good are all those medicines you brought home? If they didn't work in Philadelphia, how can we expect them to work here?"

He gave a little shrug. "We have to do our best, Rosie."

†††

I slept easier that night for the first time in days, and I awoke feeling rested and ready to help my husband serve the people of Sawmill. While John shaved and got dressed I told him about what I'd put into the little pouches I'd distributed to our neighbors. He laughed aloud, then seeing my embarrassment, he planted a kiss on my forehead.

"You made a worthy effort, my dear Rosie. I could expect nothing less from you. It was my fault you didn't have any medicines. I simply ran out of everything faster than I'd expected. As it was, I waited too long to go to Philadelphia." He ran a brush through his hair. "But you were very resourceful, darlin', and who knows? Perhaps some of those herbs and powders might have helped someone. Maybe they've already recovered because of your good deed. They may not need my services at all."

"We'll soon find out, won't we?" I said, a flicker of hope nagging at the back of my mind.

Here I was, a trained nurse, and I'd given out folk remedies. I longed to find out I'd been right to do that little act of kindness. Somehow I needed to redeem myself, but more importantly I needed my neighbors to know I cared about them and wanted to help them.

Since Amy appeared well enough to help out with the children during my absence, I prepared my nurse's kit for my walk with John. Joy filled my heart as I put each item inside the bag. Then I went next door and called on the widow Schmidt. When I told her about my decision she agreed to look in on the children later that morning.

"So your husband has returned. I vill be happy to check on your children. Now you, get to verk."

Gone was the cranky old woman who used to glare at us from her kitchen window. Gone were the accusations she once spewed from her front porch. Greta had once again become a surrogate grandmother to our children and a lifesaver for me. Now I could do what God had called me to do from the time I watched my eldest sister's baby come into the world. For the past 16 years I'd let my nurse's training fall by the wayside. Now I could pick up where I left off. I could entrust my family to God, and I could accompany my husband in his life-giving mission to our friends and neighbors.

Not that I didn't love taking care of my children, but something had been missing in my life, and now I'd found it again. Olive was right. She'd insisted that a woman can tackle both challenges—a job and a family. So why couldn't I go out for a few hours and practice my healing skills and then come home and spend time with my children? Men did it, so why not women?

I hadn't taken the time to unpack the bag I'd planned to take to Philadelphia. I pulled out my nurse's uniform, ignored the wrinkles—I could iron it later—and quickly dressed. It still fit. I skipped the old nurse's shoes with the one-inch heels and chose my fur-lined boots instead. I put on my coat and a mask, then I reached in my pocket and felt for the nurse's pin I'd put there yesterday. I attached the pin to my collar, gave it a gentle pat, and went on my way.

John was already bundled up in a wool coat and scarf and was waiting at the door for me with his medical kit in his hand. His eyes looked greener than ever as they peered at me over the top of his mask.

We waved good-bye to the children who were immersed in their studies at the dining room table, and we stepped out the front door into another brisk autumn day. The clear blue sky and the crisp, clean air belied the fact that a virulent disease was hovering over our village.

As John had agreed we went directly to Emma Wilson's house.

I hadn't seen my friend since the day I tried to hand her a bag of herbs. She'd shut the door in my face, just like I had done to her a couple of days before. She hadn't yet acknowledged the little pouches I left on her porch, never came to thank me.

"Do you think she'll see me?" I asked John as we approached her front steps.

He pursed his lips. "I don't know, Rosie. Why shouldn't she?"

It was time I confessed. "She came to the house the day you left for Philadelphia. I didn't let her in, John. Her two boys were sick. I was afraid for our children." More shame washed over me. "I shut the door in her face and told her she'd have to wait until you returned."

There on the sidewalk, just a few steps from Emma's door, I began to weep.

John stopped walking. He set his medical kit on the pavement and wrapped both arms around me. Resting his chin on the top of my head, he murmured softly. "There, there,

Rosie. You did nothing wrong. This flu has made all of us a little nervous. We get protective, maybe even a little irrational. What could you possibly have done for Emma anyway?"

"I could have let her in. I could have hugged her, shared whatever I could from my pantry. Instead I gave her advice through a crack in the door and turned her away to solve her own problems."

He backed away from me, his eyes filled with compassion. "You did not bring the illness to Emma's house, and thank God you did not allow her to bring it into ours. If there was one thing I learned while serving at the hospital it was the importance of separation. Our patients didn't begin to get well until we started putting a distance between those who had mild symptoms and those who were near death. In a way, you did the same thing right here in Sawmill. Now you must rid yourself of this guilt. Didn't you say the same thing to me a short while ago? Listen to me, Rosie. An influenza pandemic has swept through the entire world. Our job is to do what we can to stop its transmission, and if it means locking people inside their houses for a short time, then so be it."

I brushed the tears from my face. My husband was right. I had behaved like everyone else, protective of my own. Though it must have appeared to Emma that I had turned my back on our friendship, the truth was my own heart broke that day. The greater loss was mine.

"Now," John stated with firmness. "Pull yourself together and come along. We don't want to waste another minute on past hurts. We have a job to do." He picked up his bag and continued with a slight limp up Emma's front steps and onto her porch.

I hurried to get in step with him. This was a determined

man, the same one I had worked beside in the worst of conditions, maneuvering through garbage heaps in dark alleys and bending close to strangers who reeked of vomit. Back then we didn't welcome them into sterile hospital wards. We visited the sick in their backwater flats and rundown tenements.

"So you gave her one of those little pouches?" John said with a chuckle.

"I gave her two." I giggled along with him. My innocent attempt must have sounded ridiculous to this accomplished man of medicine. I became defensive. "What's wrong with what I did?" I jabbed his arm. "My mother trusted in those home remedies. Sometimes they worked. Sometimes they didn't. We could say the same thing about the medicines you brought home with you. And didn't some of them also come from herbs and seeds and the bark of trees?"

His eyes sparkling with impish incredulity. "You're a nurse, Rosie. A nurse will use whatever she has on hand if she's any good."

His remark eased my mind. But here we were, on Emma's front porch and I was about to come face-to-face with my old friend. John gave the door a good knock. My heart was pounding in time with his rapping. I trembled, nervous about seeing Emma again.

My friend opened the door. I held my breath and waited for her to say something. She peered back at me over a white mask, her tired brown eyes ringed with dark circles, the upper part of her face as pale as a pile of ashes. Her shoulders slumped under the strain of caring for her entire household even as she continued to grieve the loss of her youngest.

She stared at me with coldness in her eyes. She didn't smile, didn't acknowledge my presence at all. I was about to speak when she raised her eyebrows and shifted her attention to John.

"*You* can come in John." She raised a hand. "But not her."

I stepped back in shock.

"Are you certain?" John said. "Rosie can help."

"I don't need her help. Only yours."

He turned toward me and sighed. "Sorry, Rosie," he whispered. "Perhaps it's best if you wait here."

I looked imploringly at my friend, but her image blurred amidst the moisture that filled my eyes.

"Emma, please—"

She turned away from me. "Are you coming inside, doctor?" Her voice was crisp, emotionless.

He nodded, stepped ahead, and left me standing there alone on the porch.

The door shut in my face. I understood how Emma must have felt that tragic day when I refused to let her into my house. The world was a cruel and lonely place out there on a cold front porch. How much worse had it been for Emma who'd come seeking my help and didn't get it? How could I ever repair the harm I had done? I'd do anything to go back in time, to take back that moment and respond to my friend as I should have, with open arms and a kind word.

Those pouches I'd given out were worthless attempts at what? Making people think I cared? Most likely all of my neighbors had shaken their heads in disgust. They knew I'd been a nurse. But what had I given them? Useless folk remedies I had scraped together in a last minute surge of conscience.

Sobbing, I settled on the top step of Emma's porch. I turned to look at the door. It stood as a barrier between me and my longtime friend. I wished for that door to open again; wished for Emma to come back out and invite me inside.

Chapter Nineteen

I accompanied John to several other houses. Though everyone welcomed me inside, they were warm toward John, but they eyed me with a hard, cold stare. It was as if they suspected John had dragged me along without my really wanting to be there.

None of them mentioned my little gift bags. Had they even used any of those items? My question was answered during one visit when I went into the kitchen to dispose of an empty pill bottle and discovered one of my pouches inside the pail. I lifted it out, found it still packed with all of my little remedies, my note of helpful advice ripped to shreds. My heart broke. My neighbors had needed medical care, and I had given them junk. I'd brought shame to my profession.

These people weren't like my mother. They didn't rely on folk remedies, and those who did certainly didn't need the ones I provided. They had looked to John and me as medical professionals. They'd depended on us to stay tuned to the latest advancements.

I stood quietly by each bedside as John's comforting hands brought refreshing hope to his patients. They seemed to recover simply by having him present. Somewhere along the way I had lost the essence of my profession, the tender loving care nurses were known to provide even in the absence of a doctor. I struggled to hold back a rise of tears, couldn't wait to leave each dwelling, and when we hit the street again, I let the dam burst. I wept silently, hoping that John didn't notice. He was absorbed in the list of names we still needed to visit. He read aloud my notations regarding their medical complaints. By the time we reached the next house he already had an idea what he might use to help the people inside.

In some of the homes, John needed my assistance more than in others. I followed his instructions, went through his medical bag for whatever he needed, helped a patient get into or out of bed, emptied a urine bottle—whatever helped the doctor continue his work without incidental interruptions. I did little to bring comfort to the patients or to their worried family members. It was John's efforts that brought them relief. Though trained in the art of healing, I'd somehow misplaced the very basics of my nursing career. Did John notice? He didn't seem to. He smiled sweetly and gave me gentle reminders. "A little more gauze, Rosie," or "The aspirin, dear, the aspirin."

Nevertheless, I stayed with him for the duration of the day. I was glad I did. Otherwise I would have missed the joy of seeing several of his patients start to recover. Then there were the more serious cases. The disease had definitely found its mark, leaving a few of our friends and neighbors bedridden for several days after our first visit. Several more neighbors, upon hearing that the doctor was back in town, began to call for him at all hours of the day and night.

During John's first week home, we lost two patients. Patrick Philips' wife, Mae, and one of the Sawmill brothers, Ed Wilcox. I cried with their spouses.

In many households, one person got well and someone

else came down with the flu. People constantly traded places. One was in bed, the other in the kitchen. Then they switched.

Those who followed John's orders and kept the healthy ones apart from the sick fared better. Still, we kept running from one house to another and from one sickbed to another, many times within the same house. As days passed, my former training began to click in and I stepped up as if I'd never forgotten. As in our early days together, I began to anticipate John's orders before he ever spoke a word. He smiled at me with appreciation. We were a team again.

Of course, we both were swathed in cloth from head to toe—white medical gowns, caps on our heads, four layers of gauze over our mouths and noses, and disposable gloves. Upon returning home each evening, everything except the gloves went into a washtub filled with soap and bleach. The gloves went into the garbage. It was only a matter of time before we ran out of disinfectants. At one point we stopped at the general store and bought what was left of David's bottles. We hoped more supplies would come in from his providers out west. Now that the germs had overtaken Chicago and St. Louis, the rail shipments had slowed.

That first morning on the streets we'd gone out with a list of 24 families and by the end of the following week we'd seen 50 more. Many of our patients rallied, to my surprise. Most of the dead were under 40 years old, which I still found quite disturbing. We were horrified when we discovered one poor woman lying in bed next to her deceased husband. She was too sick to move him off the bed, and too ill to find somewhere else to lie down. A great many others were unable to bathe and feed themselves. While John moved on to the next caller, I stayed behind and took care of them.

Then I caught up with my husband and the scene repeated itself many times over.

Every day I returned home exhausted. After I kicked off my boots and hung up my coat, I threw my clothes in a tub of soap and bleach and put on a fresh change of clothes. Then I collapsed on a chair in the living room. As she had promised, Amy put together a fine meal every evening, so I didn't have to cook. But I found the long hours in the village extremely tiring. I wasn't accustomed to the pace. And, something else began to trouble me.

I came home every day to discover our table was set for six people instead of five. No sooner had we freshened up for supper when Daniel came knocking at our door. It was as if he'd been watching for our return. The Duncan mansion, situated on the hill, gave Daniel a wide view of most of the town, including our front door. Fortunately, he obeyed the rules of propriety and didn't put one foot inside our house until we were there to chaperone.

So it was that Daniel came, like clockwork, one evening. At the sound of his knock, color rushed to Amy's cheeks, and a sparkle came to her eyes. I noticed a few other changes in my daughter. On this particular day, she'd done her hair in an upsweep, leaving a few tendrils trailing down the sides of her face. She'd never fixed her hair like that before. Another shock, she was wearing one of my dinner dresses, which, I had to admit, looked better on her than it did on me. Then I peered closer. Had she gotten into my lipstick?

I was still trying to assimilate all of that when a delectable aroma of roast lamb caught my attention. Amy had pulled a leg from the freezer and had roasted it to a juicy sizzle. She set the platter on the table then buzzed around the kitchen, scooped potatoes into a bowl, and grabbed two loaves of bread from a tray on the hearth.

Then she spooned a double portion of everything on Daniel's plate, and set a tumbler of milk and a cup of coffee before him, a meal fit for a king.

I shook my head in awe. Things were moving way too fast with those two. Though I held onto my concerns, I found myself delighting in seeing young love blossom right there in my kitchen. It brought back memories of my own budding love affair with John almost 20 years ago.

My husband also kept a wary eye on the young couple. After all, Amy was only 16. Daniel was almost 19. He might be ready for a serious relationship, but our daughter was just stepping out of childhood. She still had much to learn about life and responsibility and commitment.

While we ate supper, Daniel entertained us with stories about his training. He told us he'd enlisted in the military in January 1917.

"That winter was the coldest on record," he began as he plunged his fork into a slice of lamb. He took a bite and savored the juices. It appeared that the boy had starved himself all day just so he could stuff himself at our house. He went on with his tale between voracious bites of food and long drags of milk.

"I don't know how it happened, but somehow they must have miscalculated our numbers," Daniel mused. "We were jammed into barracks they'd built for half as many men. We ended up sharing beds in shifts. One guy used the cot in the morning, then he'd go out to train, and I'd lie on it in the afternoon, then when I left, someone else came in and slept on the same used-up mattress throughout the night. We also shared cups and forks that had been quickly washed. We passed around all kinds of germs—colds, of course, also head lice, scabies, and who knows what else?" He gave a little shrug and scooped up a helping of potatoes. "We were better off than the guys who lived in tents. But we might as well have been living outside. The barracks didn't have heat, and the flimsy clothing they gave us didn't keep us warm."

He swallowed another mouthful of potatoes and then used a piece of bread to sop up the lamb juices. "A couple of guys came down with the measles," he said, snickering. "They were a sight to see." Then he lost his smile. "The measles are serious, you know. You can die." He looked around the table at us, then he stuffed another piece of sopping bread in his mouth. "Then there were the head colds. Almost everybody was coughing and sneezing. Before we transferred out, we all had fevers and runny noses. I've never experienced anything so uncomfortable in my life. That is, until I got into the trenches."

Amy listened wide-eyed. She hung on every word Daniel said, didn't seem the least bit offended when he talked with his mouth full. I had to admit, Daniel had a way of telling a story that also kept me captivated. By the time dinner was over, I couldn't remember if I'd eaten anything. If not for the tiny scraps that remained on my plate I might have wondered if I'd even taken a bite.

Daniel's monologues covered pretty much everything he'd encountered during his military training. He rambled on about doing calisthenics at six o'clock in the morning, marching 10 miles over rocky terrain, and crawling through mucky swamps. He bragged about shooting a weapon and taking care of his own personal rifle. He talked about the friends he'd made—George, Jimmy, and the guy they'd nicknamed Mouse, who would die in the war—the tricks they played on each other and on their sergeant, and the disciplines that turned them from boys into men.

Young Johnny was taking it all in, his eyes as wide as saucers. He gawked at Daniel like he'd just stepped out of an adventure book. Lily paid more attention to the food on her plate. Between every bite she served an imaginary spoonful to the doll on her lap. Meanwhile, John allowed Daniel to ramble on, like a benefactor of sorts, applauding a young warrior who'd just returned from the battlefield. My husband had never served in the military. His leg injury had kept him out. Now he hung on every word that came out of Daniel's mouth.

Eventually, Daniel's dramatic accounts moved past his training experiences and on to the reality of war.

"There's nothing more frightening than being in a foxhole sometimes up to your knees in muck, in the middle of the night," Daniel continued.

Supper had ended, and I swapped out the dirty dinner plates for servings of my strawberry jam-topped sponge cake. The young man's eyes lit up when I set the platter in the center of the table along with a pitcher of milk. I served the first piece to John and the second to Daniel. Then I created plates for the children.

Our loquacious soldier took a large bite, savored it, and went on with his tale. "We were living like animals, hadn't had a bath in days, couldn't even change our underwear." He flashed an embarrassed glance at Amy. "We were under the constant threat of poison gas, bombs, shells, and getting tangled in barbed wire. My buddies and me—we talked about all the dangers we'd encountered during the day. As we hunkered down for the night, we knew we might have to face those same dangers tomorrow. We'd have to dodge more bullets and take refuge in another waterlogged ditch. And you haven't lived until you've crawled on your belly over ground littered with stones and sharp blades of grass that tear up your clothes and prick your face."

Daniel told his stories with such nonchalance he worried me. Was he ready to take on the responsibility of marriage and family? Hopefully, he would give my daughter a couple of years to grow up.

He scraped up the rest of his cake and held out his plate for another helping. "One of the guys in my platoon carried a Bible in his pack," he said. "We called him *the Preacher*, 'cause he was always spoutin' off some verse of scripture or telling us about God and heaven. I've never been a regular church-goer, except when Aunt Grace made me go, but I listened with a willing heart. Once you've looked into the dangerous end of a rifle something changes inside you, and you want to know everything there is about God."

The rest of us watched him eat and held our breath, waiting for his next account. Needless to say, the young man was entertaining.

"The Preacher read from Psalm 91 to us, where it says that God is our refuge and our fortress and our shield, and that angels are protecting us and we can be victorious over our enemies. He called it *The Trench Psalm*. He said lots of other soldiers were probably reading the very same words in foxholes all over France and Germany." Daniel looked around the table. "Ain't that an awesome thought?" he said, raising his eyebrows at each of us. "All of a sudden, we knew we weren't alone. Thousands of other American soldiers were watching our backs while we were watching theirs."

Amy's lips parted in a sweet smile. "Tell us more about the fighting."

Daniel's back straightened. He frowned with such intensity, I feared he was about to launch into a frightening tale about death and destruction.

"Hold on, Daniel," I said. "I need to find something else for the little ones to do."

He nodded his understanding and went back to his cake. I ushered Johnny and Lily into their bedroom and settled them down with a deck of Old Maid playing cards.

"You take charge, Johnny," I told my son. "No cheating, but give Lily a chance to win once in a while, okay?'

He bobbed his head with innocence and started dealing out the cards.

Satisfied they'd be entertained for at least a half-hour, I returned to the table. Amy was brewing a fresh pot of coffee. John pushed his chair back from the table and propped his feet on another chair. Daniel was digging into his third piece of strawberry jam-topped sponge cake.

I grabbed a chair next to my husband and waited for the young man to entertain us further. His stories had become a staple at our meals. We were experiencing what was happening in other parts of the world without ever having to leave Sawmill. The newspapers certainly didn't provide all the details Daniel wove into his stories.

He scraped his plate clean, held out his coffee cup for Amy to fill it, and began to share his most exciting moments of the war.

"We faced danger day and night," he said, his eyes darting

about the room like he could sense the enemy lurking behind the sofa or springing up from the inside of the fireplace. "In the early morning hours, a party of twelve of us men were hunkered down in a ditch when one of the guys caught sight of a cloud of gray smoke at the horizon. It rolled across the barren landscape—mostly dry soil with tufts of grass here and there—and it billowed toward us." Daniel was a natural-born storyteller. "My friend Jimmy called out, 'chloride gas,' and we all scrambled for our respirators." He snickered. "We didn't really need them. That cloud was creeping along. We gathered up our stuff and simply outran it."

A ripple of relieved chuckles went up around our table. Daniel beamed with satisfaction, like a variety show comic, appraising his audience.

He added a half pitcher of cream to his coffee, stirred it well, then took a sip and prepared for the next episode in his wartime saga.

"To make a long story short," he said. "I'll give you the highlights of my journey into hell. During the day we kept our eyes on the tree lines and the cornfields for any sign of the enemy. We listened for the rattle of machine guns and the blast of grenades. At night we looked for flashes of artillery. We took bets on how close they were.

"I remember one afternoon when the enemy was on us in seconds. I barely had time to attach my bayonet when they charged us. Our sergeant yelled, 'Three-two-one—ready? Let's go!' I froze for a second. I was thinking about the guy I'd killed with the butt end of my rifle and how I'd vowed I'd never do that again. Then I looked around me at the dead— some ours, some theirs. They were staring back at me with dull, unseeing eyes. I knew then it was either kill or be killed.

Screaming, I lunged out of the foxhole and into the fray."

Daniel's voice broke and for the first time since he'd been telling his stories, tears flooded into his eyes. "My friend, George, died that day."

Our young soldier bent over and put his face in his hands. He sobbed like his heart was breaking.

My daughter caught her breath, then bowed her head and wept along with him. When she looked up her lashes were damp and her face was flushed a deep pink. She and Daniel stared at each other, the way John and I used to, long before we married.

At that moment I knew without a doubt I could do nothing to keep those two apart. Their hearts were already locked together, and there wasn't a person on earth who could break that tie. I had no hope of slowing the pace they'd already begun.

I left the table, my head swimming with questions about their relationship. They'd already moved past the budding stage and had plunged headlong into the throes of a full-fledged commitment. Why did I know this? Because within two months of working by John's side in south Philly, I couldn't think of spending my life without him. Now I was witnessing the same kind of unspoken dedication in my daughter.

I slipped out of the room, went to my bedroom and shut the door. I opened the trunk where I'd stored my nurse's uniform along with my children's baby clothes and numerous quilts I'd knitted over the years. From the top of the pile I lifted my wedding gown, white and wrinkle-free as the day I'd worn it. I could envision Amy walking down the aisle in it one day. Now, with the two of them spinning out of control, it was time John had a serious talk with them. But first, he needed to confront Daniel about his intentions.

Carefully, I folded the gown and placed it back in the trunk on top of everything else. Then I wiped the tears from my cheek and I closed the lid.

Chapter Twenty

I didn't have to wait long for John to talk to Daniel. In fact, John didn't bring up the subject. Daniel did. The very next Sunday morning he came to the house and said he needed to talk to Amy's father.

Since the church had closed its doors for the time being, we were conducting services in our living room. I was surprised to see Daniel walk in. By this time he knew this was our normal Sunday ritual. He'd claimed he wasn't a church-goer, yet there he was, dressed in one of his uncle's tailored, three-piece suits. It fit perfectly, but he kept craning his neck, like he was terribly uncomfortable in the high-cut collar and knotted tie.

John welcomed him inside and pointed to a chair on the other side of the living room away from Amy. That didn't stop the young man from staring at her and winking.

We sang a couple of hymns, then John launched into a message about not being unequally yoked, believers with unbelievers. It wasn't the same message he'd shared with me the night before, the one about tithes and offerings. Instead, he chose a passage of scripture from 2 Corinthians Chapter 6. Then he talked about how two people should not enter a relationship lightly, especially if they didn't share the same faith.

"That means any relationship," John said, his voice a little brusque. "Not in business, not in intimate friendships, and definitely not in marriage." He shot Amy a piercing glance.

I looked at Amy, who was frowning, and then at Daniel, who still had his eyes on my daughter. It seemed as though he hadn't heard a word my husband had said. I prayed that somehow God might get a hold of that young man. Otherwise my daughter's heart was destined to break.

After the service ended, we settled at the table for tea and scones. We kept the conversation light. Afterward, John picked up his Bible and invited Daniel out to his private place on the front porch.

Later that night, my husband shared the details of their talk with me, as I sat on the edge of our bed wringing my hands. John paced the floor a couple of times, then he settled on the bed beside me and grabbed my hands in his.

"No need to fret, darlin'," he said, grinning. "Amy's young man has asked for permission to court her. He's promised to treat her honorably and to see her only under our supervision. Best of all, he asked me to help him find faith in God."

I relaxed a little then, and breathed a sigh, but I still had to ask, "Does he understand what that means?"

John nodded emphatically. "He had a few questions and confessed he was troubled about the men he'd killed in the war. I helped him to understand God's forgiveness. I'm confident Daniel will be joining us for church services from now on. And he said he wants to be baptized."

One other concern pressed on my heart. "Amy's only 16," I said. "Do you think she's too young to be courted?"

He scrunched his lips, like he was trying to think of a response that would satisfy me. Then he nodded with assurance.

"She's going to be 17 in a couple of months. If they court

for a year, she'll be 18 when they wed. That's plenty of time, Rosie, don't you think?"

I still had some doubts. "We hardly know him, John. I remember him as a little boy visiting the Duncans every summer, but apart from that, this is a grown man who's come to our home asking for permission to spend time with our daughter. He's been gone these many years. He's been serving in the war. Who knows what kind of trauma he's experienced and how it's affected him mentally and emotionally."

"There isn't anything strange about him," John said with confidence. "If nothing else, his time in the military has helped him mature a little faster than most young men, perhaps even guided him to a more certain path for his future."

"What about his future? Has he mentioned anything about a job? More schooling, perhaps?"

"Yes. He told me he wants to go into his uncle's business. If you recall, Tom Duncan made a fortune selling hand soaps. Lifebuoy is one of his biggest sellers. He rarely left Sawmill to promote his products, probably went to Philly and Pittsburgh maybe once or twice a year at the most. He managed the rest of his sales by mail. You've seen his little catalogues. They've proven to be a real boon to businesses like his."

I breathed another satisfied sigh.

John fixed his emerald eyes on my face. "Stop worrying about Amy. She's a sensible girl. When the time draws closer, you can talk to her about a wedding. And, of course, you'll be responsible for telling her what to expect in the bedroom."

"We've already had that talk," I confessed. "She started asking questions when she was 10."

John chuckled and patted my hand. "Relax, darlin'. Daniel is merely courting our daughter. He hasn't asked for her hand in marriage. Let's just enjoy our daughter while she's still with us and take care of everything else when it happens. There's plenty of time."

I smiled with embarrassment. "I'm such a dolt."

"No, Rosie, you're not." He wrapped his arm around me and pulled me close. "You're a great mother and a terrific wife. You've done well with our children. Amy has turned into a fine young woman. For now I think you should give more of your attention to Johnny and baby Lily. Our boy is growing up way too fast. And Lily's always going to need you."

As always, my husband was right. Other than coaching Amy through her schoolwork and providing clothes and grooming advice for her, I could wait until Daniel proposed marriage. I doubted Amy would consider anyone else.

We left the bedroom that day with another plan in place. I agreed to continue working with John in the mornings, and I'd spend the afternoons with my children. Lily still needed to progress past the alphabet, and young Johnny continued to surprise me with his own self-appointed education using his father's medical books. With my background in nursing I decided I could explain a lot of those diagrams to him and help him understand some of the terminology.

One afternoon, when my son finished his reading lesson, he went to his father's cupboard and grabbed the microscope off of the bottom shelf. He placed it on the table, set everything the way he wanted it, and before I realized what he was about to do, he pricked his middle finger with one of my sewing needles and placed a drop of his own blood on the slide.

I held my tongue, preferred instead to tiptoe up beside him and peer over his shoulder. "What do you see, Johnny?"

"Ummm. I see little red donuts."

"What else?"

"Little purple blobs."

"Really? Do they mean anything to you?"

He turned his freckled face up at me and grinned. "I think Papa might tell me."

"Well," I said. "I know a little about such things. I studied nursing, you know. Let me see."

He stepped aside and allowed me to look through the lens. "Okay," I said. "The little red donuts are red blood cells. You have plenty of them running around inside your veins. And the purple blobs are probably white cells."

He wrapped his arms around me. "Thanks, Mama."

I understood then that his thank you went beyond gratitude for basic information. My little boy was telling me how happy he was that I had taken an interest in what he enjoyed.

From that moment on, I gave my son the freedom to look through his father's medical books whenever he wanted to. He preferred to flip through those colorful pages instead of spending time in what he referred to as his *boring school readers*. He sought out his father more often too, and asked questions that went far beyond my ability to answer. I didn't mind. Already, at eight years of age, my little boy had found his calling.

As for little Lily, she was content to play with her dolls and her alphabet blocks. It became more obvious that although she was growing physically she wasn't maturing intellectually. She bore an endearing innocence that had me thinking she might always be a little girl, even after she developed into a woman.

Every morning I entrusted my little ones to Amy and the

widow Schmidt while John and I went together on a mission to heal the people of Sawmill. Gradually our neighbors warmed up to me. I was coming to them as a nurse, not as a foolish housewife with a bag of folk remedies.

For some reason beyond my understanding John never contracted the disease. If he'd had a mild case of it, he never complained. Like a driven man, he kept on working as though the world depended on his faithfulness.

Then one evening, when the two of us were returning home from ministering to the sick, a chill came over me. It was unlike anything I'd ever experienced. I felt like I'd been encased in a block of ice. I pressed my fingers to my cheek. My face was burning up. I took my temperature. It read 103. My head ached like someone had dropped a cinder block on it.

Ignoring the delectable spread of soup and sandwiches Amy had set out, I passed the supper table and went straight to my bedroom. My muscles ached, and I was certain a hammer was pounding against my temples. My throat was raw. I kept on coughing and spitting up thick mucous. Shivering, I wrapped myself in a heavy quilt and flopped onto my bed.

John had followed me into the bedroom. He leaned over me, pressed his hand to my forehead, then to my cheek. His fingers felt like icicles. I drew my legs up against the relentless spasms in my stomach, shut my eyes against the painful glare of the bedside lamp, and tried to find relief in the smooth coolness of my pillow.

"She's got it," I heard John say. *It*, like everyone knew by this time, was the Spanish Flu.

The next two days came and went with a swirl of colorful images. Shadows played above my bed. They hovered, departed, then hovered again. I knew they were people, but I couldn't determine who they were.

Someone pressed cool washcloths against my forehead. I caught the pungent aroma of vinegar. Somebody dropped a heavy quilt over me. I sighed with relief. More shadows hovered, more hands touched my forehead, my cheeks, even my feet.

"Open your mouth, Rose," a woman's voice said. I parted my lips and received a myriad of offerings. Slivers of ice. Sips of warm broth. Honeyed tea.

The minty aroma of eucalyptus leaves penetrated my nostrils. I strained to get an aspirin down. Then more shivering followed by more heavy blankets. I grew hot. I struggled to get free of the blankets, then made a mad rush to the bathroom, followed by vomiting, diarrhea, and writhing on the cold, hard bathroom floor. Big hands slid under my arms and lifted me, dragged me back to bed. The big hands departed and gentler fingers helped me into a clean nightdress.

I fell into violent coughing.

"She's spitting up blood." Amy's panicked voice came through.

"It's all right," said John, standing somewhere behind my daughter. "No need to worry. Her color is still good."

I swallowed more aspirin. The fever remained. There was the sound of water spilling into the tub. Seconds later, I was immersed in a lukewarm bath. Then clean clothes, back in bed, more shivering, and the warmth of a heavy wool blanket.

I lost track of time, don't know how long I suffered. Finally, I was able to open my eyes, but only a little. Everything was a blur. Faces came and went. I recognized a few. John's emerald eyes, filled with concern, peering at me over a mask.

"Try hard, Rosie," he murmured. "Come back to us."

Amy, shrouded and masked, holding a spoon to my lips. Her sweet voice sang a familiar hymn. "*Now thank we all our God with hearts and hands and voices, who wondrous things hast done, in whom his world rejoices; who from his mother's arms has blest us on our way with countless gifts of love, and still is ours today.*"

Another masked face, with silvery blue eyes and the creases of the elderly, joining Amy's precious song, this time in German. *"Nun danket alle Gott,"* Greta's feeble voice grew quieter and less distinct as she finished the stanza.

Then another masked face and a pair of brown eyes, spilling tears, and a familiar voice, Emma calling my name.

"I don't want to lose you, my friend." Her words were like medicine to me. "Please, Rosie, I'm not angry with you anymore. My boys have recovered. So has my husband. I want the same for you, dear friend. I want you to get well. Please, Rosie, please fight. Fight to get well."

I don't know how many days I lost or when I started coming out of that stupor. When at last I could open my eyes fully, I looked around the bedroom for the first time and found Emma sitting in a chair across the room. She was wearing a mask and was holding a little prayer book. I gazed at her and smiled. Her eyes crinkled at the corners.

She turned toward the doorway. "John! Amy! She's opening her eyes. Rosie is awake!"

My husband and daughter came flying into my bedroom, fumbling with the straps of their masks, trying to tie them behind their heads.

My bedroom exploded with celebration as more people flooded in, like they'd been waiting outside my bedroom the whole time. Johnny and Lily were there. They lunged at my bed, reached out for my hands amidst cries of "Mama, Mama."

Daniel walked in, barely limping anymore. Behind him were the Duncans, and the widow Schmidt with an apron tied around her waist. Gentle hands ran through my hair, patted my shoulders, and stroked my arms.

The men left the room, and the women helped me into the bathroom. Water flowed into the tub. Amy sprinkled lavender salts, sending a soothing aroma into the air. Tenderly, they stripped me of my soiled nightdress. I caught my image in the mirror, shocked to see a skeletal figure and a pair of deep-set eyes looking back at me. Hands braced my arms and lowered me into the tub. The frothy water rippled soothingly against my waist. Someone washed my hair and drew it up in a bun. I looked about me at the smiling faces. Emma was there, proof that I hadn't imagined she'd come. Amy and the widow Schmidt bathed me with sponges, dried my tired body with soft towels, and helped me slip into a clean nightdress. I rewarded them with a smile and a sigh.

Refreshed from the bath I went into the dining room for the first time in more than two weeks, or so they told me. Only one place was set at the table. Mine. Amy placed a bowl of potato soup and a wedge of sour dough bread in front of me. I ate with relish.

I had become ill at the end of October, had completely missed the armistice on November 11, and had come to in time to see the beginning of winter. I gazed out the front window. Icicles hung from the eaves, a powder of snow covered the ground, and the branches of the elm tree were bare.

"Where did the time go?" I said, as more flurries fell and were caught by a swirl of wind.

John came and sat beside me. "So glad you've come back to us, darlin'." His eyes sparkled with moisture. I peered into those green pools and found love there.

"Didn't you ask me to?" I said, smiling, for I remembered the urgency in his voice. "I had the flu, didn't I?"

He nodded. "A bad case of it," he said.

"How are our neighbors?"

He looked away for a second, like he didn't want me to see the pain in his eyes. "We lost a few more," he said, then he brightened slighty. "But most are recovering nicely."

My heart sank. "Who, John? Who passed?"

He hesitated, then spoke the names. "Louise Morgan, the undertaker's wife. Carl Jackson, farmer Paul's oldest son. And several people who lived a great distance from town, folks you never met."

"Are you still going out every day?"

"Yes, darlin'. It's my duty, my life."

I understood. "I wish I could go with you."

"You will. But for now you need your rest. Amy and the widow Schmidt have everything under control. Just rest, my darlin', just rest and get strong again."

Day after day, week after week, John continued to trudge through the streets, ignoring winter's bitter cold. Occasionally, he drove his truck to the outlying farms and checked on people he hadn't seen for a while. I'm certain my husband's diligence made a difference. Our little village of Sawmill recorded fewer casualties than most of the other country towns in our state.

News reports kept coming in from other locations throughout the world where the flu continued to rage. Though many people had died of complications, like meningitis, encephalitis, and pneumonia, the actual death toll had begun to decline.

News reports estimated that 90 percent of the flu victims were recovering, though many of them could expect to suffer for months or even years with different health problems.

John told me that while I was sick he wrote a letter to the Philadelphia hospital and admitted that he'd taken the medicines. In February an answer came in the mail from one of the doctors. John read the letter first, then he handed it to me.

To my honorable colleague, Dr. Gallagher,

The other physicians and I discussed your situation. We all remembered how you labored alongside us when your own people needed you at home. The money you gave helped us to acquire more supplies. We chose to accept your work hours and your financial donation as payment enough, and we unanimously decided not to take this unfortunate incident to the police. I hope you and your family are well and that all of you will come through this pandemic in good health.

You are aware by now that a third wave of influenza has surfaced. It appears to be more aggressive and likely will infect many. Because it seems to be a weaker strain, we expect there will be fewer casualties. Our most reliable scientists have not yet come up with an effective vaccine or serum, but they continue to experiment and we hope for success in the near future.

I feel compelled to share another problem with you, one that bears overwhelming sadness. The streets of Philadelphia are full of orphaned children. An untold number of boys and girls lost their parents to the flu while they themselves remained healthy but unable to care for themselves. Our city's fathers are asking kindhearted citizens to step forward to take them in. Please talk to the people of Sawmill and encourage them to receive some of these children.

Sincerely, your friend and colleague,

Dr. Harold Sefferin

John and I looked into each other's eyes. A silent message passed between us. John smiled, and I simply nodded.

John left the next morning in Thompson's truck. He never said how many, only that he did not plan to return empty-handed.

Sure enough, that evening my dear husband came home with a truckload of frail, dirty-faced children with no possessions except the clothes on their backs. There were twelve in all, seven boys and five girls. We bathed each of the little ones and allowed the older teens to wash themselves. Then we gave them clean clothing and fed them chicken soup and brown bread. While Amy and I took care of those needs, John went to see Mayor Barnes. Together they put out word that we had acquired a dozen children who needed homes.

Emma Wilson and her husband were the first to respond. They welcomed a nine-year-old girl into their home. The widow Schmidt accepted a teenage boy, saying he could help her with chores on the property, and in return he'd have a place to live until he was ready to go out on his own. Mayor Barnes and Mildred, who were childless, took two boys and one girl. Felina Gray took a girl the same age as her daughter. Patrick and Mae Philips added two boys and two girls to their brood of six. Patrick claimed they had plenty of room in their three-story farmhouse, plenty of food in the pantry, and plenty of chores to divide up among them. In the end, John and I invited two boys into our small cottage. To make more room, my husband agreed to turn our attic into a loft for Johnny and our adopted sons.

"Hopefully, they won't make the same mistake I did as a boy," he said, wincing from the memory of his leg injury. "No hanging over the side."

Ultimately, the erroneously named Spanish Flu—or as the French called it, *la grippe*—came to an end. Just as no one could pin down a specific origin, the pandemic of 1918 left the same way it came—mysteriously. No one had figured out the cause, and as hard as the scientists tried to find a cure no one succeeded. While the casualties from the Great War were high—more than two million Germans and 116,000 Americans, the figures didn't come close to the number of those who had died from the flu. Scientists later estimated that 50 million to 100 million people perished worldwide. Third world countries, which were hit the hardest, were unable to provide accurate numbers. As it was, entire communities suffered great losses, among them several Eskimo villages where there were no survivors.

In America, the state of Pennsylvania had the highest death toll in the country with 60,000 casualties. The City of Brotherly Love was one of the hardest hit municipalities with more than 12,000 dying.

John and I were both worried about our families. My husband went to Cowell's store and phoned his brother. He learned his father had died of heart failure. I wept with him, and together we told our children.

When I was able to get out and walk a few blocks, I also used Cowell's phone to call my sister Betty.

"Angelo's gone," Betty said with tears in her voice. "The *influenza di freddo* got him. He couldn't fight the flu, had too many health problems already."

"Angelo? The flu?" Tears rushed to my eyes and my throat tightened. As much as I wanted to kill my brother at times, I would miss him.

"Mama wailed for days," Betty told me. "All those years

she called him a stupid head and cursed at him in Italian, but she loved Angelo. She would never have admitted it, but I think he may have been her favorite. He was the one who needed her most."

My sister broke down then. "Oh, Rosie, they wanted us to put his body by the curb to be tossed with the others on the undertaker's wagon. Mama wouldn't hear of it. I called Tommy to come and help. He was sick too, but he promised to bring a shovel and a heavy blanket so we could wrap Angelo in it and give him a halfway decent burial."

I wept loudly with my sister, unconcerned that David was nearby moving things around on a shelf. A host of memories flooded into my mind. Angelo, sneering at me over the dinner table, pulling my hair out of my meticulously formed bun. Angelo, cracking jokes about the nursing profession. Angelo, walking me down the aisle on my wedding day when Papa was too sick to come to church.

Betty continued to sob into the phone. She said my mother and two of our sisters, plus several of my nieces and nephews had come down with the flu. They all survived. Betty and my younger sister, Annie, had somehow avoided infection. Though she was still a teenager, Annie had stepped up to help take care of everyone.

"Like a nurse in training," I boasted, wiping a tear from my eye.

Talking about my family drew me back to the days when I made regular visits to Little Italy, the scene of block parties and festivals, birthday celebrations and anniversaries, and family reunions that bound us all together like glue. Now the flu was wiping away everything I held dear.

I left Cowell's store that day feeling more depressed than

ever. But the dark cloud that had settled on us had a silver lining. It came a few months later when the flu mysteriously vanished and we began to rebuild our lives. Businesses reopened. Schools held classes. Church bells announced Sunday services. My sewing club got together again, and John started going to Rotary Club and city council meetings. We threw out our masks—or put them away in case we might need them again someday.

Though on the surface everything appeared normal again, we all behaved differently. I washed my hands more often. I stopped hugging friends when I ran into them at the market or on a village street. Nobody shook hands anymore. Most of us continued to stay home, especially those who experienced the slightest sniffle. We kept our distance from others who were sick, and we were prepared to don a mask again—anything to keep from living through another nightmare like the one in 1918.

I caught the flu and recovered. But millions of other people caught it and didn't survive.

President Wilson's wife, Edith, became ill in February, 1919. The president followed in April, became violently ill, and was confined to his bed for a while. Though he tried to conduct business from his bedroom, he tired easily. Word was he'd lost some of his cognitive abilities. He gave in to the demands of foreign nations, and he stopped addressing the American public. During the following summer Wilson suffered a debilitating stroke and remained under the full-time care of his physician. He never fully recovered.

The influenza of 1918 struck other people who would one

day become well-known. Among them was John Steinbeck, Pulitzer Prize-winning author of *The Grapes of Wrath*. Steinbeck was 16 years old when he caught the flu. He suffered with lung problems for the rest of his life.

Walt Disney also was 16 at the time. He lied about his age and signed up with the Red Cross Ambulance Corps. When he caught the flu, he didn't get to serve in the war effort. He didn't recover until after World War I ended.

Other notables who caught the flu and survived were actresses Mary Pickford and Lillian Gish, England's Prime Minister David Lloyd George, Franklin D. Roosevelt, German Kaiser Wilhelm II, General John J. Pershing, Ethiopia's Haile Selassie I, Edvard Munch, painter of *The Scream*, and Winston Churchill's wife, Clementine, whose daughter's nanny, Isabelle, died from complications of the flu. Then there was novelist Katherine Anne Porter, who years later gave a graphic account of what it was like to suffer with the flu in her historic short story, *Pale Horse, Pale Rider*.

It appeared no one was immune. Influenzas are not selective. Though third world countries suffered the greatest losses, no one on the entire planet could escape the monster's tentacles. For a while it appeared that the influenza had won.

But it hadn't. The warring nations ended the military conflict and joined forces in a different kind of war. Now they were battling a common but invisible enemy. Some of the world's greatest medical minds worked day and night to come up with a vaccine and a cure. They risked their own lives experimenting with virulent cultures while handling the blood and sputum of the dead. They worked long hours in private labs. Then they came together and shared what they had learned. Some believed a vaccine could upset the natural balance of a person's immune system. Others plunged ahead to develop one. Other theories arose over what kind of germ had caused the flu in the first place.

Prominent individuals kept appearing in the news—like Dr. Paul Lewis of the Phipps Institute and Canadian researcher Oswald Avery. Their efforts and those of a multitude of other scientists helped pave the way for future research.

A decade later, while some of us were still grieving our lost loved ones, we entered the Great Depression, then World War II. And, as sure as the weather has its natural cycles, it seems worldwide pandemics do too, which we were to discover this year when the Asian Flu reared its ugly head.

Chapter Twenty-One

December, 1957

Over the past four decades we lived through the Spanish Flu, two world wars, and the Great Depression. Scientists continued their labors and developed serums and antibiotics. In 1928, Alexander Fleming developed penicillin. The first flu vaccine became available in 1938 when Jonas Salk came up with an effective formula.

Forty years ago our gardens turned into graveyards. It took years for us to rise from the ashes and start over again. Then the graveyards began turning back into gardens and flowering landscapes promised "the purest of human pleasures," as Sir Francis Bacon said.

Now we've been hit by another pandemic, the Asian Flu. The first signs of it occurred in Hong Kong in February, supposedly from a mixture of strains, both human and avian, possibly ducks. More than 250,000 Chinese contracted the disease. Many of them either recovered fully or they lived to spread the germs through various modes of transportation—trains, buses, planes, and even smaller conveyances like taxis, rickshaws, and canal boats. Then there were the Americans who traveled to areas rife with epidemic and brought the germs home with them.

A *New York Times* story warned that the flu was coming our way. People in the big cities panicked. They flooded into the streets and lined up at clinics and hospitals seeking antibiotics.

The good news is, we now have two weapons that weren't available in 1918. Antibiotics and vaccines. And thanks to the efforts of microbiologist Maurice Hillman, more than 40 million doses of a new vaccine became available even before the Asian Flu reached the United States.

Like most influenza pandemics, this one went through a brief lull, which gave us a false sense of security. It was thought to be less lethal than the one that struck in 1918, but it's far more aggressive, passing from one person to the next with the speed of a bullet. Last month a second, more virulent wave struck. Scientists are suggesting the need for a new vaccine.

It's no wonder then that I stand here and look out over my backyard with mounting concerns. I breathe deeply of the fresh, cool air. Mounds of snow cover the ground where the roots of summer's plants lie dormant. In a few months they'll rise to new life. Hopefully, so will we.

Releasing a sigh, I step off the back stoop and start pulling our laundry off the line. The length of rope runs from the house to a T-shaped pole at the far end of our yard. Flossie used to graze back there. She died during the winter of 1920. We never bought another horse.

John got several years of service out of Thompson's truck. He replaced it in 1928 with a Ford Roadster.

I glance with fondness at the house next door where the widow Schmidt used to live. She died in her sleep in 1927, probably from old age. Her adopted son buried her in a common grave beside Oskar. A young family lives there now. After all this time, Greta's bed of poinsettias is bursting with color, the only bright spot amongst an array of grays and blacks and browns on our block.

As I drop the wooden pins into the cloth bag, they strike the pile with resonating *pings* in the crisp morning air. Piece by piece, I lower the freshly laundered clothes into a large wicker basket. The bed sheets crumple stiffly in my hands. Now bleached a brilliant white, an hour ago they reeked of sickness, stained with my husband's urine.

I enter our bedroom huffing under the weight of the basket and plunk it down on the floor. John's sitting in a chair next to the bed. He winks at me. Over the years, the luster of green has faded from his eyes, dulled even more by his recent illness. His parched lips separate in a weak smile. My heart softens with love for this man who spent his entire life caring for others. Now it's his turn to be the patient. There's no telling how long I'll be able to keep him in bed. I've heard that doctors make the worst patients.

The poor man already lost most of his red crown of glory. Over the last couple of days I've picked stray hairs from his pillow and from his shoulders. His rosy cheeked face has paled. The strength of muscle has left his arms and legs. Sprawled like he is on that chair he looks like one of Lily's limp rag dolls.

Speaking of Lily, she still lives with us, never matured past the third grade. Though John and I both refused to take the vaccine, saying we'd rather leave the limited supply for the young folk, we made sure Lily got hers. Our little girl is coming up on her 45th birthday. She still plays with alphabet blocks and a growing collection of dolls, and she recently added a fully furnished dollhouse and a stack of coloring books and crayons to her special corner of her bedroom.

After Amy graduated from high school, she married Daniel. The Duncans passed away last year and left them a small fortune. Daniel had already given up selling soap and had purchased a Ford dealership. He and Amy moved with their four children into a high-class neighborhood in Philadelphia.

As we all expected, Johnny pursued an education in medicine. He's now a medical research scientist in Boston. He's married to Nancy, a lovely young woman who runs a shelter for abused women. They have two children.

Our two adopted sons, Philip and Andrew, moved back to the city, where Philip became a lawyer with a large firm, and Andrew joined the city police department. Both are married and have families of their own. They never did find out what happened to their relatives after the flu annihilated many of Philadelphia's residents.

Several people who'd lost loved ones suffered from depression and guilt over the years. They wanted to know why one family member died while they escaped unharmed. Many survivors mourned for months and suffered physical and psychological trauma. A few found peace through their faith. Others sought counseling. In time, healing came, and people moved on with their lives, allowing an occasional reflection on the pandemic of 1918.

Humming, I move about our bed and cover the mattress with fresh sheets, tuck in the ends, and smooth the wrinkles. As I help John out of the chair I'm reminded of my own frailty. The years have taken their toll on me too. The day I contracted the Spanish Flu I lost some of my strength and never got it back again. A persistent cough has stayed with me for four decades, and I tire easier these days.

Bracing myself, I slip one hand under John's armpit and

press my other palm against his back, guiding, lifting, and coaxing him into bed.

He rewards me with another weak smile. "Thank you, Rosie."

I pat his shoulder. "It's okay, John. I don't mind looking after you. One day very soon, you'll get your strength back."

The amused crinkling of his face tells me he knows I'm lying. He doesn't say anything, but we both know the truth. Seventy people have died in Sawmill since this new influenza hit. Seventy out of a population of about 1,800. Sadly, the number of deceased goes up every day.

The one doctor in town took ill and had to go for treatment at one of the hospitals in Philadelphia. He left a month ago and hasn't returned.

Many of my old friends have passed on, not from the flu, but through the natural course of aging and illness. David Cowell died from a heart attack while restocking the shelves in his store. He was creeping up on 98 and hadn't taken a day off in his life.

Felina Gray survived a bout with the flu. She married a traveling salesman and moved with him and her two little girls to the city. Mayor Ed Barnes retired from office. His adopted son was elected in his place. Frank Wilcox passed the sawmill operation to his sons and retired to Florida.

My sisters and their children survived the pandemic of 1918. Mama passed a few years later of unknown causes. Annie found her in bed, a smile on her face, like she was ready to go. Speaking of Annie, she's now the head nurse of pediatrics in a Philadelphia hospital. She married a surgeon. They have three children.

Now 81 years of age, my husband was weakened by a heart attack two years ago. Pretty much overnight, I turned from loving wife to devoted caregiver. At last, I understand what carves worry lines on people's faces. I like to call them marks of experience, but they're really the trials of life.

On a more positive note, I was able to enroll in a nursing school and get my much desired diploma. The hospital where I had trained had burned down along with all its records. I was a few weeks from graduating when they dropped me. Then this second chance came along, and John encouraged me to go for it.

"You've earned it," he insisted. "You've put in several decades of working in the field. If anyone deserves to have a nursing diploma, it's you."

I look at my husband now, and the worry bug bites me again. He came down with the flu about ten days ago. In the beginning he complained that his legs felt weak. Then he started shivering. He dropped into a chair and asked me to bring him a quilt. I hurried to get a nice thick one and wrapped it around his shoulders. He insisted he was freezing, but his forehead was ablaze. He ended up in bed, and he's been there ever since.

Mainly, I've been keeping alert for signs of pneumonia, but he hasn't coughed today, not even once. And his fever is gone. He's lying there now, a smile on his lips and looking fairly comfortable.

"How about some chicken soup, dear?" I offer.

He nods. "Sounds good, Rosie. And bring me the newspaper."

That morning's edition reported the casualties. Nearly 68,000 Americans have died of the flu, and the death toll is nearing 2 million worldwide. I've been sheltering my husband from the reports. Now he's asking for the newspaper.

I make a pretense of straightening his blankets, which

don't need straightening at all. By smoothing out non-existent wrinkles I can avoid the questioning flicker in my husband's eyes.

"I want the paper, Rosie." Irritation has altered his tone.

"The newspaper?"

"That's what I said." He sounds a little gruff for as sick as he's been.

"Whatever do you want with the newspaper?" I tug at the bottom of the spread. "It's all junk, nothing that should interest you."

"Junk or no junk, I want to read it. Now are you going to bring me the newspaper, or do I have to get out of this bed and get it myself?"

I dare to stare at him. He challenges me with narrowed eyes and lips pressed stubbornly together.

"I wrapped the chicken bones in it and put it in the garbage." I lie, but I'm planning to do that very thing as soon as I leave the room.

The wrinkles on John's brow relax and he chuckles. "Oh, Rosie. I can see right through you. Stop trying to protect me. I need to know what's going on in the world. Believe me, I can handle it."

I release a sigh. "If you hadn't gone out in the cold, you wouldn't be stuck in this bed right now. Why on earth did you leave the comforts of home to lug that medical bag around like you were still 40 years old?"

He's shaking his head. "Rosie, Rosie. You knew my calling when you married me. I'm like the postman—neither sleet, nor snow, nor ice, or whatever. Dr. Savage took ill and left town. Our neighbors needed medical care, and they couldn't wait. I had to do *something*."

I give him a little smirk and leave our bedroom to get his soup. Hopefully by the time I return he'll have forgotten about the newspaper.

He doesn't mention it when I come in carrying a tray with a steaming bowl of chicken soup and a plate of saltines. I hurry out of the room to clean up the kitchen.

Fifteen minutes later I return to the bedroom expecting to find John asleep. Instead, he's sitting on the edge of our bed pulling on a pair of wool socks. He follows with pants and a flannel shirt, then a pair of fur-lined boots.

With amazing agility he springs off the bed and hurries to our clothes closet. "Okay, where is it?"

"Where is what, John? And what do you think you're doing?"

"My medical coat. Where did you stash it?"

I take a firm stance and put my fists on my hips. "I threw it out. That thing was older than the hills. It's time you stopped limping around town looking like a kid dressed up on Halloween."

He flushes a deep pink. "You shouldn't have done that, Rosie. I still need it."

I cross my arms. "Well it's gone now, and what you *really* need is to get back in bed."

"Harrumph! Try and stop me."

He pushes past me and heads for the living room. I follow him. He grabs his overcoat off a hook, dons a wool hat and gloves and fumbles around in his cupboard for a face mask. Over the years his pharmacy shelves have gone from fully packed to almost empty. Three of them now serve as storage for my needlework projects.

I stand in shock. My stubborn husband is stuffing his beat-up, old medical kit with bottles of aspirin, Tylenol, Vicks

VapoRub, and cough syrups—common drug store products anyone can buy. He hasn't had a license in years. Couldn't order a prescription drug if his life depended on it.

It's all I can do to keep from laughing. "What do you expect to do with those things?"

He closes his bag and juts out his chin. "I can give comfort, Rosie. The same thing I did three weeks ago. If nothing else I can determine who needs to go to the hospital." He lifts his bag from the floor and straightens his tired body with a grunt. He starts to turn away, then pauses and looks me in the eye. "Didn't you do the same thing 40 years ago? Didn't you go out there—" he bobs his head toward the door "—with a wheelbarrow full of herbs?"

I blush, now speechless.

John opens the front door and leaves me standing there with my mouth open. Hunched with age, he shuffles awkwardly down our front steps then pauses at the end of our walk as a flatbed trailer rumbles past. It's laden with sawed boards for the undertaker—a stark reminder of the horse-drawn wagon that passed our house in 1918, loaded with roughly built coffins for the bodies that would go into them, sometimes two or three at a time.

John turns and gives me a wave, then he stumbles off down the street, determined to save as many as he can. I shake my head. *What on earth does that feeble octogenarian think he's going to accomplish out there?*

But how can I expect anything less of this man? He's the same person I worked beside on the back alleys of Philadelphia, ministering to poor souls who couldn't pay. The same devoted physician who trudged up and down the streets of Sawmill during the worst pandemic in history. The same brave man who raced to the city to buy medicines and ended up staying there to help. Dr. John Gallagher hasn't changed. He's older, yes. But inside him lives the same, selfless young man who refuses to quit.

I'm still standing in the open doorway. John's almost out of sight now. I need to make a decision. I can shake my head in selfish pride and hole up in my home like I did 40 years ago when I turned my back on friends and neighbors who needed me. I can live the rest of my days in boring indifference, a lonely old woman making crocheted buntings for her grandchildren. Or I can absorb a little of John's indelible spirit.

A fire erupts within me. Suddenly, I'm 12 years old, and my older sister, Marilyn, is giving birth to her first son. Then I'm 14, and I'm helping the midwife deliver Betty's baby girl. Then I'm delivering Annette's baby while the midwife looks on. Like a whirlwind, I'm in nursing school, following my long-held dream, and then I'm traveling around the tenements beside John, doing what I was called to do.

I turn away from the door and quickly grab my winter coat and scarf off the hook. I slip on my boots and check my pockets for a pair of gloves. I hurry to the bedroom and search my jewelry box for the little nursing pin with the red-and-white striped ribbon. I proudly fasten it to my coat. Then I quickly grab a mask, and I head into the street after my husband. He's already turned the corner. I pick up my pace. There he is. My boots crunch against the packed snow. He hears my footsteps and turns around. He smiles, and his eyes shine emerald green again. He's standing straight and tall, like a younger man.

I draw close to his side and slip my hand in the crook of his arm. Then we start off down the street together—a doctor and his nurse on a medical mission—like we used to do not so very long ago.

Acknowledgements

W hile this book is a work of fiction, I've woven through the text a good amount of factual information based on an actual event that happened a hundred years ago. Besides setting the scene for the 1918 Spanish Flu, the details bear a shocking resemblance to what the world has been experiencing with the recent Covid pandemic.

There are too many similarities to ignore the lessons we can all learn from how the world reacted to a worldwide pandemic that may have killed as many as 100 million people. As of the date of this writing, the Covid virus has killed a little over 2.5 million throughout the world. Of course, today we have vaccines, antibiotics, and serums they didn't have back then. But just like us, the people wore masks, they practiced isolation, and multiple businesses, churches, and schools shut down. They just didn't do so long enough. In many cities the lockdowns lasted for only a month or two.

Like with all my books, I depended on multiple resources and also several individuals to bring this work to completion.

Many thanks go to my beta readers, Charles and Delores Kight, and my daughter, Joanna Jones. I also want to thank Dr. James Kuhn of Trinity Health Care for reviewing the medical information, also Brigitte Shultz, John Naftzger, Gretchen Naftzger, and Sylvia Marten for proofing Greta's German accent.

Thanks go to my publisher/editor, Mike Parker of Word-Crafts Press, for his diligence in making my work shine. And, last but not least, my eternal gratitude to Jesus Christ, my Lord and Savior, and the guidance of His Holy Spirit for bringing me through another labor of love.

Resources

BOOKS

Diseases in History—Flu by Kevin Cunningham, Morgan Reynolds Publishing, Inc., Greensboro, N.C., 2009

Influenza—The Hundred-Year Hunt to Cure the Deadliest Disease in History by Dr. Jeremy Brown, director of the Office of Emergency Care Research, NIH, Touchstone Imprint of Simon & Schuster, Inc., N.Y., NY., 2018

Flu—The Story of the Great Influenza Pandemic of 1918 and the Search for the Virus that Caused It by Gina Kolata, Farrah, Straus and Giroux Pub., New York, 1999

The Great Influenza by John M. Barry, Penguin Group Publishing, New York, New York, 2004

Pandemic 1918 by Catharine Arnold, St. Martin's Press, N.Y., N.Y. 2018

The Devil's Flu by Pete Davies, Henry Holt & Co., LLC, N.Y., N.Y. 2000

The Great War—A Combat History of the First World War by Peter Hart, Oxford University Press, New York, 2013

The Timetables of History by Bernard Grun, Simon & Schuster/Touchstone, N.Y., N.Y., 1991

WEBSITES

The Lakeshore Guardian, March 2015, The Way It Was

The Pharmaceutical Century, Ten Decades of Drug Discovery, ACS Publications

"Philadelphia Virtual Tours," YouTube video

"Imagining the Bounds of History," by Shannon Selin, shannonselin.com

"The Medical and Scientific Conceptions of Influenza," virus.stanford.edu

Library of Congress, U.S. History, loc.gov/classroom-materials/united-states/history

"America in the 1900s," Democrat & Chronicle Newspaper, Money Column, June 7, 2014

ONLINE RESOURCES

https://philadelphiaencyclopedia.org/archive/typhoid-fever-and-filtered-water/

https://www.onlyinyourstate.com/pennsylvania/philadelphia/philadelphia-in-the-1900s-pa/

https://www.onlyinyourstate.com/pennsylvania/philadelphia/early-1900s-philadelphia-pa/

https://www.history.com/topics/world-war-i/world-war-i-history

https://www.worldwar1centennial.org/index.php/practice-of-medicine-in-ww1.html

https://www.thehealthy.com/home-remedies/15-harmless-folk-remedies-worth-a-try/

https://www.healthline.com/health/folk-remedies-passed-down

https://www.history.com/news/spanish-flu-pandemic-response-cities

https://www.cdc.gov/flu/pandemic-resources/1957-1958-pandemic.html

https://www.ncbi.nlm.nih.gov/pmc/articles/PMC3291411/

https://www.britannica.com/event/1957-flu-pandemic

https://www.britannica.com/science/influenza#ref740015

https://www.ncbi.nlm.nih.gov/pmc/articles/PMC2714797/

https://www.thelancet.com/journals/lancet/article/PIIS0140-6736(2031201-0/fulltext

https://www.history.com/news/1957-flu-pandemic-vaccine-hilleman

https://www.google.com/search?q=lyrics+to+I+Love+You+Truly&oq=lyrics+to+I+Love+You+-Truly&aqs=chrome..69i57j0i22i3015.6297j0j15&sourceid=chrome&ie=UTF-8

https://www.bbc.com/news/education-37975358

https://www.claddaghdesign.com/ireland/irish-proverbs-and-what-they-mean/

https://www.fluentin3months.com/italian-sayings/

https://www.britannica.com/event/Battles-of-the-Isonzo

https://www.facinghistory.org/weimar-republic-fragility-democracy/politics/casualties-world-war-i-country-politics-world-war-i

https://www.spokesman.com/stories/2019/jan/20/the-doctor-and-the-pandemic-spokanes-1918-fight-ag/

https://www.theguardian.com/world/2020/apr/05/nurses-fell-like-ninepins-death-and-bravery-in-the-1918-flu-pandemic

https://www.melinadruga.com/1910s-slang/

https://www.encyclopedia.com/history/culture-magazines/1900s-glance

https://fraser.stlouisfed.org/title/union-scale-wages-hours-labor-3912/union-scale-wages-hours-labor-may-15-1921-492986?start_page=51

https://mainlinetoday.com/life-style/the-history-behind-some-of-the-main-lines-most-iconic-estates/
https://nursing.vanderbilt.edu/news/florence-nightingale-pledge/
https://mcgillins.com/history/https://www.theirishstore.com/blog/26-common-irish-sayings/
https://www.mentalfloss.com/article/58376/14-famous-people-who-survived-1918-flu-pandemic
https://www.goalcast.com/2018/02/08/inspirational-florence-nightingale-quotes/
https://nursegrid.com/blog/list-nurse-rules-early-1900s
https://www.nursing.upenn.edu/history/publications/calm-cool-courageous
https://www.mentalfloss.com/article/57987/9-unfamiliar-things-youd-see-hospital-1900

About the Author

Pulitzer Prize nominee in the field of journalism, Marian Rizzo has won numerous awards, including the New York Times Chairman's Award and first place in the 2014 Amy Foundation Writing Awards. She worked for the *Ocala Star-Banner* newspaper for 30 years. She also has written articles for *Ocala Style Magazine* and Billy Graham's *Decision Magazine*.

Several of Marian's novels have won awards at Florida Christian Writers conferences and Word Weavers retreats. In 2018, her manuscript for *Muldovah*, another suspense novel, was a finalist in the Genesis competition of American Christian Fiction Writers.

Marian earned a bachelor's degree in Bible education from Luther Rice Seminary. She trained for jungle missions with New Tribes (now ETHNOS 360), and she served for two semesters at a Youth With A Mission training center in Southern Spain.

Marian lives in Ocala, Florida, with her daughter, Vicki, who has Down Syndrome. Her other daughter, Joanna, has blessed her with three wonderful grandchildren.

Also Available From

WordCrafts Press

Girl with a Black Soul
  by Jennifer Odom

The Five Barred Gate
  by Jeff S. Bray

A Black Horse
  by Michelle A. Sullivan

Ill Gotten Gain
  by Ralph E. Jarrells

The Mirror Lies
  by Sandy Brownlee

www.wordcrafts.net

Made in the USA
Las Vegas, NV
18 August 2021

28331760R00177